THE
ASSIGNMENT

MASSEY SECURITY DUET BOOK ONE

S. NELSON

The Assignment/ S.Nelson.—1st edition

ISBN-13: 9781096243175

There is a bit of me in every tale that bears my name.
When my hero laughs, I also smile.
When he falls, I wince with pain.
When he does wrong and suffers for events that I have planned,
I feel his hurt, his grief, his shame.
And side by side we stand.
So, if someday, by chance, the world proclaims him as
immortal, I shall share the glory.
It was I who pushed him through the portal.

~ Georgetta Nelson

PROLOGUE

Ford

Smoke filled my eyes and temporarily blinded me, the soot burrowing into my nostrils before descending into my lungs. Suffocating me, threatening every breath I struggled to take, I scrambled along the concrete, the pads of my fingertips desperate to touch anything other than twisted metal and jagged pieces of glass. Tiny pricks that would've normally made me wince, spurred me on, the pain driving me to keep searching.

"Where is she?" I cried, the evening breeze stealing my words and whisking them away, my pleas dying as soon as they left my lips. People had gathered around the wreckage, but damned if I could see anyone. I heard murmurs, voices talking over one another so quickly I couldn't make out a single word.

Crawling closer to what I thought was the front seat of the vehicle, I reached forward but couldn't find the handle. As I searched, my lungs screamed for oxygen, and although I didn't want to remove my hands from the crushed metal, I had to find some sort of breath or I'd be no good to her. I snatched the bottom of my shirt and pulled it over my mouth, the fabric of my clothing giving me a small reprieve from my burning lungs.

Sirens sounded in the distance while I crawled along the ground. "Julia!" I shouted, moisture clouding my vision. I couldn't determine if the glassiness was caused by my impending anguish or if it was from my body's response against the smoke. Either way, I could barely see.

Flashes of memories bombarded me. Seeing the pride on her face when I'd removed her training wheels, and she rode down the driveway without incident. Splashes of water hitting my shirt when she did her best cannonball into the deep end, her airy laughter infectious when she resurfaced and saw my faux-annoyed expression, the quirk of my brow making her giggle even more. The sad look in her eyes when I told her I would be leaving to serve our country. The pain in my chest when she latched on to me, linking her fingers behind my neck because she didn't want me to go. My mind only pulled the fond memories but none of the bad.

I clutched the pendant hanging in the middle of my chest before continuing my search. When I finally located the door handle, I wrapped my fingers around it and pulled with all my might. All hope was dashed for an easy entry when nothing happened. Again, I tried. Still nothing. It wasn't until I moved my hand farther up the door I realized the window had been shattered. Hope surged through my veins as I reached inside, my arm dancing wildly around inside the car. But I touched no one. Acting on instinct, I leaped to my feet and practically dove inside. What I hadn't seen, or felt seconds prior, was although the window had been shattered, a single piece of glass remained, off to the right, nestled in tightly. The tip of the shard sliced me deep while I struggled to heave my large body inside. The burning sensation distracted me for a brief moment, carrying me away from the fear building inside.

Once I cleared the opening, falling clumsily inside, blood trickling down my side from the jagged cut, my gaze landed on a body slumped over but still secured by the seat belt.

Julia.

My kid sister.

Guilt slammed into my chest. Blame planted itself firmly right next to it. The way I treated her when I thought I was helping. The way I cut her off for months at a time because I didn't want to be an enabler. For the things I said to her right before she hopped in her car and sped off down the road.

A single breath of relief passed my lips, but as quickly as it mixed with the contaminated air around me, I sucked it back in. I'd found her, but as I fumbled to release the clasp pinning her in her seat, I knew she was gone.

CHAPTER
ONE

Ford

"I told you I'm not interested. Now stop asking me," I barked, the half-empty bottle of beer slipping through my fingers and hitting the wall across the room. The remnants dripped down the gray-colored drywall. Okay, so maybe it didn't slip from my fingers so much as I hurled it through the air. Pretty close to my brother's head, in fact. Although, to be fair, if I wanted to hit him with it, I would've. My aim was spot on. More so when I was sober, but that was neither here nor there.

"I told you I need your help with this one, man. Besides, you can't keep yourself locked away in this godforsaken place." His narrowed eyes shouted he believed his tough-love spiel would change my mind. As if I could forget everything that had happened in the past six months and jump right back into another assignment. Maybe my little brother was the one who'd been drinking. "Besides, this place fucking stinks. Ever hear of a garbage can?" He trudged through the clutter, kicking clothes, shoes, and old cartons of Chinese food out of his way.

Owen called a couple weeks back and practically begged me to help him out with a high-profile gig. I didn't bother getting any details because I told him it was out of the question. My surliness obviously did nothing to deter him from pestering me about it.

We owned our own security services firm, Massey Security Inc., and while it was small, only employing a half-dozen men, we'd already built a solid reputation for ourselves. Even in my drunken state, I knew I'd let him down, relying on him to run the firm while I wallowed in despair and liquor. He'd experienced the same loss, yet he forged ahead, and I had no idea where he pulled the strength from.

"You wan... wanna clean it up f... for me?" Scrambling off the couch, I swayed a few times before I righted myself, the room spinning all around me. When I closed my eyes, my dizziness intensified. Shit! I saw three of my brother when I pried open my lids, all of them glaring at me in disapproval. Approaching the one in the middle, I bumped his shoulder with mine as I walked by, intent on drowning myself in more alcohol. I tipped the bottle to my lips, but before I could taste the cool liquid, it was ripped from my hand. I reached to snatch it back, but my reflexes were shit, obviously.

"Give it back." I took two slow steps toward him. The spinning worsened. "Now!" He circled me, making me even dizzier. "Goddammit, Owen! Gimme my fucking drink." Leaning forward, I rested both my hands on my thighs, trying to catch my breath. All this exertion was for the birds, and for what? A beer? I had more where that one came from. I attempted to sidestep him, but he moved in front of me, and because I wasn't fully upright, I stumbled to the side and fell over before I could catch my balance.

"Sad." He tutted. "Just sad." I watched his feet move across the room toward the front door, the hurried steps messing with my vision. "I'll be back tomorrow." He twisted the handle but didn't open the door. I assumed he turned around to look back at me lying on the floor because the trajectory of his voice changed.

"Clean yourself up and be ready to go at noon. And Ford?" The silent pause told me if I didn't answer, he'd stand there until I did, and I wanted him out of my place so I could continue getting drunk. Well, drunker than I already was.

A frustrated breath left my lips. "Yeah?"

"Don't think I won't bring by reinforcements to drag your ass out of here, drunk or not." He snapped open the door. "Be ready at noon," he repeated, stepping into the hallway. "And make sure you take a fucking shower," he shouted over his shoulder before the door closed behind him.

CHAPTER
TWO

Ford

"You look like hell, man." My response to my brother's keen observation was to flip him off, striding ahead of him to gain the distance needed so he'd stop talking.

Sure enough, he showed up at noon, not a minute past, banging on the door before annoyingly ringing the doorbell repeatedly. When I whipped open the door, clutching the side of my head because the chime from the bell hurt like hell, he snickered before jumping back a step. He knew damn well he was gonna get hit if he stayed close.

Walking toward the driver side, I gripped the handle and pulled the door open. As I attempted to fold my tired ass in the seat, Owen shouted behind me, the chirp of his car alarm making a god-awful sound.

"No way. We're not showing up in that rundown piece of shit you call a car." Baffled, I looked over the roof of my Chevelle and scoffed.

"This is a fucking classic." Years back, I'd bought a red, 1966 Chevrolet Chevelle SS 396, and while it needed a complete overhaul, bumper to bumper, I'd fixed her up all by myself, damn proud of how she turned out. I changed the color to black and poured my heart and soul into every detail. My car

7

was the only thing that seemed to make me semi-happy these days.

"It's a piece of shit," he countered, smirking because he knew his insult would rile me.

"It's worth more than that foreign hunk of junk you have."

"Maybe, but we're not showing up to this job with you looking like you do, and in some loud, unpredictable muscle car.

"She's not unpredictable. She's just temperamental… like all females tend to be."

Owen shook his head before getting in his car, beeping the horn when he'd decided I was taking too long. I took my time crossing the fifty feet between us and sauntered to the passenger side. Once seated, my brother tossed a pair of dark shades in my lap.

"Keep those on when we meet this guy. You'll draw enough unwanted attention to yourself as it is. I don't need them freaking out over your eyes." He laughed, although the sound was laced with a bit of jealousy. My brother had always been envious of the attention I'd received growing up because of my eyes. I had what was referred to as heterochromia iridium. Two different colored eyes, and not just that… they were piercing, as my mother would often say. My right one was a medium shade of blue, and my left one was amber in color.

"Green is not a good look on you, brother."

"Neither is red, which is why I don't wear either."

"It's too early in the day to try and decipher your coded bullshit." I leaned my head against the headrest and closed my eyes, the sunglasses he'd thrown at me still in my lap.

Taking a new job had been the last thing I wanted to do, but my brother would've hounded me until I gave in. There was only so much resistance I could exert before I relented. We both knew it, and I was sure he was grateful he didn't have to gather a few of our friends to come and drag me out of my house.

I hadn't questioned Owen about who our new employer would be or how long the job would last. Questions were for people who cared... and I didn't. I simply wanted him to get off my back because he'd been pestering me for months to rejoin the land of the living. I should be grateful he gave me those months to myself, cut off from the rest of the world. Shit, I'd still be holed up at my place, shades drawn, and phone battery drained if he hadn't forced his way inside. Well, forced was maybe the wrong word since he did have a key. Still, Owen was a pain in the ass when he wanted, or needed, to be.

Shoving all thoughts of the impending meeting aside, my memories pulled me back to months prior. When my world had been normal. Images flashed, one after the other, but they weren't what I wanted to remember; instead, they were recollections I wanted to forget. The arguments. The constant worry if she was okay or not. The unanswered phone calls. Some memories of her I would always keep close to my heart, but the bad seemed to push their way to the forefront.

"I forgot you had that." Owen reached over and touched the cross hanging from my neck. My eyes flew open just as my hand swatted his away.

"Don't," I growled, clutching the metal between my fingers to protect it.

"Sorry."

"Just keep your eyes on the road and your hands on the wheel," I instructed, my voice raspy from lack of hydration. Owen fumbled with the radio, to which I swatted his hand again.

"What the hell?" he griped.

"Just don't." I leaned my head back once more and stared

out the window, the next two hours of the ride traveled in silence. We both lived in Connecticut, not far from each other and apparently, we had to drive to New York to meet the guy. I hated road trips, but I'd already given my brother enough shit about the job. I wasn't about to complain about the ride, too. We'd see how I felt on the way back home.

The car finally slowed, coming to a stop in front of an upscale restaurant, one equipped with valet service. Good thing Owen insisted he drive because there would've been no way I would've handed off my keys to some young punk.

"Come on. We're gonna be late." He left the engine running and exited the vehicle, passing the valet his keys before stepping in front of the car only to leer at me through the windshield. It was his way of trying to hurry me along. And because I wanted to get back home as soon as humanly possible, I exited the passenger side without complaint.

It would be an asinine question to ask where we were because obviously, we'd arrived at our destination, about to meet the person who'd hired us for this godforsaken job. I still had no idea who we were going to be working for or who we'd be assigned to, and I couldn't muster up enough of a fuck to care. The only thing I prayed was that the gig was short. As in a few days short, but something told me from the fat smile I witnessed on my brother's face as I walked up next to him, it was going to be anything but.

"Should I even bother to ask?" I mumbled, walking through the door ahead of him, my sunglasses still in place and tinting my vision once inside.

"You wouldn't believe me if I told you."

Every muscle in my body locked up from his tone. "This better not be something long-term, man." My gripe fell on deaf ears, and instead of stressing myself out any more than I already was, simply from not being diligent enough to ask a goddamn question beforehand, I took a deep breath and allowed him to walk a few paces ahead. Otherwise, I feared my leg just might catch his, and while the image of him tripping and falling made the corner of my mouth twitch, I wasn't that surly. Yet. But I sure as hell was well on my way.

CHAPTER
THREE

Ford

"**S**top breathing down my neck," he murmured, turning his head toward me and trying to be as discreet as possible. The man behind the podium cleared his throat, and Owen gave him his full attention. I knew my brother was itching to warn me to be on my best behavior, but we were ushered across the crowded restaurant before he could turn to give me one of his signature annoyed looks, the one with the inwardly slanted eyebrows, his most famous one. Come to think of it, he flashed me that expression quite a bit, but not as often as I snarled at him, as of late.

"Mr. Dessoye," the host announced. "Some of your party has arrived, sir."

"Thank you."

My brother blocked the view of the man we'd been announced to, but as soon as he took a step to the side, I saw who sat at the table. Walter Dessoye, one of the most famous movie producers of our generation.

"It's nice to see you again, sir," my brother greeted, extending his hand.

"And you. And please call me Walter. None of this sir nonsense." Walter smiled before turning his attention toward me, taking a step around the table to come closer, an action that was

12

both polite in nature but also unnerving somehow. Maybe it was because I was a fan of multiple movies of his and was a bit star struck, or maybe my slight unease was because his presence was larger than life. Whatever it was, I didn't have time to decipher any of it before he reached out to shake my hand. "You must be Owen's brother."

"Ford," I offered, pumping his hand a couple times before breaking the connection.

He gave me a curt nod before returning to his seat, gesturing with the sweep of his arm for us to join him, which we readily accepted. Once situated, we placed our drink order with the waiter. I wanted to tell the guy to bring me some whiskey, but the voice in my head, the one struggling to remind me to be responsible, yelled at me to just have water. So that's exactly what I ordered. I knew if I acted any way but reserved and professional, I'd never hear the end of it from my brother. And listening to him chastise me again, for the entire car ride home, especially, was the last thing I needed.

I leaned back in my chair and kept my gaze straight ahead, still not believing I was sitting directly across from Walter Dessoye. The first movie I'd seen of his, Star Gazer, was when I was just thirteen years old. A few buddies and I skipped school and snuck into a matinee at our local theatre, and since I was forbidden to see R-rated movies, I had to keep my excitement all to myself. I knew if I told Owen, he'd use it against me at some point and either blackmail me or just flat out tell our parents, to which I was sure I'd be grounded.

For as famous as the man was, he seemed down to earth, His attire was casual, a bit too casual for the type of restaurant he'd picked to meet us, but I had no doubt the place didn't bat an eye when he showed up. Owen and I were dressed in slacks and dress shirts because we wanted to make a good impression. Well, Owen did. I couldn't care less, but my brother had threatened me to ensure I dressed the part.

When the waiter returned and placed our drinks on the table, he fidgeted with his writing pad, his eyes glued to the famous customer before asking us what we wanted to eat. I declined, as did my brother, but Walter ordered some dish that contained sea urchin and cauliflower. The image of it alone enough for me to be thankful I'd just have my water.

"Has your brother filled you in on the job?" Walter asked, taking a slow sip of his drink, looking at me with something akin to amusement dancing behind his eyes. Or was I reading his expression all wrong?

"Not yet."

"Oh." He turned to look at Owen before glancing back in my direction. "Can you remove your sunglasses, son?" Him calling me son would've pissed me off had he not been at least thirty years my senior, his full head of dark-brown hair screaming the opposite. That, and he was Walter fucking Dessoye, after all.

Not a word left my lips as I removed the shades before placing them on top of the table. I waited for him to make some sort of remark about my different-colored eyes, because everyone always did, but instead, he gave me a slight nod before opening his mouth to speak. Before he could say anything, however, a flurry of movements distracted him, and he rose from his chair before I realized what was going on.

"I thought maybe you were going to stand your ol' man up again." The airiness to his tone momentarily distracted me from a flutter of memories that came barreling into my overactive brain. With the mention of "ol' man," I remembered he had a daughter, possibly two. The one I definitely knew about was a diva socialite, at least that was what was always branded all over the tabloid news. Not that I intentionally sought out that type of information, but I'd catch it every now and again, whenever I flicked through the TV channels or logged onto the Internet.

I started to put two and two together, realizing why Owen hadn't readily offered up the details of the job assignment. He knew if he told me who we'd be protecting, I would've told him to shove the job up his ass.

"Are you ever going to stop throwing that in my face?" A blonde-haired woman approached, but before she made eye contact with me, I put my shades back on. The last thing I wanted to do was draw her attention. Besides, my heart picked up its pace, and a flush crept up my neck. Not because the woman hugging Walter was gorgeous, because she was, but because I was furious with my brother for putting me in this situation. I'd naïvely thought this job was routine. Low profile. How stupid of me.

Leaning back in my chair, restraining myself from kicking Owen under the table, I watched the interaction between Walter and his daughter. For the life of me I couldn't remember her name, but soon enough, I was sure we'd be introduced. He leaned in to kiss her cheek before holding her chair out for her. She adjusted her leopard-print jacket before accepting, dropping her huge purse on the chair beside her, and exhaling before finally looking at the two strangers at her father's table.

She looked bored, flicking her poker-straight hair over her shoulder. "Who are they?"

"That's why I asked you to lunch today. I thought it was the best time to introduce you to Owen and Ford Massey." He parted his lips to continue speaking, but his daughter's rudeness poured forth.

"Why?" Not a smile. Not a flicker of interest. Nothing but a look of contempt shot our way.

"I've told you and your sister that I have some concerns, and until those concerns are dealt with, I've hired someone to watch over the both of you. It's just for a short time." Her brows knitted seconds before her eyes widened, whipping her head to the side to stare dumbfounded at her father.

"You want us to deal with bodyguards?" Her question was laced with disdain, as if the mere notion of having to "deal" with someone watching over her was just beyond the scope of what was appropriate. "That's why you wanted to have lunch. Out in public. So I wouldn't make a scene." She crossed her arms over her chest, mirroring the actions of a petulant child. "Isn't it?" She raised her voice a level with the reiteration.

"Calm down, Cara." *That's right. Her name is Cara.* Walter attempted to place his hand on her shoulder, but she moved away before he made contact. "It's for your own safety. I don't know what I'd do if anything ever happened to you or Emily."

"What about Mom? Did you hire someone to hover over her every move?" Her quick temper tantrum had me shaking my head, my annoyance with the way she treated her father pissing me off. Here he was trying to protect his family, and she reacted like this? It appeared as if her reputation had been well deserved.

"I've made arrangements so that your mother doesn't go anywhere without me." When he saw she was going to make another argument, he interrupted. "I can't watch over all three of you. I wish I could. Hell, I wish I could lock you up so that I know you'll be safe, but I can't push it that far." Something told me he would do just that if permitted. "This is happening, honey. You may as well get on board and not make this any harder than it has to be." His tone switched from apologetic to stern, the straightening of Cara's posture indicative of someone who knew she'd lost the fight.

"Fine. But they better not get in my way." She stood abruptly, grabbed her purse and hurried away from the table without another word.

"Please excuse me for one moment," Walter said before rushing after his daughter. If I peered to my left, I could see the two of them out on the sidewalk, her arms flying all around her while he stood firm. I couldn't help but take her in, appreciative of the way her fitted black dress hugged her curves, but I quickly chastised myself for my thoughts.

Her father looked like he was having a hell of a time dealing with her, shaking his head in response to whatever she said. A moment later, she threw her hands in the air, turned on her heel and walked away.

"Let's go," I growled, rising from my seat and heading toward the exit. Owen was right behind me, but before I could yell at him, I approached Walter, feeling bad for the guy that he had to deal with such an ungrateful daughter. Didn't she know how lucky she was to have someone who cared about her enough to go to any lengths to make sure she was safe?

"I'm sorry about all that." He looked embarrassed.

"Don't worry about it," Owen spoke up. "It's understandable she'd be upset." My brother tried to justify her behavior, which the guy seemed to appreciate.

"Well, I suppose you now know what the job is." His statement was directed toward me. I nodded. "So, how does this work? Do you decide who watches who, or do you take turns?"

"To make it easier, we'll assign ourselves to each of your daughters." I held my breath while Owen continued to talk. "That way we know who we're responsible for at all times."

"Can I make a request, then?"

"Sure."

My lungs seized up because I had an odd feeling I wasn't going to like what he was going to say.

"Ford." *Here it fucking comes.* "Can you be the one to watch over Cara?"

My pent-up breath rushed from my mouth in one quick exhale. I silently counted to three before I answered. "Sure."

"And I'm assuming you have weapons."

"Of course," Owen responded, flicking his gaze to me briefly when I remained silent.

"Good. Now that that's settled, come by the house tomorrow around noon, and I'll show you both where you'll be staying." He looked at Owen when he said, "I'll email you the address." As we shook hands and Walter walked away, my brain tried to register his parting words. For some reason, my comprehension was delayed, but then it hit me full force that not only was I going to be assigned to a pain-in-the-ass diva, but we apparently were also going to be living on site and for God knew how fucking long.

Owen refused to look at me after the guy left, a telltale sign he knew I'd be pissed off. While we waited for the valet to bring his car around, I hauled off and punched him on the arm. Hard.

"What the hell!" He rubbed at the affected area.

"I'm going to kill you." The menace in my voice was enough to make him take a step to the side.

CHAPTER
FOUR

Cara

"But I don't understand why I have to have someone watching every move I make, Mom. It's not fair," I grumbled, slapping the top of the kitchen island in frustration. I'd had less than twenty-four hours to come to grips with what my father wanted. I knew he had his rules, especially when we were growing up, enforcing curfews and spending budgets, etc., but nothing so invasive as to what he shoved down my throat this time. I was going to be twenty-five years old in three weeks, far too old to have to listen to my *daddy* like some teenager.

"It's for your own safety, sweetheart." My mom rounded the island and came to stand next to me, pulling me close. With her hands on my shoulders, she smiled, erasing some of my rising temper. "Don't fight your dad on this one, Cara. He loves you. We both do. And until he finds out exactly what's going on, we want you and your sister to be safe. I don't know what I'd do if anything ever happened to you." Tears filled her eyes, her chin beginning to quiver. "Please just go along with this." One lone tear escaped and traveled down her cheek. "Please."

There had been three previous threats against my family over the years, but nothing ever came of them. For a short time, after each one, Emily and I had to adhere to a strict curfew until my dad was satisfied we were no longer in harm's way. All of our after-school activities were closely monitored, and we weren't allowed to go anywhere without one of my parents, even to our friends' houses. Looking back, they were doing what they thought was best in order to protect us, but I'd felt trapped, a circumstance I never wanted to experience again.

I hated seeing my mother upset, so with gritted teeth and a steely posture, I gave in. "Fine." Gone was the glassiness in my mom's eyes, the water receding as soon as I uttered my compliance. *Oh, she's good. Guilt will get me every time.*

She pulled me into a hug. "Thank you, honey. You've made me so happy knowing I can rest easy that someone will be watching out for you. That you'll be sa—"

I cut her off, her flair for the dramatic outweighing my own. "Okay, I get it. You win." She gave me a wink before releasing me.

The front door to the house I shared with my sister opened and closed, heavy footsteps sounding down the hallway telling me my father was here. And sure enough, he appeared in the doorway of the kitchen seconds later, looking from me to my mother and back again.

"Everything okay?"

"Yes. She's agreed to the security detail." She practically sang her answer to my dad, walking up to him and throwing her arms around his neck, pecking his lips before whispering something in his ear. She was probably telling him how she mom-guilted me into agreeing to have strangers surround me all day long. The thought I wouldn't have a private moment to myself irked me, riling up the inner temper tantrum I was going to throw if I didn't get a hold of myself.

I'd been told I was a diva, a bitch, a spoiled brat, and everything else you could think of. None of those names came from my parents, but I saw the disapproving looks they threw my way from time to time, especially after seeing a picture or a headline in one of the many gossip magazines or plastered on the internet sites. I stopped trying to explain my actions. Most times those occurrences were blown way out of proportion just so they could make a sale. I wasn't claiming I was innocent, but I wasn't as bad as I was portrayed to be either. Most times, at least. Emily, on the other hand, was painted as the good sister slash daughter, her many volunteer projects evident she had her head on straight, unlike her twin sister.

"Have you told Emily about this?" I repeatedly tried to get in touch with her last night, but I couldn't reach her. I leaned my hip against the edge of the counter and drummed my fingers on top of the marble. "Or are you going to surprise her with it like you did me?" I couldn't keep the bitterness from my tone, no matter how much I tried. Okay, to be fair, I hadn't given it my best effort.

"I just called her," my dad responded. "She's on her way home now." As the last word left his mouth, the doorbell rang, which was odd since I wasn't expecting anyone, and Emily wouldn't ring the bell to her own place. My dad looked at me with a mixed expression of suspicion and worry before disappearing to answer the door. I heard him speaking to a man, then another voice sounded, and I had a sneaking suspicion the two men from the restaurant yesterday were standing just outside. My suspicions were confirmed when I saw two guys following my dad back into the kitchen, my mom stepping in front of me to greet our *guests*.

I snatched my phone from my purse and texted my sister.

Me: where are you?

Emily: I'm on my way home. Why? Where are you?

Me: I'm here with Mom and Dad. Hurry up.

Emily: Is everything ok?

Me: Just get here.

I tossed my phone back inside my purse, my attention now on the looming forms of our new bodyguards. They both had short cuts, but the taller of the two's hair was a darker shade of brown. His lips were full, his bottom plumper than the top and he sported a fresh scruff, whereas the other guy was clean-shaven.

"Honey, these are the men I hired to watch Cara and Emily. Owen and Ford Massey." He turned toward the men. "This is my wife, Diana."

They all exchanged pleasantries, Owen stepping closer to my father in order to continue talking. I was curious as to what he was saying but not enough to interrupt and find out. I busied myself with looking through the fridge, even though I was only doing it to waste time. While I was turned away from the others, I had an uneasy feeling someone was staring at me. I should get used to that awareness since I was going to have my own shadow for a while. Regardless, something made me search out the cause for the goose bumps that had broken out all over my skin. When my eyes landed on Ford, who stood a few feet from the others, I drew in a breath. I couldn't tell if he was staring at me because of those damn shades, but my skin prickled with a touch of unease. I wasn't creeped out, per se, but a strange feeling rolled through me nonetheless.

A car door slammed out front, then thirty seconds later I heard my sister walk into the foyer, calling out to me as soon as the door closed.

Owen had been blocking the entryway to the kitchen, moving to the side when Emily appeared, her eyes flitting from him to Ford to me then to our parents. She smiled nervously before uttering her hellos.

"Emily, there is something I want to talk to you about," my dad started. He pointed to one of the bar stools. "Have a seat."

"You better stand for this one," I warned, rolling my eyes before I could stop myself.

"Okay…." She looked how I felt. Uneasy. Again, she peered at Owen and Ford before glancing back to our dad. At least Owen gave her a smile. Ford, on the other hand, appeared standoffish and broody, two qualities which admittedly would've normally intrigued me, but my inner voice told me to steer clear of him. As much as I could, given he'd apparently be invading our personal space from here on out.

"I'm not going to go into too much detail, but I've received a threat, and until I find out who is behind it, I've hired these men to watch over you and Cara." My dad glanced at me quickly before returning his attention to Emily.

"What kind of threat?" she asked.

My dad reached out and rubbed her arm. "Don't worry about that."

"Well, if they threatened to torture and kill us, I think we have a right to know," she suddenly blurted, lowering her voice once she saw my eyes widen. Emily was normally calm and reserved, even in sticky situations. So, to say I was surprised by her response was an understatement.

My dad's expression morphed from shock to irritation to worry, all within the span of several seconds. "It's nothing like that, but it was enough to make me want to do something extra to ensure your safety." He turned toward the two men behind him. "Speaking of. Owen will be assigned to Emily and Ford will be watching over Cara."

My sister peeked over at who seemed to be the friendlier of the two while I gawked at Ford. The words barreled out of my mouth before my brain could filter them, to figure out a different way to say what I was about to.

"I don't want him," I scoffed, my hands finding their place on my waist in a show of defiance. "I'll take Owen."

"No. I've already made my decision."

"But I. Don't. Want. Him," I repeated, glaring at my dad in hopes he'd give in just so he wouldn't have to listen to me complain. My tactics normally worked, and I prayed this time was no different.

Ford took a step closer and opened his mouth, but Owen seized his arm and stepped in front of him. He whispered something to him before stepping away. Ford's jaw clenched as well as his hands, but every second our stare down lasted only heightened my nerves. I swore I saw him smirk, but I couldn't be sure.

"It's done, Cara. Get on board."

"I don't understand what makes this threat any different than the ones before. Nothing ever happened with those. So why are you going to this extreme?"

"Well, for starters, you two are older and more in the public eye. Which means whoever is making the threat has a better chance of following through on it." My dad's poignant stare told me he wouldn't budge. When he put his mind to something, he was stubborn, a trait of his I inherited.

While I continued to physically show my displeasure with sighing and head shakes, my sister was calm—stunned, but calm, sneaking a peek at Owen every now and then, when she thought

I wasn't paying attention. "There's something else." *What other demand was he going to lay on us?* "I want your car keys."

"Whose?" I asked, looking at Emily as if she had the answer.

"Both of yours."

"Why?" my sister asked, sounding genuinely confused, as was I.

"Because they'll be accompanying you two wherever you go. So to eliminate the possibility that you'll take off without them, I'm giving them your keys." My dad squared his shoulders and held out his hand, patiently waiting until both of us handed over our fobs. Emily did so quietly, but I was the opposite.

"I don't want anyone driving my Porsche except me." I clutched the device in my hand.

"I'm sure he's a fine driver, honey. Nothing is going to happen to your vehicle." My dad's hand was still stretched toward me, patiently waiting for me to concede. I did so with an exaggerated squint of my eyes.

"Oh, there's one more thing." He walked through the kitchen and opened the French doors which led to the patio. "These men will be staying in the guest house until further notice."

CHAPTER
FIVE

Ford

A barrage of expletives swirled in the air behind me as Walter escorted us to the guest house, where apparently Owen and I would be staying until the job was over. I'd read my brother the riot act the entire way home yesterday, even telling him I wasn't going to accept the job, but he begged me to stay on. He'd pleaded with me, something he rarely did, explaining that Walter Dessoye would be a huge client for us, and his referral would go a long way for our security company. He could've had one of the other guys help him out, but he insisted it was me he needed.

I'd finally relented but warned him that if he ever pulled this shady shit again, he'd regret it. I kicked him out of my house while he sported the biggest grin of appreciation.

"And this is where you'll be staying," Walter announced, as we passed the biggest inground swimming pool I'd ever seen. Once through the sliding glass door entryway, he gave us a quick tour of the place. It was close to one-hundred feet away from the main house, the space bigger than my current home, with every amenity I could imagine.

It boasted a spacious living room, white walls and furniture, bone-colored tile covering the entire floor.

The kitchen was also white. White cabinets. White marble

countertops. White speckled, marble tile. The stainless-steel appliances were the only things to break up the color, or lack thereof, depending on how one described it.

Various art hung on the wall, but I couldn't care less about the décor, still wrapping my head around the fact I'd have to stay on the premises until the job ended.

There were windows everywhere, letting in ample amount of light, something I wasn't used to seeing since I always had my curtains drawn. I preferred the dark, but it looked like I didn't have much of a choice in this place.

Three bedrooms and two full baths completed the guest house, but for the life of me, I couldn't understand why this place existed at all. With the size of the main house, which was beyond the scope of what ten people would require, let alone two twentysomething-year-old women, who the hell needed this place, too? But I supposed, if you had the money... why not?

We came to a stop back in the living room after the tour, Walter taking a seat on the couch and encouraging us to do the same.

"Do you have any questions?" He reclined against the sofa. His wife, Diana, had just walked in, quickly followed by their two daughters.

From my research online the prior night, I'd discovered the women were not only sisters, they were fraternal twins. However, they seemed to be polar opposites. Emily was involved with multiple charities, spending most of her time helping others—from animals to the elderly to the homeless. Cara, however, was a completely different story, one painted with alcohol, partying, and everything else that went along with that scene. The stereotypical rich girl who didn't have anything better to do than spend her old man's money. And of course, I'd been the one allocated to watch over her.

I took a seat opposite him and leaned forward, my forearms resting on the tops of my thighs. "Does the main house have cameras?" I saw my brother, who sat to my left, nod after my question.

"There is one in the front of the house, on the porch. One near the French doors coming from the house to the patio, and... I think that's it." I was surprised with all their wealth that they weren't better prepared, for safety's sake. They lived in a gated community, but in case someone got past the security guard posted near the entrance, there was no protection once they reached the house.

"So, there are no cameras inside the house?" My surprise prompted Cara to throw in her unwanted two cents.

"Of course not. And there won't be any, either." She refused to sit with the rest of us, not even next to Emily who'd chosen to sit next to her mother.

I declined to give her my attention, instead focusing solely on Walter. The man calling the shots.

"I want cameras in all rooms of the house, except for the bathrooms. Then everything will be linked up to mine and Owen's phones so we can monitor the activity around the clock, if necessary."

"That *won't* be necessary," Cara interrupted once more.

Again, I ignored her, but I could feel the heat of her stare.

"I have a friend who specializes in this type of security. We could have it all set up tomorrow," Owen offered. "All I need is your approval."

"Dad!" Cara was still insisting he listen to her, but thankfully the man forged ahead and allowed us to do what he'd hired us to: keep his family safe, no matter how much one of them refused.

"Go ahead," Walter agreed. "You have my approval. Whatever you need." He stood, reached for his wife's hand and helped her to her feet. "Ford. Owen. Come with us. I want to have a few words with you before you settle in."

We followed them outside until we reached the corner of the patio, disappearing inside yet another building, this one smaller. The pool house.

Walter released his wife's hand and took a step toward my brother and me. "Listen, I don't want there to be any misunderstanding between us. I've hired you to watch over our daughters. My little girls," he emphasized with a raised brow. "That means you keep your distance but be close enough to jump in if anything happens." He advanced closer. "Do you understand me? Are you reading between the lines, fellas?" Gone was the laidback, casual man from yesterday's meeting. Hell, even from moments ago. Standing before us was a father warning two men to keep their hands to themselves, to do the job they were hired for and nothing more. If possible, I had even more respect for the man because he held nothing back.

"Loud and clear," Owen and I responded simultaneously.

He nodded before turning around and walking out, Diana shaking her head and flashing us a small smile before she followed him.

The next day was lost to a flurry of activity. Owen contacted our buddy Seth and managed to convince him to work on a Sunday, something he normally didn't do. And since he was used to setting up high-tech systems for the rich and famous, this job was right up his alley.

It took all day to complete, but the result was peace of mind, not only for Walter and Diana but for Owen and me. The women, not so much, although Emily adapted quickly, realizing her father was only doing what he felt he should in order to keep them safe. The other one, though, gave resistance at every turn, and I couldn't envision her yielding to any of the intrusive behavior anytime soon.

Motion detecting cameras were placed in every room of the house, except for the bathrooms as I'd instructed. Additional ones were installed by the front door as well as by the back. And there was one on each end of the patio. We even had them installed by the entrance to the guest house, as well as inside, again skipping the bathrooms. We couldn't be too careful. After the threat was found and eliminated, the family could remove the ones they wanted or keep everything in place.

There was an alarm system already in place inside the main house, but neither one of the women used it. They rarely armed it when they left or while they were inside, proving how easy they would be to get to if someone had half a mind to do so.

Seth replaced their existing system, going over in detail how to use it. He ensured it was easy to understand and left it up to Owen and me to make sure they enabled it. All the damn time. All four of us had the code. Five, if you counted Seth, but we trusted him implicitly.

We'd retrieved the essentials from our places and set up in the guest house. The drive back was at least three and a half hours, depending on traffic, so we grabbed as much as we could.

This was to be our new home for the foreseeable future. I could only hope the culprit would be found soon, ending our employ but at the same time, I was grateful for the money we'd receive for the job. I'd left the running of the business to Owen, a selfish thing to do I realized, but I was in no shape to watch over others when I could barely function after what happened. He'd kept the business afloat, but it was time I stepped up and did my part, even though my instincts told me to run far away.

Sunday blended into Monday, and since we both took our jobs seriously, we made the first of three rounds inside the main house, checking every room thoroughly, Owen taking the downstairs while I ventured up to the second floor. For the upcoming nights, we were assured the security guard on duty would walk the premises at least three times, no doubt being paid extra by Walter.

Closing the door to one of the spare bedrooms, I cursed under my breath because the next room I had to check was Cara's, and based on our prior encounters, she wasn't a fan of mine. I knocked on the door, but there was no answer. It was early, close to eight in the morning, so I assumed she was still sleeping and didn't hear me, and because I couldn't leave without checking things out, I rapped against the door once more. Still nothing. Turning the handle, I pushed it open until I cleared enough space for me to enter, quickly scanning the area for any unwanted guests. All clear.

My eyes found Cara's bed empty, but before I could wonder where she was, knowing she hadn't left the premises because I would've known, the bathroom door flung open, a burst of steam billowing in. I tried to announce my presence, but she caught me standing there before I could say anything.

"What are you doing in here?" she shouted, clutching her towel, her wet strands sticking to the tops of her shoulders. I should've felt bad for scaring her, but all I could do was take in the sight of her. With a face free of makeup and water droplets glistening on her skin, she looked innocent, and I'd forgotten for a moment that her personality belied the illusion which bombarded me.

"I'm doing my rounds." I averted my eyes so as not to appear as some sort of creeper.

"You're what?" She stood taller and dropped her arms to her sides, watching me like a hawk.

I moved farther into the room. "Making my rounds." The frown on her face caused me to elaborate. "We have to check every space in this house three times a day." I walked toward the walk-in closet. Opening the door, I stepped inside, shaking my head at the sheer amount of shit she had in there. So many clothes, piles heaped in the corners because there wasn't enough space. To be clear, any normal person would've only needed half the space with what they owned, but as I suspected, Cara had gone overboard. From the little I knew of the woman, I guessed overindulgence in many areas was common for her.

"But this is my bedroom. Don't you think I'd know if someone was in here with me? If I was in danger?" Her voice trailed off as I emerged from her closet, kicking a pair of shoes out of the way before I tripped over them. "Hey, those heels cost more than you probably make in a month."

"I don't doubt it," I mumbled, not in the mood for her attitude so early in the day. I approached her bed and crouched down, peering underneath.

"Hello?"

I didn't answer, continuing about my business, thankful I was almost finished.

She clapped her hands. "What the hell? Helloooo?" I swore if I continued to ignore her, she'd probably stomp her foot. I walked past her, and because she stood so close to the bathroom, my next venture, my shoulder brushed hers as I passed. "Where are you going? I just came out of there."

"Just making sure." A quick check and I was finished, heading back out and across the room.

"Hey." I kept on walking. "Ford!" I stopped and turned my head slightly to the right, refusing to give her my full attention. Several seconds of uneasy silence passed. "Are you ever going to take off your sunglasses?" Her question surprised me, but what was even more shocking was the tone she used. It seemed, dare I say... sincere and not at all bitchy.

I never answered, instead walking into the hall and toward the top of the steps. She mumbled something under her breath behind me and slammed her door.

It just so happened that during the second time we checked the house, Owen and I switching floors, Cara was planted on the sofa as I passed through. I stopped in front of the TV to check the cameras from my phone, completely engrossed with confirming they were working properly. What I didn't realize was that she had been watching a show and she wasted no time in telling me what she thought. Any normal person would've politely asked me to move, but not her.

"I can't see through you," she barked. "I can't believe I have to put up with you until God knows when. This is so unfair." I heard every fucking word, even though she griped to herself. I wanted to shout that dealing with her spoiled and bitchy ass wasn't my idea of time well spent, either, but I kept my mouth shut.

Once satisfied everything was in order, I waltzed into the kitchen, stumbling on Owen and Emily. They'd been talking about something but stopped as soon as they saw me, Owen giving me a small smile before he checked the mudroom. He reentered twenty seconds later.

"You good?" My question to my brother was answered with a nod. I returned the head jerk and walked back into the living room, being sure not to stand in front of the TV again. "Are you planning on going anywhere in the next hour?" I asked Cara, my eyes on her, watching, waiting for a response.

She never looked at me. "No."

I rolled my eyes when I passed my brother. Since I couldn't abandon my post and go for a walk, leaving the women without added protection, I chose to take a swim.

Quickly changing, I strolled to the other side of the pool and dove in the deep end, but I hadn't finished a full lap before I heard her voice.

"I changed my mind. I need to go shopping."

I should've just released the air in my lungs and sank to the bottom of the pool. It would've been a better fate than having to deal with that woman for one more second.

CHAPTER
SIX

Cara

I didn't realize Ford was in the pool until I walked out onto the patio, hearing the splash and drawing my attention toward the deep end. I watched as his arms sliced through the water then disappeared underneath, only to resurface seconds later. From the little that I saw, the man had amazing arms, but because I didn't want to give him the satisfaction of staring, I looked away, only speaking when I knew he'd hear me.

"I changed my mind. I want to go shopping." I never waited for his response before walking back to the house. Already showered for the day, I dressed, threw on some makeup and swept my hair up into a strategically styled top bun. Twenty minutes later and I stepped outside, covering my eyes with a big pair of shades. Ford was dressed and ready, leaning against the bumper as I brushed past him and reached for the driver's door handle, but I was halted with a growl.

"Not gonna happen," he said, stepping up next to me, my keys in his hand.

"What? So, you're my driver now, too?" I smirked when the muscles of his jaw tightened.

"I'm not your driver in the conventional sense."

I retreated and stood by the back door. He looked in my

direction, although I couldn't tell if he was looking at me. *Damn shades.*

"What?" he asked, tilting his head to the side.

"Aren't you going to open the door for me?" I over batted my eyelashes.

He ignored me and disappeared inside, and it was then I had a decision to make. I could sit up front with him or ride in the back, keeping a safe distance between us. It didn't take me long to make a choice.

Safe distance.

Heading to Main Street where some of the cutest shops were located, I refrained from asking many questions. There was a good chance he'd ignore me. While I was curious about Ford Massey, I didn't want to appear as such, so I kept my mouth shut and pulled out my phone. I scrolled through social media, and when I became bored with that, I typed out a few quick texts to some friends.

Ten minutes into the ride, however, there was a pressing question I just had to ask. "What happens if we shut our phones off and decide to go somewhere without either of you?" A simple enough inquiry, so why did my words cause his shoulders to tense?

My dad gave them the authorization to put trackers on our phones so they could monitor our whereabouts at all times, even though the plan was for us to constantly be connected at the hip.

"We can track you even if your phones are off." Curt and poignant response, and one that pissed me off. Of course, I thought about ditching them at some point. Emily and I had plans for flying out to California for our birthday in a few weeks and hitting up a few clubs. And having two men, who didn't quite blend in with our group of friends, shadow us, wasn't my idea of a good time. Besides, there were some things I partook in that I didn't want getting back to my parents. I was grown, and I could do what I wanted. I didn't need someone snitching on me.

"How is that even possible?"

"There's a way."

"What if we decide to call Uber?"

"We'd know."

"How?" Silence. "How would you know?"

A loud sigh escaped his lips, and I could only imagine what he was thinking. "We have your calls monitored."

"So, you can listen in on our conversations?" A flush rushed through me at the reminder we had absolutely no privacy whatsoever.

"Your calls are monitored," he repeated, not directly answering the question.

As I opened my mouth to argue, knowing damn well I wouldn't get anywhere with him, we arrived at our destination. I directed him to park outside a nearby shop I wanted to visit, and once he'd stopped, I jumped out and rushed toward the store, not waiting on Ford to catch up.

I was already rooting through some of their clothing when he walked up behind me, standing a little too close for my liking.

"You need to wait for me." His warm breath hit my cheek, and a shiver shot through me. I couldn't decipher if it was because he'd been invading my personal space or because of something else.

"That wasn't me trying to lose you. Trust me, you'll know when that happens." I carried on as if there wasn't a huge man looming over me, seemingly watching every freaking move I made. There were only two other customers present, and the one clerk who was busy behind the counter sorting out silk scarves.

I swore I heard Ford grunt then complain about something under his breath, but I kept on browsing, turning to catch a sneak peek of him every so often.

With multiple pieces of clothing flung over the crook of my arm, I lost myself in the thrill of the hunt, trying to focus on what I wanted to purchase for my upcoming trip and not on the man in the sunglasses, hanging out toward the front of the store.

"Can I help you find anything, Miss Dessoye?" Sometimes it was an advantage when people recognized me.

"Nothing in particular. Just browsing," I answered. I stretched my arms toward her. "But you can start me a room."

"Of course." She smiled and took the articles of clothing before walking toward the back where the dressing rooms were located.

When I'd finally made my way through most of the racks, selecting a few more pieces, I glanced over my shoulder only to find Ford still standing in the same place, arms crossed, and his head held high, face void of expression.

I said nothing as I disappeared in the dressing room the clerk had started for me, figuring he'd be close behind since he wouldn't be able to see me from the front door. Heavy footsteps sounded against the dark hardwood floor, closing in on me as I escaped behind the red curtain.

"How long are you going to be?"

"As long as it takes." Pulling my dress over my head, I hung it on the hook before I tried on my first choice. A black, sequined silk dress from an up-and-coming designer, Victoria Altosh. With a deep V-cut in front and a hemline just above my knee, I'd wear a pair of my red-bottom heels and be dressed to kill. A few accessories and I'd be ready to hit the town. I hung it on an empty hook, my "must purchase" pile. The next several items, two dresses, a silk blouse, and a mini skirt, I tried didn't quite flatter me the way I thought they would, but the fourth item, a blood-red dress hugged my body in all the right places. It was another one of Altosh's designs, a designer who was quickly becoming a favorite of mine.

"Hey," I called out, unzipping then removing the red dress. I'd seen a pair of dark skinnies and a cute graphic tank, that said *Perfection*, on a rack just outside the dressing room, but I needed someone to hand them to me, so I didn't have to get dressed just to retrieve them. "Helloooooo?" I enunciated the word, my frustration clipped on the last syllable.

"She's busy," a gruff voice answered, and I had no doubt Ford was most likely rolling his eyes, not only from boredom but from impatience.

Clutching the curtain, I opened it slightly. I found Ford standing guard, leaning against the wall. Dressed all in black, including those damn shades, he looked regal, but his entire demeanor screamed don't-come-near-me.

"Hand me those jeans and that tank top." I snapped my fingers and pointed toward the items, and I thought for a split second he'd help me out. But my hope was dashed when he stared straight ahead. "Well?" I shifted my feet and opened the curtain another inch. He still didn't make a move. "What? You're gonna completely ignore me now?"

"Are you almost done?" He finally spoke.

"No, I'm not. I need to try on those two things,"—I pointed again toward the articles of clothing—"so until they're in my hand, I'm not going anywhere." Several seconds passed, and he refused to move. "Why can't you just hand me what I want?" There wasn't so much as a flinch of a movement to indicate he'd help me out, continuing to remain quiet as well. I swore his silence irritated me more than any words he could've spoken.

A rush of heat swirled through me and all the words forming in my brain became strangled in my throat, so many things I wished to say died before my breath ever gave them life. On a huff, I flung open the curtain, narrowed my eyes at him and snatched the items I wanted from the nearby rack. In my anger, any kind of modesty I possessed, which wasn't much, fell away. I had my bra and panties on, so it wasn't like I was naked, but I was grateful the dressing rooms were located in a more secluded section of the shop, away from prying eyes, with the exception of Ford, of course.

Once back inside, I closed the curtain, wishing it was a door instead so I could slam it.

"Do you ignore all your clients like this? Or is it just me?" I pulled up the jeans, turned around to check out how they made my ass look, and smiled, my expression falling when I remembered I was in the middle of my rant. "Are you in such high demand that it wouldn't matter if my father fired you?" I pulled the *Perfection* tank over my head, and once I deemed it, well, perfect, I removed it, snagging my dress from the hook and quickly getting dressed. "That mysterious and broody image you have is just annoying," I spat, continuing to ramble.

Flinging open the curtain, I stepped from the dressing room and almost smacked right into him. His closeness rattled me, but I refused to give my reaction a second thought, chalking it up to being angry. I brushed past him. "And what's with the damn shades, Ford?" I never allowed him to answer, deep down knowing he wouldn't, before finding the clerk so I could pay for what I'd selected.

And I was right. Ford never said a word, the drive back home silent between us.

CHAPTER
SEVEN

Ford

Count to ten. Shit! Count to a hundred. Do what you have to in order to calm down. I reminded myself I was a professional and I'd dealt with tough clients before. *I can do this. Just continue to ignore her.* The tension swirling around inside the vehicle was thick enough to choke most people. Luckily, I wasn't like most, although I barely held on to my restraint. What I wanted to do was drag her out of that fucking dressing room, clothed or not, through the uppity store, and throw her into the back seat. Hell, if I had duct tape, I would've used it on her. Her mouth... my God... her mouth. And let's not forget about her attitude.

I blew out a breath before taking another big inhale, the muscles of my jaw sore from frustration. As I was about to entertain more internal ramblings, thoughts pinging from one to the other, most of them not making any sense, my phone rang. A ringtone indicating my brother was on the other end.

"What's up?"

"Where are you?"

"On our way back to the house. Why?" My heart had started to slow to its normal beat, only to pick back up again from Owen's short pants of air hitting my ear through the cell.

"Walter received another note. He's on his way over, so get

here as soon as you can." Owen never waited for me to confirm before he hung up.

Due to heavier traffic than when we ventured out earlier, it took me closer to a half hour to get back to the house, my brother rushing outside to meet me as soon as I threw the vehicle in park.

"What the hell took you so long?" He barely waited for me to exit the driver side before he tossed another question at me. "What were you two doing all this time?" I didn't appreciate his tone. Not one bit. As if Cara and I had been doing something we shouldn't have. Or maybe I read too much into the question. My irritation at wasting a large part of the day babysitting her while she needlessly shopped for clothing she didn't need, more than annoyed me. Then to have to deal with her uppity ass on top of it put me in an overall sour mood. Owen was experiencing the aftermath of said mood.

I pushed past him, walking quickly toward the main house, my brother hot on my heels. He started to speak again, but I cut him off, my nerves frazzled enough for today.

"If you ask me one more goddamn question, you're gonna regret it." I didn't mean to sound so harsh, but, like I said… sour.

In my rush to get away from Owen, I hadn't even bothered to check whether Cara had exited the vehicle. I got my answer when she brushed past me, the bags she carried hitting my side as she hurried on by. She mumbled something under her breath, but I hadn't been close enough to hear, nor did I care.

"What did the note say?" I asked when Cara had disappeared inside.

"I don't know. He just said to meet him here." Moments later, we walked into the living room where Walter and Diana were seated on the couch with Emily. Cara was nowhere to be seen.

Walter stood and walked toward me, pulling me into another room and away from everyone else in earshot. "Did something happen with you and Cara?" His question wasn't veiled, his angry tone mixed with a touch of confusion.

"No."

"She didn't seem so happy when she walked in here," he accused, the narrowing of his brows telling me he didn't believe me.

"To be honest, sir, your daughter seems to always be in that mood. From my short experience in her presence, at least." He stared at me, and I was man enough to admit Walter Dessoye pulled off intimidation well. He could switch from laidback and friendly to sharp and overpowering in the blink of an eye, especially when he felt the need to be protective, like he was right then about his daughter. Silence was his tool, and the tactic was enough to make me uncomfortable, so much so, I needed to say something, anything, to break the stifling air forming between us. "I swear, nothing happened. I accompanied her while she went shopping, and then we came back here." He finally took a step back.

"Okay," he acquiesced with a slight nod. One word switched his manner back to friendly, although concerned, which was the reason we'd been called to meet. I followed him back into the living room to join everyone else, Cara still not present.

"Do you want me to go find Cara?" Emily rose from the couch and looked at her father.

"No. Don't bother her. Besides, I don't want to add to her foul mood." Walter and Diana sat on the sofa, Emily retaking her seat next to them. Diana placed her hand on her husband's arm in a show of support. I took the seat next to my brother on the couch opposite of the family, intent on hearing about the new note Walter had received. The reason my brother and I had been hired in the first place.

"Initially, I'd received a note that said, *'You destroyed my life, so I'm going to return the favor.'* And while I had no idea what that meant, or obviously who it was from, I had a gut feeling it wasn't a prank. Which is why I hired you both." He glanced at his wife before giving us his attention again. "I just got another one today."

"What does it say?" I asked, leaning forward.

"'Everything you love will vanish.'" After expelling the words, Walter leaned back against the sofa.

"Dad." Emily's voice was soft and unsure. My brother shifted to move, no doubt to comfort her, but I stopped him with a firm grip on his knee. He turned to look at me, but I kept my focus on Walter. Thankfully, he hadn't noticed because if he had, there was no doubt in my mind he would've raised a brow in question. After we were done with our meeting, I'd have to remind Owen not to get involved, more than making sure Emily was safe. Anything beyond that and he was playing with fire. Not only for him personally but for the state of our business.

Walter reached over his wife for Emily's hand, to which she readily accepted. They exchanged silent comfort before he vacated his seat.

Owen and I both stood, as well. "Can I see the note?" I extended my hand in preparation that he'd allow me to see it, which he did, pulling it from his back pocket. It was a half sheet of plain paper sealed in a plastic baggie. I'd been on enough jobs in my day to know that not all threatening letters were made with cut-out letters from magazines. Some were typed. Some were handwritten. I'd even seen some written in blood. This one was handwritten in sloppy penmanship. It appeared to be a man's handwriting, but it could have just as easily been done by a woman, using her non-dominant hand. Nothing should be ruled out at this point.

There was a mark in the top right-hand corner. It looked to be a part of a symbol or an emblem, or maybe it was nothing at all. I handed Walter the note back and waited for him to give us a directive.

"I have a team working on this, but since I'm not any closer to finding out who is sending these letters, I'm going to need you to be on your guard." He looked right at me. "I know Cara can be a handful, but don't let her rile you. Don't let her distract you, giving her an opening to do something foolish, like trying to take off on you."

"But you know I can find her if she does pull that shi—" I stopped myself. "If she tries to ditch me, I'll find her."

"I know you'll find her, but the time in between is what I'm concerned about."

"Don't worry about a thing, sir." I wanted to chastise him and tell him that maybe if he'd disciplined her better, she wouldn't be such a spoiled brat.

"Did you need anything else from us?" Owen took the lead that time, sensing my mood hadn't improved much since I'd gotten back.

Walter and Diana gave Emily a hug goodbye before heading to the front door. "If anything else comes up, I'll let you know."

Moments after they left, my phone alerted me that Cara's cell had been shut off. Would she dare try to sneak out just after her parents left? Or had she already left, exploiting the fact we were heavily engaged in conversation? A discussion which involved her personal well-being?

"Shit!" I headed toward the stairs, telling myself to check every room of the house before I flew off the deep end.

"What's wrong?" Owen followed, Emily not far behind him as we all rushed up the stairs. My heightened demeanor affected theirs, the closed mouths and tight lips telltale signs they were concerned.

"Cara's phone just turned off." I rushed down the hallway toward her bedroom, flinging open the door as soon as I wrapped my fingers around the handle. Empty. I crossed the threshold and took several steps until I reached the bathroom. That door was also closed, so I pushed it open with force, a hurried state to my search. Only this time, the room wasn't empty. Cara was sunk down in the large jetted tub, eyes closed, her hearing smothered by the white earbuds she wore. I hadn't meant to stand there motionless, but the sight of her disarmed me. Her blonde hair was darkened from the water, pushed back so I could see her entire face. She was stunning, especially when her mouth was closed. She looked... peaceful. Approachable. Odd sentiment, but there it was.

The calmness of the moment shattered when Owen and Emily came up behind me, shouting out their relief she'd been found. We'd all prematurely jumped to conclusions when I should've searched the house before thinking the worst. Their abrupt shouts alerted Cara she had visitors, and to say she wasn't happy about her intruders was an understatement.

She sank lower into the tub, the bubbles quickly evaporating. "What the hell are you doing in here?" she screeched, the sound making me stick my finger in my ear and wiggle it around. Damn, the woman had a high octave range. Owen and Emily had backed away out of view, but I continued to loom in the doorway, silent and stock still. "Get out!"

Instead of complying, I wanted to know why my phone was alerted that she turned hers off. "Where's your phone?"

"What?"

"Where is your phone? I got an alert you turned it off. I thought we already went over the rules. You're not to turn your phone off. Ever." I spotted the device on the edge of the vanity, and instead of giving Cara her privacy, I stepped into the space and swiped her cell. Nothing except a black screen. I tapped on the side buttons, but still, it didn't turn on.

"Ford!" I finally met her icy stare. "Get. The. Hell. Out of here." I turned to leave. "Close the door," she yelled, right before I heard a splash of water. From the corner of my eye, I saw her start to rise out of the tub but slammed the door before I saw any more of her.

"She's pissed," Emily confirmed.

"Is she always this volatile?" Owen scratched the back of his head, clearly uncomfortable.

"We did just walk in on her while she was in the tub. Naked." Emily restrained a small smile. "I'd be pissed if I had an audience, too." She glanced at Owen, then shifted her attention to the floor, a pink tinge coloring her cheeks.

Sensing my frustration with Cara's cell, Emily grabbed it from my hand and strode toward the nightstand, placing it on the charger without saying a word. "I told her it's time for a new one. This just doesn't hold a charge anymore."

It died. Of course.

I was confused as to why that possibility hadn't occurred to me before then. I'll chalk it up to... what? I had no idea, but before images of Cara in that damn tub started to filter in, I complained under my breath and left her bedroom. I needed a stiff shot. Only one, just to erase the sharp edges of my nerves.

CHAPTER EIGHT

Cara

Toweling off, all I kept thinking about was how Ford scared the hell out of me when I'd opened my eyes. My heart rammed against my chest right before fire burned in my veins. I'd gone from fright to anger in mere seconds, screaming at him for making me feel... everything.

I had no idea why he stood in the doorway to my bathroom, and I should've been creeped out by him watching me, even though his eyes were hidden, but I wasn't. A notion which disturbed me on a whole other level. I wanted more than anything to remain unaffected by him, but the man stirred up all sorts of conflicting emotions inside me.

If I wasn't thinking about the different ways to get under his skin just to get a reaction out of him, I was wondering if he thought about me, other than as a client. None of it made any sense because simply put, I didn't know him. I didn't know anything about him, except his first and last name and that he had a brother, Owen. And it wasn't as if he was forthcoming with any personal details. Although, I was sure I had something to do with that. Okay, I had a lot to do with that. I flat out threw a fit when I found out my dad hired someone to watch me, or out for me, as he would say. Then when he assigned Ford to me,

I spouted out that I wanted his brother instead. Then earlier, at the shop, I treated him as nothing more than hired help

Maybe I should be nicer to him, not be so salty every time he was around. It would certainly make it easier for when I did have to pull the old disappearing act when we went to California. Maybe if he thought he could trust me, he wouldn't be all up in my business as closely as he was now.

I ran a brush through my hair and threw on some yoga pants and my *Perfection* graphic T-shirt, dismissing all the varying thoughts swirling around inside my head and deciding that I needed to forget about Ford and see if Emily wanted to veg out and watch a movie. Normally, I'd get dressed up to hit the town, lose myself to a few drinks, and whatever other party favors were present, but that night I wanted something different. And no, it wasn't because there was a broody bastard nearby. A man who confused me just by sharing the same space with me.

"Get over yourself," I mumbled as I went in search of my sister. I checked her bedroom, then the first level, but I couldn't find her. Venturing outside to check the patio proved fruitless, as well. The only other place to look was in the guest house. Where *he* was.

Opening the door, I peered inside, but no one was present. Hmm… I should've just called her cell. I could've made this a whole lot easier, but it was too late now. My phone was charging and in the other house. May as well continue the search in here.

"Emily? Are you here?" I had no idea what she would've been doing in the guest house with our security detail, but since she wasn't in our house, and our vehicles were still out front, I wasn't left with many options. "Emily?" I repeated, venturing up the stairs and down the hallway toward the bedrooms. I called out for my sister two more times, but no one answered. There was only one more room to search, and as I turned the handle to open the door, an awareness prickled over me. But I ignored it, sure I was being ridiculous. I had no idea if anyone was inside that room, let alone which one of the men occupied it.

The space was empty, but I stepped inside anyway. Walking toward the window, I looked outside, and sure enough, both vehicles were in the driveway. I thought possibly I'd been mistaken, but there they were, staring me in the face. *Where the hell is Emily?* I needed to see my sister, suddenly feeling disturbingly alone.

"What the hell are you doing in here?" *I spoke too soon.* I jumped, startled by his voice even though I should've expected there was a chance I'd run into him. His gravelly tone sounded raspier than usual.

When I turned, I was surprised, not only by the fact that Ford stood in the middle of his room in nothing but a towel, but he wasn't wearing his sunglasses. I swore those damn things were glued to his face and seeing the absence of them had me taking a step closer without even realizing I'd moved.

I'd concocted numerous reasons why he shielded his eyes.

A nasty scar.

He was blind, even though that one didn't make sense seeing as how he drove.

One of his eyes drooped.

But none of those were the reason.

He hid them because… well, I didn't know why, other than he had two different-colored eyes. Eyes that were mesmerizing. Piercing. They were the first thing anyone would notice about him; the reason people would want to walk up to him and just stare into them.

I drew closer, but he backed away, shaking his head slightly, like he viewed me as some sort of threat.

"I asked you a question." His posture belied his tone. He sounded angry, yet his breathing was slow and steady. His shoulders lacked tension and his arms hung by his sides. "You trying to even the score?"

"I... uh...." I swallowed my words, momentarily forgetting how I ended up in his bedroom, of all places.

"You... uh... what?" His brow rose, his face devoid of emotion, making it difficult to read him. But something told me Ford Massey wasn't an easy man to read in any situation, that he kept his secrets closely guarded.

It was he who advanced on me that time, taking two long strides toward me, his eyebrow stuck in that damn sexy arch. My breathing picked up, his closeness unsettling me. I'd only been around the man a handful of times, but I had never experienced the mixture of unease and excitement I did right then.

His right hand twitched, and for a moment, I thought he was going to attempt to reach out and touch me, but nothing happened. Maybe I was only hoping he would make a move, or maybe I prayed he'd back up and give me some room.

Everything confused me.

My feelings.

My thoughts.

The way my heart slammed against my chest.

The overwhelming urge to stay yet flee.

I averted my attention and stared at my feet, but not for long because I refused to allow this man to intimidate me, and I had no doubt that was his intention.

I picked up my head and swore he'd come closer, even though he hadn't moved. From this angle, however, I could see the different shades of his eyes. The left was a beautiful shade of amber, flecks of gold sprinkled around the pupil. And the right was an amazing shade of blue. Not ice and not dark, but more of an ocean blue, a speck of brown close to the black of his eye.

"Has anyone ever told you how gorgeous your eyes are?" He didn't answer, the silence spurring me to blather on when it should have made me shut my mouth. I didn't fawn over men. They tripped over themselves to get *my* attention. "Of course they have. How stupid of me. I'm sure you get that compliment all the time from women. Although I'm sure you'd rattle quite a few men with those peepers." *Peepers? Why am I still talking?*

His brow finally relaxed, and I swore I saw the corner of his mouth curve upward, but only for a second. So fast, I could've imagined it. But I hadn't imagined him parting his lips, the tip of his tongue swiping over his full bottom one. And just when I thought he was going to say something, other than to ask me for the third time what I was doing in his room, Owen appeared out of nowhere, walking in on the odd exchange between us.

"Wait until I tell you what happ—" Owen stopped midstride when he saw the two of us standing so close, neither one of us speaking. It looked like we were engaged in something intimate, although not by choice.

Sure, I'd come into his room unannounced.

Sure, I didn't leave when he appeared in nothing but a towel.

Sure, he'd distracted me.

Sure, I'd babbled on about nonsense.

But the scene of us together looked like something it wasn't. Plain and simple.

"Do you want me to come back?" Owen asked. I turned to look at him, and his eyes pinged from Ford to me, then back again, and if I wasn't mistaken, his mouth began to turn up at the corners. I didn't want him to think something was going on, so I stood straighter and took a deep breath.

"You're not interrupting anything. Trust me," Ford grunted, taking me in from head to toe before turning his back on me and disappearing into his bathroom. He slammed the door behind him in what seemed like anger. Although, I had no idea what the hell he would be so upset over, other than me invading his personal space. I hadn't been rude to him during our short encounter. In fact, I'd paid him a compliment, something I now regretted because I'd given him the upper hand.

CHAPTER
NINE

Ford

Hours had passed since the incident in my room. Incident. Maybe debacle was a better choice of a word. Why had she been in my room? Had she been looking for me? Or had she wanted to go somewhere and needed me to take her? Either way, her presence had surprised me, although I'd tried my hardest not to react. I believed I succeeded.

Entering the kitchen in the main house, I stumbled on a scene, one which made me shake my head in disbelief.

Emily was pressed against the refrigerator, Owen trapping her in place with his hands pressed against the cold stainless steel on either side of her. She smiled at something he'd said, but her lips straightened when he leaned in, her eyes widening before slowly closing.

"Owen," I barked, the incredulity in my voice halting him from closing the deal. He mumbled something before pushing off the refrigerator, Emily averting her eyes from me as she passed by and left the room. Once we were alone, I let him have it. "Are you fucking stupid?" He opened his mouth to respond, but I halted him with a flick of my hand. "What are you thinking? Do you know what'll happen to you if Walter finds out you're fucking his daughter? Especially when he warned you to keep your hands to yourself? Warned us both?"

Owen stepped toward me with a fire in his eyes. "We're not sleeping together." He stopped talking. He looked like he wanted to say more, but then thought better of it, trapping his secrets behind his lips.

"Well, you're doing something inappropriate." I rounded the island, the space between us disappearing. "Don't play off what I saw as nothing."

"It's none of your business."

"That's where you're wrong, brother." I crossed my arms over my chest. "It *is* my business. You're the one who asked me to take this job with you, and now you're gonna fuck it up because what… she bats her eyes at you? She probably does that to everyone." From the little I knew about Emily, both personally, and what I'd read online, she didn't appear to be that type of person, but I needed to insinuate it to get a reaction from him. A reaction which would tell me everything, even if he didn't verbally affirm my suspicions.

"Don't talk about her like that." He mirrored my body language, defensive as could be.

"And you're gonna stand there and tell me nothing is going on?"

"Let it go," he warned, brushing past me on his way out of the kitchen.

Owen was a grown man, and if Walter found out something was going on between him and Emily, my brother would have to be the one to deal with the consequences, both personally and professionally.

The next couple of days passed without incident. Simple pleasantries occurred when I saw Emily and a curt nod from me was directed at Cara. Sometimes, she'd ignore me and turn her attention toward something else, and sometimes she'd purse her lips and stare at me. I had no idea what the woman was thinking, and I didn't possess enough emotional energy to try and figure it out. So when she decided to throw an impromptu pool party in the middle of the week, I should've been delighted she'd be occupied with her friends. But that wasn't the case. Because we had no idea who'd been sending the threats, we couldn't rule out anyone, including someone in her close circle. I tried to talk her out it, but she dismissed me with a flick of her wrist before walking away from me.

With thirty people in attendance, I had my work cut out for me. Standing next to the entrance to the guest house, with my sunglasses firmly in place, I not only had to focus on Cara but on her friends, as well. My eyes pinged from person to person and it didn't take long before the muscles in my body locked up with tension, a semblance of a headache starting to form.

There were more women in attendance than guys and while, as a red-blooded male, I should've delighted in all of the exposed skin, my attention stayed on Cara, the most scantily clad of them all. There was a difference between a bikini and whatever it was that she wore. She had a great body, and apparently, she wanted everyone to appreciate it.

Two vertical strips of red material shielded her nipples and nothing else, while a small piece of fabric covered her lower half. The straps connected to the material were clear so it looked like she'd somehow simply pasted the material over her private areas. And when she turned around, only the crack of her ass was covered. I'd never seen anything like it.

While some people chose to drink, others smoked, some doing both. When a pungent haze of pot assaulted my nose, I wanted nothing more than to intercede, but what the hell would I say? Everyone was grown. Besides, I doubted Cara would take kindly to me berating her friends.

At one point during the party, I had to use the bathroom. Owen had left with Emily earlier that morning, so as I hurried inside to relieve my bladder, I brought up the app on my phone so I could view everything that happened outside on the patio.

As I washed my hands afterward, my eyes still glued to my phone, I saw a guy walk through the back gate and approach Cara. Approach was the wrong word. He looked to be sneaking up behind her, his steps slow and steady. Cautious. I slammed the faucet lever down and rushed outside.

As I hurriedly approached, intent on tackling the fucker, Cara turned around and squealed, jumping into the guy's arms and planting a kiss on his mouth. My steps slowed but I continued to walk toward her, deciding enough was enough, and we needed to have a little chat.

Experiencing a beautiful summer day in the Hamptons was what most people could only dream of, but right then, I'd rather be anywhere else. I ignored the whispers as I passed by countless women. *Who is that?* Was the most common one, but I had no time to entertain any of them. One woman was my sole focus.

Cara chatted up her newest guest, oblivious to the fact I was striding up right behind her. One of her friends, who was close by, stumbled up next to her and touched her arm, jerking her chin toward me. Cara turned around, and as she did so, she almost fell over. Taking a quick peek at my watch, I saw it was only 1:15. Just barely after one and she was already tipsy. The joint in her hand didn't help.

"Oh, it's you," she scoffed, turning away from me and back toward her guests, but not before looking me up and down, focusing on my waist several seconds too long. In my haste to rush outside, I hadn't realized that bottom of my shirt was bunched and that I'd forgotten to button the top of my jeans.

The way she visually devoured me pissed me off. If I was even the tiniest bit interested, her blatant perusal would've caused me to act. To accept her invitation and prove the consequences of her visual assault were indeed something she didn't want. I realized my thoughts weren't logical and were all over the place, but as long as I didn't voice them, or give in to them, which wouldn't be a problem considering who the recipient was, I was fully within my right to think what I wanted.

With a quick flick of my eyes, I assessed the guy didn't appear as shady as he had on camera, but I couldn't be too careful.

Cara's hair was pulled into a high ponytail, so there was no doubt she heard me when I leaned in and spoke into her ear. She flinched when she felt my breath on her skin.

"I need to talk to you. Alone."

She ignored me, but the guy glanced over at me. The look I gave him was enough for him to make a beeline toward a group of women across the pool area. The aggression wafting off me affected everyone within a hundred-foot radius. I could feel their stares, heard their mumblings, but my only focus was the woman in front of me.

"What the hell?" she muttered, turning around to face me, but she did it so quickly she stumbled forward. I grabbed her arms to steady her, and instead of her shouting for me to release her, she looked up at me and licked her lips, taking one final drag of her joint. She flicked it to the side right before she blew the smoke in my face.

Her eyes traveled from my face down the length of me and back up again once she'd apparently had her full. Again. I could've come off with some smartass comment, asking her if she liked what she saw, but I knew that was a line I didn't want to cross. Even in faux jest.

While Cara was busy assessing me, I was doing the same to her, keeping my face void of expression so she couldn't read me. The woman projected an I-don't-give-a-shit attitude, especially toward me, but there was a dusting of pain hidden deep behind her eyes. The alcohol and drugs swirling through her veins couldn't hide it. Instead, it highlighted her vulnerability. I dared not focus on the state of her undress for fear my body would react, and there was no explaining that away.

My hands were still wrapped around her upper arms, the feel of her skin burrowing into me, so I abruptly released her and took a step back. "Let's go." I tried to be respectful, but what I wanted to do was chastise her for being so careless.

"I'm not going anywhere with you."

"I just want to talk to you," I rebutted through gritted teeth. "Then you can rejoin your guests." Keeping a calm demeanor when I was fighting the urge to shout at her tested every bit of my crumbling reserve.

"No." She folded her arms across her chest, pushing her tits up until they almost fell out of her barely there top. One wrong move and everyone would see what was underneath, although there wasn't anything she'd left to the imagination.

Her refusal triggered me to take a deep breath. I'd never put my hands on her to forcefully remove her, but I could ruin her party.

"I'm giving you one more chance to reconsider." I emulated her body language, silently warring with her.

"Or what? You can't do anything. You have to just stand there like a good little boy and watch me." She dropped her arms to her sides and drew closer. A little too close for my liking. "But I bet you like that, don't you? Watching me?" She ran the tip of her tongue over her bottom lip. "Do you get off on it, *Ford*? Do you jerk off to the image of me in bed? It's not like you have to imagine me. You get to watch me through the camera." Before I realized what she was doing, she trailed one of her nails over my bicep, flashing me a fake, flirty smile.

"You're drunk." I shrugged off her touch.

"Don't forget stoned." She laughed, the sound forced and uneasy.

Ignoring her pathetic attempt to rile me, I tried to get her alone again. "Just a few words then I'll let you get back to your party."

All too aware there were multiple sets of eyes on us, I focused on one objective. All I wanted to do was pull Cara away from her party to let her know… what, I wasn't completely sure of. Yes, what she'd done was stupid, whether she knew it or not. And yes, she was putting herself in a vulnerable position by drinking and getting high. But I was hired to protect her. To watch her and interfere when necessary. This was one of those times, right? The line was blurred, and I didn't want to overstep my bounds, but I had to do something.

Just when my brain started to tire of the internal back and forth, I spotted Owen and Emily coming through the gate, a relieved rush of air escaping knowing I had back up.

They both rushed over, and as soon as they were close enough, I dragged Owen to the side, leaving Emily with Cara. "Where the hell have you been?" My aggressive tone surprised him.

"I had to go with Emily to the shelter." He said it like I should know their schedule.

"Well, while you were off traipsing around, I was stuck to deal with this shit," I barked, lowering my voice once I'd seen a few people look our way.

Sensing I was more than a little annoyed, Owen gave me a curt nod before walking back toward Emily, leaning down and whispering something into her ear, proving once again they were becoming too close for what was deemed professional.

Emily led her sister over to the makeshift bar and handed her bottled water. Once she drank it, her sister handed her another. The rest of the guests carried on about their business, goofing off in the pool and lazily lounging about as if they didn't have a care in the world. And most of them probably didn't if they were anything like their hostess.

After several hours, the impromptu party finally died down, the last of the stragglers leaving just before five o'clock. Of course, they'd left a mess.

I saw Cara return after she'd walked the last of her guests out, stopping to talk to Emily who was busy collecting beer bottles and glasses. Owen was close behind with a garbage bag and a smile.

Cara threw me an annoyed look before sauntering back into the main house, her ass cheeks on full display. She slammed the door behind her, not a care in the world that she left her sister to clean up.

Even though it was the last thing I wanted to do after the afternoon I had, I helped Owen and Emily get rid of the garbage. And as I worked, I couldn't help but wonder if my interactions with Cara would ever change.

CHAPTER
TEN

Cara

As I washed away the day, my brain wouldn't allow me to wipe away the scene that happened earlier. When I had the idea to throw a last-minute pool party, it was because I'd been feeling down and needed a pick me up. Truth was, my protection detail was the last thing on my mind. It seemed ridiculous since Ford was always there, but he wasn't the center of my world, or my first thought, despite how aware of him I was when he was close by.

With each interaction we had, most of them not pleasant, I seemed to crave his attention. Even if it was negative. The man rattled me. Plain and simple.

"Watch me, Daddy." I twirled around in the pink and white tutu my mother had bought me. *"I'm gonna be a ballerina someday. I'm even gonna make my own dress."* On film, my dad watched me dance with the biggest smile on his face, a smile I hadn't seen directed toward me in years. Admittedly, that was partly my fault. I loved my father, both of my parents, and they'd given me a wonderful childhood, but I hadn't been the easiest daughter to love. Not in over a decade.

I watched my ten-year-old self on the TV screen, the innocence of that girl making me sad when it should've brought me some sort of happiness. I'd been a dreamer, thinking the world was a magical place and that anything was possible. I was different back then, which I knew every adult could say, but most people retained a sliver of optimism from their youth. A piece of themselves that was hopeful that believed they'd be safe from monsters. Little did I know, did she know, that in two short years, I'd be changed forever.

I pulled the blanket up toward my chin, nestling into the couch as the rest of the home movie played. On screen, Emily emulated every move I'd made. Her giggles spurred my own. I took her hand in mine, and we danced around, falling to the ground when we'd spun too fast. A single tear trickled down my cheek, my sadness at having lost sight of the younger me too much to contain.

My sister had looked up to me back then. Not so anymore, not that I could blame her. Instead, it was me who'd become envious of her. I never spoke the words. In fact, I mocked her enthusiasm for goodwill. I cringed at the way her eyes lit up when she spoke of helping others. I had no room in my life for anything but my own selfish needs.

As the movie ended, and I wiped away another tear, I heard the rustling of paper behind me. I'd been so wrapped up in my thoughts and the past that I was unaware anyone else was in the room with me. I turned to look in the direction of the noise and was surprised to find Ford looking at me. His face expressionless as usual. He wasn't wearing his sunglasses, and I supposed that was because I'd already seen what he hid beneath them. Therefore, no need to keep up the mystery.

It wasn't until he picked up a piece of paper from the table he'd been leaning against that I jumped up from the couch and rushed over.

"Do you mind?" I snatched the sheet from his hand, unable to contain my anger at the invasion of my privacy, again. "Don't you know it's rude to go through people's things?" I turned my back to him and grabbed the rest of the drawings. My drawings. It was a hobby of mine. I hadn't been lying when I told my dad I was going to make my own dress someday. I wanted to create my own line of clothing. When the time was right. Until then, I was content doodling the many images whirling around inside my brain.

"Did you draw those?" he asked.

I'd been so flustered he'd not only snooped at my work but had the audacity to ask about them that I never answered, several sheets of paper slipping through my fingers. When I turned to face him, my eyes searched out his. Maybe I thought he'd put my ego at ease and tell me I had talent. Though if he offered such words, my typical defense mechanism of bitchiness would prevail.

Or maybe I thought he'd apologize for prying, and bend to pick up the papers strewn at his feet. He did neither of those things. Instead, he simply returned my stare. As the seconds passed, I became flustered, a feeling I hated because it meant I wasn't in control of the situation. But I was quickly learning that whenever Ford was around me for too long, my mind and body warred with each other. Not having the strength to decipher what was going on inside me, I bent down and gathered the sheets of paper, crumbling some of them in my haste to get away from the man as quickly as possible.

As I stalked from the room, I shouted over my shoulder, "Next time, don't touch stuff that doesn't belong to you." I had no idea if he smirked or if his face continued to be blank. And I hated that I cared.

CHAPTER
ELEVEN

Cara

"We're gonna have so much fun." I paced my bedroom, my phone glued to my ear as I listened to my best friend, Naomi Horan, ramble on about all the clubs we needed to visit when we went to California for mine and Emily's birthday. Twenty-five was staring us in the face, and we had to celebrate right.

Naomi came from money much like I did, her parents spoiling her every way they knew how. Her dad had invented some device that NASA used for their space shuttles. The man was legit smart. But unlike me, Naomi hadn't given her parents as many heart attacks as I'd given mine.

"Even with your bodyguards around?" Good question.

"I'll figure something out," I promised, although I had no idea if what I said was the truth. Ford had proven to be relentless. Unyielding. He'd barged in on me while I was in the tub, and all because my phone had died and sent him an alert it'd been turned off. Then he all but ended my pool party earlier than I wanted because he stood nearby and watched me like a hawk, making everyone else feel uncomfortable with his domineering presence. A clenched jaw and hands that tightened into fists every few seconds would make anyone uneasy. Throw in a few sneers, and it didn't make for a party atmosphere. And that wasn't me guessing that's why my friends had left early. They told me as much.

"Why don't we talk about it more tonight?"

"Looking forward to it." I disappeared into my closet and mindlessly looked through clothes while we talked. "Did we ever decide on a place to go?"

"Yeah, The Avenue."

"That's right. I can't believe I forgot."

"And don't forget it's Kurt's birthday. He'd be heartbroken if you didn't remember."

"I doubt that. Besides, even if I had forgotten, he'd be just fine." Kurt was Naomi's cousin, and we'd hung out a handful of times. On several occasions, he'd tried to lay claim to me, chasing off other men who'd approached me, and because we had fun together, and he was my best friend's family, I let it slide. "We'll try and nail down some of the places we want to hit in Cali, then go from there."

"Okay," she answered. "See you soon."

After ending our conversation, I spent the next hour and a half primping, picking out the perfect outfit and styling my hair in big loose curls. I was looking forward to a night out where I could lose myself a bit and forget all about the unwavering tension between me and Ford. An unease that made me second-guess all my intuition and rational thought. Okay, so maybe not all my thoughts were rational, but they were mine, and the last thing I wanted to do was dissect them.

Putting the finishing touches on my makeup, I was startled when my bedroom door flung open, Emily appearing in the doorway with a smile that seemed to have taken up permanent residence on her face as of late.

"You're lucky I didn't screw up my lipstick," I chastised,

looking at her in the reflection of the mirror. Her goofy grin made me shake my head, whatever annoyance I'd felt at her intrusion quickly evaporating. I could never stay mad at my sister, and she knew it all too well.

She entered farther into my room and picked up one of the dresses I had laid across my bed. The one item of clothing strewn about that wasn't ready to be worn. It was one of my first designs, a dress I'd been working on for the past month. I couldn't seem to get the stitching on the sides just right.

"This is beautiful." She handled the lace bodice with care. "And I love the color." I'd chosen a deep purple, a shade that flattered almost every skin tone. "When will it be finished?" She glanced over at me, meeting my eyes in the mirror.

"Soon, I hope." I flashed her a quick smile in appreciation.

"Well, *soon*," she reiterated the word, "you'll be the talk of the fashion industry." She held the not-quite-finished dress up in front of her and twirled around, winking at me when she'd come full circle. "And I'm gonna get all the free clothes I want. Closets of them."

I couldn't help but laugh. "Is that right?"

Before she could answer, someone appeared in the doorway. I could only see a dark suit, and as quickly as my shoulders tensed, they loosened because the man who stood there was not the infuriating brother. But rather the younger sibling, the man who seemed to have the hots for my sister. As she appeared to have for him. I was all about letting loose and having fun, as my friends could attest to, and I'd be the last person to get in Emily's way of letting her hair down and taking the plunge into a well-deserved romp, so I said nothing as she stepped closer to him. He leaned down, gave me a quick smile then whispered into her ear.

A flutter of want swirled in my belly. A longing I hadn't known existed erupted inside me, but I tamped it down before I gave in to the silly fantasies of wanting someone to look at me the way Owen looked at Emily. It was just lust, right? No way it could be anything more than that. They'd only known each other a short time, not long enough for anything else to reside between them.

Not to get me wrong, men looked at me with lust all the time, and I at them in return. Well, some of them. But that was the only emotion I allowed myself. It was safer that way. No need to get my heart all twisted up into something that would no doubt splinter it apart. I had no time for that shit.

I'd never been in love, and that was the way I'd like to keep it.

Owen coughed, drawing my attention back to the two of them huddled near the doorway. It was Emily who spoke, though.

"We'll meet you at The Avenue if you don't mind. I need a drink." My downturned brows and open mouth made my sister laugh. "What? I can have a drink every now and again."

"I didn't say anything," I retorted.

She stepped away from Owen and closer to me. "You didn't have to." Suddenly, her smile vanished as well as her bottom lip, her teeth going to work on the soft flesh. "Do I look okay?" she whispered. My eyes drifted over her, and although she wasn't wearing anything overtly sexy, she looked enticing. A black tank top paired with a gold belt around her middle gave her a subtle, sexy accent, the pair of dark skinny jeans she'd chosen hugging her smaller curves. She topped the outfit off with a classic pair of black Louboutins. Sexy but not overdone. Subtle. Not blatant. Not like me.

There were many differences between me and Emily, even though we were twins. She was an inch shorter than my five-foot-eight frame, her hair a rich chestnut shade. Other than our thin builds and family resemblance, we didn't share a single similarity.

Her eyes were brown.

Mine were blue.

She was small chested.

I was decently endowed.

She strived to help others.

I couldn't be bothered.

She was conservative.

I pushed the line so far, most times I'd lost sight of the damn thing.

Her smile was genuine.

Mine was forced.

I nodded and gave her a wink, my approval bringing back her smile. "I'll meet you there," I shouted after her as she and Owen walked back out into the hallway.

CHAPTER
TWELVE

Ford

The encounter with Cara earlier had ended badly, as was typical. But what happened before she flipped out surprised me. When I first came into the room, she was busy watching an old home movie, and while I should've done my rounds and left, I stood there watching right along with her.

To see her as a child, and how happy she looked, made me smile, an occurrence I didn't even think was possible where she was concerned. Then I looked down at the table, something catching my attention from the corner of my eye.

Many drawings littered the tabletop. Dresses. Business suits. Bathing suits. All detailed and colorful. When I picked up one of the papers to look underneath that was when Cara jumped up from the couch and rushed toward me. Her eyes were glassy, and she looked like she'd been crying, but I didn't have time to decipher if that was indeed true before she started yelling at me.

Afterward, I understood why she'd been flustered and upset. I'd snooped through her private things, although, to be fair, I hadn't known they were hers.

Maybe there was more to the woman than she allowed others to see.

Focusing on the present, I paced in the kitchen of the main

house, the back and forth doing nothing to calm my nerves. Instead, I inhaled and blew out breath after breath in a shitty attempt to calm my rising irritation. I didn't feel well and going to a club was the last thing I wanted to do, but I couldn't leave Owen to protect both sisters. My stomach flopped, a dot of perspiration appearing on my brow.

I opened the refrigerator to look for something to drink that would help, and thankfully there was an unopened bottle of ginger ale. When I turned around to search for a glass, I quickly forgot all about my upset stomach. I almost dropped the bottle of soda. I couldn't focus on much more than the woman standing in front of me. But as soon as it registered in my brain that my eyes were assaulting her, running the full length of her, I closed them and exhaled another breath, making sure not to be too obvious.

Turning back toward the cabinets to grab a glass, avoiding her altogether, the hiss of the bottle's cap filled the silence of the space. I took two large gulps of soda before turning to face Cara once more, schooling my features to ensure she couldn't read me. I'd become quite skilled in the art of avoidance and aloofness.

We stared at each other, her eyes narrowing while she appeared to be studying me. After several moments, she finally spoke. "What?" She cocked her head slightly to the right. "You don't approve of what I'm wearing?" The smallest smile lifted the corners of her mouth, but her expression wasn't genuine. She was goading me. Looking for a reaction. The queasiness in my stomach intensified, and I briefly closed my eyes. When I opened them, I saw that her lips were pursed, and she had a hand on her hip. She emanated cockiness.

"I don't care what you wear." Her smile faltered. "If you

wanna look desperate, that's up to you." Her mouth fell open, and I swore her brows hit the edge of her hairline. My response was as much of a shock to me as it was to her, but I sure as hell wasn't about to apologize. *I'll blame it on feeling like shit.*

The scrap of black material she called a dress barely covered her, yet she appeared surprised by my reply. Maybe surprised was the wrong word. Offended? Pissed off? Whatever emotion ran through her kept her lips parted wide.

The plunging neckline barely hid her tits, which were going to pop out if she moved the wrong way, and the sad excuse for a hemline fell just below her ass cheeks. The dress looked more like lingerie, and that comparison was a generous one. To make the ensemble more obvious, she had on heels that tied all the way up her calves, making her legs look like they went on for days, and making her dress look even shorter. If that was at all possible.

"Desperate?" Her voice rose an octave. Maybe two.

I'd already said too much, so without another word, I snatched the keys from the table and strode toward the door. Stepping over the threshold, I turned to see if she was following behind me. It was then I saw her mouth was still wide open, her eyes so big I was surprised they hadn't fallen out of their sockets. "Are you coming?" I asked, the boredom in my voice apparent, as if I hadn't just insulted her.

I was sure not many people talked to Cara so candidly, but I wasn't like most people. I gave up caring what other people thought a long time ago. I'd censored myself before, and bad things had happened. Never again. My fingers wrapped around the cross hanging from my neck, and for a moment, I closed my eyes and pictured my sister's face. I was content to lose myself to memories but was wrenched back into the present by an angry voice.

"How dare you speak to me like that? Who do you think you are? I will not let you disrespect me like that again." Her voice level rose once more, her hands clenching into tight fists as she glared at me. Her skin tinged pink in anger and amusement bubbled in my chest, especially when my smirk fueled her fury.

"Are you done?" I twisted to face her and tilted my head.

Her chest rose with the inhalation of air, but before she spewed any more words my way, I turned away and walked out the door, her gasp following behind me. The chirp of the alarm signaled I was done with our short interaction.

I was soon bombarded with regret, though. Regret for taking this assignment. Regret for letting her get to me, for making me respond at all to the question about her outfit. Regret for not being able to suppress the distaste for her choice of clothing. I should've stayed silent and walked out of the room at the first sign that she wanted to irritate me.

I found Cara attractive. I'd have to be blind not to, but that was as far as it went—an appreciation for her physical attributes. But as soon as she opened her mouth, to me or to anyone else, I saw her for the spoiled brat she was. Nothing more. Nothing less. And I had no time in my life for such people, not that anything would or could go any further than the current arrangement between us. Eventually, I'd move on without a second thought for her or her family.

Releasing a puff of air, I attempted to rid my body of any stress where she was concerned. It just started to work when I realized she still hadn't come out of the house, refusing to make things easy on me, especially when I wasn't feeling well, although, she didn't know I was under the weather.

Two minutes passed and still she remained inside, no doubt cursing me up and down, trying to figure out what she was going to say to me as soon as she got her ass out here. I sat inside the Porsche SUV, waiting for her, and as the seconds ticked by, I became more irritated.

"Just forget about her," I mumbled to myself. "Just relax." Her absence plucked the edges of my last nerve, and deep breaths mixed with talking to myself barely restrained the urge to march back in there and throw her over my shoulder just so she'd leave the goddamn house.

Another minute passed.

Then another.

Still no Cara.

A text alert interrupted my mood, and thankful for the distraction I swiped my phone open.

Owen: *What the hell is taking you so long?*

My brother and Emily had gone ahead of us, against my advice of us all traveling together. Emily never seemed to give my brother a hard time like her sister did with me. How I wished I'd been assigned to the more easygoing daughter instead. My life and stress level would be much more manageable.

Owen: *Hello?*

My patience dwindled as my fingers flew over the keyboard of my phone.

Me: *I'm waiting on her Highness to get her ass out here.*

Owen: *What's the problem?*

Me: *She's pissed off. Not shocking.*

Owen: *What did you do?*

Why did it have to be something I did, although he'd guessed correctly? Still, it would've been nice if my brother had given me the benefit of the doubt. My logic was fucked up, I knew. I didn't directly answer his question; instead, I skated around his inquiry.

Me: I feel like shit and she's making my job harder.
Owen: Whatever. Just hurry up.
Me: I would've thought you'd want some alone time.

No response. He knew how I felt about him getting involved, or whatever the hell he was playing at with Emily, but I
couldn't help myself. Since I was in a foul mood, I enticed him
to join me.

Contemplating going back inside and throwing her over
my shoulder, I thought better of it. Manhandling her would
be crossing the line, although what I'd just said to her could be
construed as line crossing, as well. Inappropriate. Then again,
we'd engaged in a few inappropriate situations. Besides, I didn't
need to add to the list of things she could complain about to her
father.

Every part of me twitched to throw her over my knee and
give her the spanking her parents obviously never gave her.
While she wasn't disrespectful to her parents, not over the top,
at least, there was a level of obedience that was lacking. Closing
my eyes, I shook my head. "She's not a kid," I grumbled into the
silence of the garage, "although she's acting like one."

I became borderline volatile, and instead of continuing to
calm down and wait Cara out, I slammed my hand down on the
steering wheel, every expletive I knew flying from my mouth in
anger right before I hopped out of the vehicle and stalked back
inside the house.

When she saw me reappear, she took a step back, and I
wasn't sure if it was because she was furious with me, as she
often was, or if it was because of the way I appeared. My shoulders were squared and rigid, my jaw so tight it felt like it would
shatter if I didn't relieve some of the pressure, and soon. My
steps were hurried, invading her personal space until the tips of

my shoes pushed against hers. We were literally toe to toe. Her little temper tantrum was the last thing I wanted to deal with, but unfortunately, I had all night. She didn't, however. I'd learned that, for as much as a diva as she could be, she didn't like to be late. And as if on cue, her eyes drifted to the clock on the wall.

"I can stand here all night, *sweetheart*." The hue of her irises darkened. The clench of her delicate jaw mirrored mine, although the bravado she projected wavered the more our breaths mingled.

"I can't stand you," she seethed. Locked in a stare-off did nothing but push my anger to another level. The woman was stubborn, and it was almost unbearable. In any other circumstance, I may have found her insolence admirable, but not right then. Right then, she was doing everything to aggravate and piss me off. Right then, she didn't have a care in the world for the inconvenience she bestowed on me or for those who were waiting on her.

"How you feel about me doesn't matter," I countered. "What matters is that I keep you safe, something you seem to want to disrupt." My eyes drifted over her from head to toe again. The way she was dressed was certainly going to rile up unwanted attention, and it was going to be my job to intercede, of course.

She took a single step back, the contempt on her face seizing her expression. The huff of her breath and the crinkle around her eyes told me everything, as if I didn't already know how she felt about me. Hell, she just told me she couldn't stand me, which was fine with me because that meant I didn't have to deal with her hitting on me or trying to convince me I could keep her safer if I shared her bed. I saw the way she watched me from time to time. The way her eyes roamed over me, a little too slowly every now and again. And the way she sometimes fixated a little too long on my mouth.

"I'll tell my father you mistreated me," she threatened, arching a perfectly manicured brow in wait.

A condescending laugh escaped me. I couldn't help my reaction, because although I hadn't been employed long by Walter, I was aware he knew all too well the antics of his daughter.

"Go ahead. We'll see whom he believes." She gasped at my sheer audacity. "Now, let's go." I extended my arm and waited for her to precede me, but she remained frozen in place. "You're gonna be late." Soon after, she walked ahead of me, mumbling incoherently.

Striding toward the driver side, I passed her standing by the vehicle. As I opened my door, half my body disappearing inside, I turned to look back at her. Her exaggerated sigh echoed through the space, and again, I wished I'd never let my brother talk me into this goddamn job.

"You need to open my door." Her arrogant tone pushed my last button, but instead of telling her exactly what I thought of her attitude, I counted to five and folded the rest of my body inside the black SUV.

"We've already gone over this. I was hired to protect you, not open your doors." The rattling of the window as I slammed my door prompted her to rip open her own and finally situate her pompous ass inside.

CHAPTER
THIRTEEN

Ford

As I waited for the garage door to open, I flipped on the radio, the soothing sounds of Sinatra filling the air. I could already feel some of the stress ebbing away, that was, until the woman sharing the space with me complained.

"What is this?" Finding her eyes in the rearview, I smirked, although she may not have seen. I didn't answer, instead turning the volume up two notches. "Turn this off and put something from this century on," she demanded, fidgeting with the hem of her flimsy dress. When I still didn't comply, busying myself with entering the address into the navigation, she leaned forward and snapped her fingers next to my ear. "Hello? Did you hear me?" She fell back against her seat, attempting to lengthen the material which barely covered her. Maybe my comment somehow made her second-guess her choice of clothing. Or maybe she was so frustrated that in order to stop her from physically lashing out at me, she fiddled with her dress instead.

Although I probably should've shut off the radio altogether, I let it play, the crooner's voice soothing me yet irritating the hell out of Cara.

Ten minutes passed while I weaved in and out of traffic, dealing with incompetent drivers who made no qualms about texting while barreling down the road at eighty miles an hour. Muttering under my breath had become the new norm, and while I had no problem using expletives at the drop of a hat, I curbed the need to scream at everyone slamming on their brakes or failing to use their turn signals.

Cara was quiet, but I could sense her brooding temper was on a slow simmer. Every now and again, I'd catch her looking at me, or out the window or down at her phone. Someone was texting her, and it wasn't until I caught a glimpse of a smile did my mind wander. Who was texting her? What were they saying? What made her smile? She seemed reasonable with others, yet her attitude toward me increased. As question after question rattled my brain, I became annoyed with myself for caring at all.

"My grandfather used to listen to this." Her voice startled me. "He was eighty. What's your excuse?" I caught the roll of her eyes before she returned her attention to her phone. Her fingers flew over the screen with ease, the corners of her mouth turning down ever so slightly.

I ignored her question and focused back on the task at hand. Getting her to the club and out of my hair. To be more accurate, she'd still be my problem, but I'd rather watch over her from afar than be the one in her direct line of fire.

I glanced at the display screen. We'd arrive at our destination in seven minutes. Seven very long minutes, but soon enough, I could dump her off with her sister and whoever else was waiting on her, and join my brother, trying our best to blend in, a feat in itself. We'd most likely also be the only ones not drinking or having a good time. And oh, how I wanted a shot of something stiff to take the edge off, but for as much as I loved to drown myself in alcohol, I'd never partake while on the job. Even I wasn't so careless, although I was sure Owen would beg to differ from time to time.

Out of the corner of my eye, I spotted a black Mercedes swerving in and out of traffic. Call it instinct or misplaced paranoia, but my attention was pricked. Heightened more than normal. Wanting to see what would happen, I changed lanes and waited to see if the Mercedes would follow. And sure enough, it did. It could be coincidence, or the car could be following us. Several seconds later, I sped up and switched lanes again, veering toward the farthest one on the right. It followed again.

"Fuck," I shouted, turning down the radio, my eyes bouncing back and forth between the traffic ahead and the bastard following us.

Cara picked her head up from her phone and sighed. "What now?" Her tone was blasé. She didn't give a shit there was a real threat out there against her family, too wrapped up in the bubble that was her life. One not born in reality. Not any reality I knew, at least.

"We're being followed."

"What? How do you know?" Her questions were rushed while she flipped around in her seat to look out the back window. The Mercedes was three cars behind, in the same lane. Since all of my focus was on ditching the asshole, I never answered her. "Ford! How do you know someone's following us?" she repeated.

"It's my job to know." I could've given her a play-by-play of how I knew, but it wasn't my job to tell her every little detail. My job was to ensure she was safe at all times. That was it. She only needed to know what I chose to tell her, and when I felt she should know. Nothing more. Nothing less.

Cara kept turning around to check but didn't witness

anything out of the ordinary because the Mercedes was still behind us, until it wasn't. Veering out of our lane, it sped up until it was two cars behind. Then one. Then it was right next to us on the left. When I turned to see who it was, I saw a young guy jabbering away. He was either singing or talking to someone over Bluetooth. No one else was in the vehicle with him. He looked agitated but sped up before I could get another look at him. I did, however, catch his license plate. RICH AF. *Rich as fuck.* What a douchebag.

When the truck in front of us switched lanes, the Mercedes swerved in front and nearly missed hitting me. I slammed on the horn and the brakes at the same time. Luckily, nothing happened except for him continuing to drive like an aggressive asshole, crossing until he exited on the right. The same damn exit we were taking.

Cara looked out of the back window once more. "Are we still being followed?"

"No."

"We probably never were," she muttered, but I heard her loud and clear.

"It's not my job to convince you of anything. It's my job to assess a threat, if present, and deal with it."

"Whatever." She went back to texting while I tapped the leather-encased wheel with my finger and silently wished we were already at our destination. Only two minutes to go then I'd be free of her eye rolls and rudeness.

A loud sigh from the back seat pulled me to look in the rearview. Visual daggers were shot my way while she worked her plump bottom lip between her teeth.

"We're almost there," I all but barked at her. Internally, I berated myself for engaging because I should have kept my mouth shut and our conversations to a bare minimum, but her cocked head and narrowed eyes demanded I say something. Anything.

I saw The Avenue, the club of choice that evening, up ahead on the right so I reached over to switch off the guidance route. I didn't know whose voice was more grating, the navi's or Cara's.

The vehicle barely came to a stop before she hopped out of the back seat, rushing toward her sister who was pacing on the sidewalk, my brother not far behind her. I jumped out of the driver side, threw on my sunglasses, and tossed the key to the valet who had suddenly appeared out of nowhere. Had my brother not been so close, I would have given her a tongue lashing for not waiting for me. For whatever reason, she didn't seem to think the threat against her family was real, and I didn't want her to have to find out the hard way. For as much of a pain in the ass as she was, my need to make sure she was kept out of harm's way was ingrained in me. She was my responsibility until further notice.

"Let's go, Ford," my brother shouted from the sidewalk, right before he ushered the ladies inside. I caught up to them in a few strides, Owen leaning in close because the music was deafening. "You sure do have your hands full with that one. Thank God Emily is the exact opposite. Sweet as can be."

"Fuck you."

Owen laughed and walked ahead of me, the sisters still well within our sights. "Can you even see anything with those damn shades on?" He wasn't looking at me when he asked his question, his focus strictly on the women, a smile appearing when I witnessed Emily make eye contact with him.

I grabbed his forearm to get his attention. "First off, you're the one reminding me that I should wear them at all times. Secondly, you better not be shittin' where you eat."

His smile turned upside down. "What the hell does that mean?"

"You know goddamn well what that means. I thought I told you to shut that down." I hadn't spoken those exact words, but I insinuated as much when I'd caught them in the kitchen. "It'll only make our jobs harder." We were locked into a visual battle. "Cut it off. Now." I moved to step around him, but he hit my shoulder with his as he brushed past me.

"You don't know what the hell you're talking about," he barked, his tone and defensiveness giving everything away. Owen was shit at hiding things from me. Always was. I was about to haul him into a nearby corner to remind him of what could happen if his guard was down, when suddenly a man, close to fifty feet from where I stood, shoved his way through the crowd with purpose. As I followed his line of sight, it occurred to me that he was headed toward Cara and Emily, the crooked smirk on his face telling me he was up to no good. His dirty blond hair was slicked away from his face, the back hitting just below his collar. His thin build was draped in yuppy, metro-style clothing, his pale pink pants a bit too snug, never mind the fucking color. His cocky swag and condescending flick of his wrist toward a passing waitress already told me everything I needed to know about him. He was an asshole.

When I locked eyes on Cara, I saw her smile, then wave at the guy, indicating she knew him. But I didn't, so I smacked my brother on the arm and jerked my chin toward the unfolding scene. With a puff of our cheeks and an annoyed look flashing across both of our faces, we rushed forward and reached the women before the culprit. Positioning myself in front of Cara, I pushed her behind me.

"What are you doing?" She tried to move me but was

unsuccessful, of course. "I know him." She grabbed my upper arm and attempted to move me once more.

I turned my head to the side to look at her. "Stop." Then I swiveled back around and placed my hand on the guy's chest as he moved forward. "No way. Not gonna happen, buddy," I said in my most menacing voice. What I wanted to do was punch him in the face before tossing him out of the club on his ass. I had no justification for such thoughts, but I had them, nonetheless.

"He's a friend of mine." With my attention still focused ahead, Cara managed to sidestep me and move next to the guy. She snatched his hand and pulled him through the crowd.

"Goddammit!" I took a few steps forward when I felt someone tug on my arm. Emily.

"She's sort of dating him," she offered, flashing me a sympathetic type of smile. One that told me she didn't particularly care for the guy. Or was I reading her expression as such because *I* didn't like the look of him?

"Doesn't matter." Again, I attempted to approach the two of them, now seated at the bar, when Owen stepped in front and blocked my view, shaking his head.

"Let it go. You can keep an eye on her from over there," he said, pointing to a corner near where they were busy chatting away. I only had two choices. I could stress myself out by cutting their *date* short, then in return have to listen to her mouth for the rest of the evening, or take my brother's advice and hole up in the corner and keep watch. I chose the lesser of two evils. If I had to contend with a pissed-off Cara for hours on end that night, I very well might drink myself into oblivion.

Two hours had passed, and Cara was drunk, barely able to sit upright on her stool, the guy she was supposedly dating doing nothing to step in and cut her off. Instead, he was too worried about scoring, his hand disappearing up her skirt, right there in front of anyone. Cara didn't appear to have a care in the world, not for herself or anyone else, for that matter.

At one point during the evening, while my eyes were glued to every movement they made, I saw him pass her a small baggie, and it didn't take a genius to guess what it was. She slyly slid it off the top of the bar, her fingers curling into themselves at her side. I'd had enough. It was one thing to get mind-numbingly blitzed, but it was another to mix drugs into that concoction.

Looking around the bar, I located my brother, standing close to Emily. Shocker. He must've sensed me staring because he picked his head up and locked eyes with me, the crease in his brow giving way to his confusion. I flicked my chin toward Cara and threw my pointer finger in the air, our signal I was going in. Owen leaned down to whisper something in Emily's ear, her eyes finding me as soon as he backed away. I had no idea what he'd told her, but afterward, she rested her hand on his forearm, her thumb sliding back and forth over the fabric of his shirt. Since I had my own situation to deal with, I shoved all thoughts of the nature of their relationship to the side as I pushed off the wall behind me and strode toward Cara and her *friend,* hellbent on calling it a night. For her and for me. Owen snaked through the crowd, joining me seconds later.

They never saw us approach. One moment, she was throwing her head back and laughing at whatever attempt of humor the asshole made, and the next she was on her feet and Owen and I had become the barrier between them.

"Wh...what the hell?" she slurred, her eyes glossing over while she tried to focus. I snatched her hand and pulled it between us, prying open her fingers before she realized what I was doing. Just as I suspected, there was a small bag of coke clutched in her palm. "What do you think you're doing?" She swayed on her feet, reaching for the edge of the bar to help steady her.

"What I should've done a half hour ago." I tossed the bag behind the counter, not caring who found it, and whipped around to face the fucker responsible for giving that shit to her. I couldn't help but wonder how many times she'd used in the past. Or was that going to be her first time? Instinct told me it wasn't the latter. "I suggest you leave," I growled over the roar of the many patrons.

"I'm not going anywhere," he countered, struggling to move around me so he could reach Cara. The last thing I wanted to do was to be involved in a physical altercation, but my hands were on him before my brain could deter me otherwise. I snatched him up and pulled him close.

"You're done." I assessed him as quickly as I could, noticing right away that his pupils were dilated, and he seemed amped up. His demeanor could be because he'd snorted that shit sometime during the night or because we were about to come to blows if he didn't back down. Either way, I needed to remove him from the situation and do it as quickly as possible.

"Who the fuck do you think you're talking to?" He squirmed to get away from me, but I held tightly.

"You stay away from her or else." My words were met with a laugh. My presence intimated most, but the bastard in front of me was probably so entitled he thought nothing bad could happen to him. I was there to set shit straight. If he so much as spoke to Cara again, I'd knock those pearly whites down his goddamn throat.

I never gave him the opportunity to test my restraint because before any of us could figure out what was going to happen next, Owen grabbed the guy from the left, and I flanked him on his right, both of us shoving him toward the exit. I thought I heard Cara shouting something behind me, but I couldn't be sure with all the other noise assaulting my ears. Music and patrons combined.

Once outside, Owen released his hold on the guy, but I tightened mine, turning him to face me so there was no mistaking my next threat.

"Don't ever come near Cara again. If I so much as see you around her, you'll regret it." Owen gripped my shoulder and squeezed. When I still hadn't released the shithead, Owen leaned in closer.

"Ford. Let him go." Several seconds passed with me glaring at the guy, imagining all the ways I'd make him suffer if he ever came near Cara again. "Come on, man," Owen prompted, "he's not worth it. Besides, no one is inside with them." *Shit!* I'd been so wrapped in removing the guy that we'd left the women by themselves inside the club.

I released the guy's shirt and shoved him backward. He stumbled a few steps but righted himself before his ass hit the pavement. He mumbled incoherently before tossing his ticket at the valet waiting nearby. Owen went back inside the club, but I stood there, and I wasn't going anywhere until I saw him drive off. Minutes later the valet drove up in a black Mercedes. The car looked familiar. Before the jackass took off, I walked behind the vehicle and saw the license plate. RICH AF. *Figures.*

As soon as he left, my heart began to slow its erratic thumping. My breaths regulated and my thoughts weren't so jumbled together. Some fresh air and I was ready to reenter the club, preparing myself for the backlash I was going to incur as soon as I saw Cara.

Striding through the space, I carefully navigated around the numerous drunk patrons, sidestepping a few of them to avoid getting drinks spilled on me. When I'd approached the area of the bar where the scene had unfolded, my brother and the women were nowhere to be seen. After scouring the entire club, I found myself in the hallway, near the restrooms, Owen leaning against the wall by himself.

"Where are they?" I asked the question but already knew the answer.

He pointed toward the women's room. "In there." He shook his head before breaking eye contact.

"What?" My patience hit an all-time low.

"You tell me." He pushed off the wall and approached. "What the hell was that back there?" I opened my mouth to speak, but he kept talking. "You were out of line, Ford. Way too aggressive. It's not our job to interfere unless they're in harm's way."

"And you don't think him giving her coke puts her in harm's way?" I rose up to my full height of six three and flared my nostrils, preparing to do battle with my younger brother.

But instead of Owen challenging me, his face relaxed. "It's not the same, and you know it." He ran his fingers through his wavy brown hair. "You can't save everyone from themselves. Cara isn't Julia."

Ignoring his comment, I looked away and attempted to gather myself. My emotions were all over the place. The last thing I needed Cara to witness was the uncertainty painted all over my face. Maybe Owen was right. Maybe I'd been a touch too aggressive, but deep down, I knew that guy was no good. A bad influence. I tried to do what was right, to interfere and hopefully steer Cara away from her bad habits. But who was I to intervene? I was just some guy who'd been hired to make sure no one kidnapped her or tried to kill her. But wasn't that sort of what he'd been trying to do? Not the kidnap part, but attempt to kill her? What if she overdosed? Or took that shit with other stuff?

Black and white melded into gray.

My time for reflection, or self-doubt, or revelation or whatever the hell I wanted to call it, was over the moment the ladies walked out of the restroom, Cara glaring at me as she passed by. I thought for sure she was going to read me the riot act, chastise me for interfering with her friend, but she said nothing as she brushed past me. Emily was holding her steady because she'd had too much to drink. With my head up, alert to our surroundings, I followed behind Owen who was a few steps behind them. We were headed toward the exit when my brother suddenly stopped walking, and because he'd given me no warning, I slammed into the back of him.

"What the hell?" I looked around him, and it was then I saw the reason we'd all stopped walking.

Emily grasped Cara's arm, but her sister struggled to break away from her, and when she did, her eyes zeroed in on me. There was no mistaking the fury in her stare, and as I prepared myself for her wrath, whatever that might be, be it verbal or physical, I stood tall.

Her steps were staggered as she approached, but in a few short strides, she stood in front of me, anger and embarrassment etched into the morphing expressions on her face. With ragged breaths and unsteady feet, her brows drew tight and the corners of her mouth turned down, a slight quiver of her chin the telltale sign she was about to erupt.

"How. Dare. You!" she shouted, a flush of red spreading over her cheeks. I didn't bother to answer because I knew whatever I said would be the wrong thing.

From the corner of my eye, I could see several people turn and look at the spectacle unraveling near them. Us. I knew none of this was going to end well, and before anyone started recording, if they hadn't already, I stepped around Cara and shouted for my brother to escort both of them outside.

Handing over our tickets to the valet, we headed toward a secluded corner of the building. Cara resisted at first, but when Emily reminded her that she didn't want any more bad publicity ending up online, something their parents could see, Cara gave up and followed her. I made sure to keep my distance.

I saw Owen headed straight for me, and because I didn't want to get into it with him again, I raised my hand to ward him off. But he opened his mouth anyway.

Adrenaline continued to pump through me, worsening the sickness I'd been battling that evening. I had a headache the size of Texas and my mouth had been watering on and off for the past half hour.

"I think I should drive Cara home and you drive Emily." Even though what he proposed was a smart idea, he looked uneasy about the suggestion. And I was sure it had everything to do with him being away from Emily.

I simply nodded, walking toward Emily's white BMW. She followed behind me after whispering something to Cara. If she said something to my brother, I didn't see, disappearing inside before slamming the door.

I wanted to say something to Emily. Anything. But while I contemplated apologizing for what happened, deep down I knew my admission of guilt would come across as insincere. The truth of it was… I wasn't sorry. Not one bit. So instead, I kept my mouth shut, allowing the silence between us to fuel my unease.

Five minutes into the ride back to the house, Emily's voice broke the quiet.

"Cara wasn't always this way." I glanced at her in the rearview, letting her know I was listening. "Growing up she was the best sister anyone could ask for. She was fiercely protective over me, coming to my defense on a few occasions when I'd been bullied."

She glanced out the window quickly before turning her attention back toward me. "Even though we're twins, we had our own group of friends. Whenever she hung out with hers, and I was alone, she always included me, and even if some of them complained, she'd tell them that if they didn't like it, they could leave. Which they never did." A ghost of a smile appeared on her face, disappearing quickly before she continued to reminisce. "We had a lot of fun together, until one day... she just changed. My mom said it was probably puberty, her hormones running rampant, but I knew it was something else, even though I didn't know what exactly. You know?" Her question was rhetorical, of course.

I remained silent. Emily appeared to take my lack of conversation as a cue to divulge more. "I've talked to her many times about the stuff she does. How it's dangerous. And stupid. Pointless. But she's stubborn and doesn't want to listen." She released a strangled sigh. "It's hard watching someone you love go down a path of self-destruction."

"Trust me. I know." My response was resolute.

Emily chewed on her the corner of her bottom lip before releasing her next words. "I'm not sure why I just told you all that, but something tells me you have her best interests in mind, even though you don't like her."

"It's... not that I—"

"You don't have to lie, Ford." She flashed me a sympathetic grin. "My sister doesn't give people a chance, especially when she knows she won't get her own way." She took a breath. "I think you're good for her."

We'd arrived at our destination before I could even contemplate asking her just what she meant by that.

CHAPTER
FOURTEEN

Ford

Emily's odd comment rattled me, but I couldn't explain why because it was ludicrous. *"I think you're good for her."* The only person who'd be good for Cara would be a therapist, someone who'd help her work through her shit. Someone who'd delve deep into why she acted the way she did, and my instinct told me her reasons weren't strictly because she was spoiled.

"What's the matter?" I strolled up behind Owen who stood by the back door of the Porsche, patiently waiting for me.

"She passed out."

I peered inside and saw Cara sprawled across the back seat, her dress hiked up to her waist. "For Christ's sake." I gripped the back of my neck before heading around to the other side of the vehicle. It'd be easier to extract her if I could grab underneath her arms.

"Do you need my help?"

"Not with this. Just open the front door." Once Cara was safely in my arms, I slammed the door with my foot before carrying her toward her house. I tried not to jostle her, but I tripped up the front step, my foot catching the edge. Thankfully, I'd been able to steady myself before I fell and dropped her in the process. She moaned something in her sleep right before her arms snaked around my neck, nuzzling her face into my neck and pressing her lips to my skin.

Despite being still angry with her and the way she behaved, making me react the way I had back at the club, I couldn't help but feel protective over her. She reeked of alcohol, and while my nose didn't appreciate the circumstance, my fingers enjoyed the feel of her skin.

Looking down at her face, seeing how vulnerable she appeared, tore at something inside me. What that was, I couldn't explain.

Careful not to trip again, I took my time ascending the staircase. Memories of me barging in on her flooded my brain as soon as I entered her bedroom. But I couldn't think about that right then. My only goal was to put her to bed safely, staying with her for a bit to make sure she didn't throw up in her sleep and choke on her own vomit.

I laid her down on her bed, untying her heels before dropping them on the floor. If she were awake, she'd probably scream at me for treating them so carelessly, making me aware of just how expensive they were.

I turned around to shout for Emily, but she was standing behind me, and I had no doubt she was looking out for her sister.

"Can you undress her and put her under the covers?" I asked, turning around to face the wall. "You can turn around, too." I pointed for my brother to face the wall, as well. He turned without a second glance.

"Sure," Emily responded, making quick work of ridding Cara of her dress. Although I was sure it wasn't hard to do considering there was barely any material. It wasn't but a minute before she said, "All done."

"I'm gonna stay here tonight."

Emily frowned before looking at Owen. "Why?" Her stare was now focused on me.

"Because I don't want her to puke in her sleep then choke on it." Plain and simple. I could tell she wanted to ask me another question, but Owen interrupted before she had the chance.

"She's safe with him. I promise."

"I know," she agreed, but I didn't blame her for being cautious. I couldn't fault her for being hesitant leaving her drunk, passed-out sister in the company of a man she barely knew. While I could bet Emily knew all sorts of details about my brother, she didn't know much about me at all.

I ushered them out of the room so that I could get situated, pulling the large, blue chair and ottoman near Cara's side of the bed. If she woke in the middle of the night and tried to get out of bed, she'd no doubt trip over me, but I couldn't take the chance of being across the room in case she did, in fact, throw up in her sleep.

After removing my shoes and jacket, I hunkered down into the oversized seat and leaned my head back, staring at the ceiling, recapping the night's events. Again.

Ten minutes after my lids became heavy and closed, Cara started mumbling incoherently, moving around so much that the covers which shielded her shifted down her body. The flimsy bra she wore under her dress moved with her, her tits in jeopardy of popping free any second. I knew I should look away because it was the respectful thing to do, but I stared instead. It wasn't my finest moment. As I leaned forward in the chair, prepared to draw the blanket back up to cover her, she kicked the material away, her matching panties sheer and hiding nothing. My eyes widened at the sight of her, and while I wanted to visually devour her physique, I cursed myself for looking.

I made quick work of covering her back up before I fell back into the chair, shutting my eyes and willing myself to keep them closed. It worked. Sleep pulled me under before I could berate myself any further.

CHAPTER
FIFTEEN

Cara

A rumbling noise interrupted my sleep, although I didn't have the strength yet to open my eyes. As the cobwebs of my slumber ebbed away, the sound—choppy, staggered sounds—became louder.

Snoring.

Was that me? Was I making that noise? Had I been so loud I'd woken myself up? I listened to the sounds of my breaths and realized it wasn't me who was sucking in air like that. And if it wasn't me….

My eyes popped open and I looked up at the ceiling, the god-awful sound coming from my right. Slowly, I turned my head to the side and found Ford slumped over in the chair I normally kept in the corner of the room. At some point, he'd dragged it close to the bed and apparently proceeded to pass out in it. But why?

Memories of the previous night faded in and out, and I couldn't hold on to one long enough to help me figure out why he'd fallen asleep with me in my bedroom. As I lay there, angry with myself that another night had gone by, a night I couldn't quite recall, a shiver coursed through me. Looking down, I saw a thin sheet was the only thing shielding me, and when I picked it up, I took notice that I only had my bra and panties on, both articles of clothing twisted and barely covering me. I quickly looked over at Ford. He was still fully dressed, sans shoes and jacket. The only difference this time was that he was no longer slumped over in the chair, but awake. And looking right at me. I stared right back.

While I'd never voice my thoughts, something about his eyes made me want to give myself over to him, to tell him every little dark and dirty secret I held close. Maybe others reacted the same when they saw him. Maybe that was why he constantly shielded himself with those damn sunglasses.

"Your sister undressed you." His voice was gruffer than usual. He sat up straight and stretched his arms above his head, his shirt rising and allowing me to catch a glimpse of his stomach. Sections of his hair stuck up, and his disarray made him appear more normal and approachable.

In all my encounters with Ford, he'd always been so serious, so to see him wake up, his hair messed, and his shirt all wrinkled, it put him in a different light. Not that I wanted to see him as anyone other than the guy who'd been hired to protect me.

"Why are you in my room?" I pulled the sheet until it was tucked under my chin, my eyes finding his, waiting for his answer. But his lips remained sealed, his stare making me uncomfortable, and I couldn't figure out why. He wasn't leering at me. He wasn't trying to see what I hid under the white linen. Hell, he hadn't even moved his eyes from my face. But the way he looked at me, it was like he was trying to search my soul.

Maybe I'm still drunk.

A breath of tension left my lungs as I stared at the ceiling once more, resigned to the fact that he wasn't going to respond. The man was unpredictable, speaking only when he wanted to.

Ford Massey was a hard man to figure out. He neither stared

after me in lust, nor did he try and get closer to me because of who my father was. I'd been the object of both in the past. Lust and opportunity. Instead, I often felt him judging me, passing it off as if he was just looking out for my well-being because he'd been hired to do so. But I knew he didn't like me. The feeling was mutual.

He shifted in the chair, drawing my attention back to him. He peered down at his watch before glancing back at me, never enlightening me as to why he was in my room.

"You better get dressed. Your father will be here any minute." He rose and walked across the room.

"Why?" It irritated me when he ignored me, more so than I let on. There was nothing ruder than someone choosing not to answer a question. Well, I was sure there were worse things, but right then, there wasn't anything I could think of.

I sat up but kept the sheet clutched to me in case he turned around, even though intuition told me he wouldn't. He promptly closed the door behind him without a word.

Twenty minutes later, I strolled into the living room and saw my parents sitting on the couch, Emily sitting next to them. Ford and Owen weren't present, and I wondered where they were. What was so important that they would leave my family alone? What topic was my father going to raise that didn't require the attention of the security detail he'd hired?

Flashes of the night before filtered in, but not enough that I could remember everything. All the memories before we arrived at the club were intact. Receiving a text from Naomi telling me she had to cancel because she thought she had food poisoning. Ford driving like a nut because he thought we were being followed. But as soon as I started drinking, living it up, my memories were foggy, then disappeared altogether.

"Cara, sweetheart," my dad started, "why don't you take a seat." The tone he used was a familiar one. He was going to broach a topic I wasn't going to like. The thought he'd received another threat disappeared as soon as it had entered my brain, because if that were the case, Ford and Owen would be standing right there with us. No, this was something else altogether.

"I think I'll stand." I looked over at my sister. "Do you know what this is about?" Emily shrugged and shook her head at the same time. I scrutinized her expression, and it appeared she was as much in the dark as I was.

CHAPTER
SIXTEEN

Cara

"This isn't going to turn into an argument. Do you understand me?" My dad paced in front of me with his hands placed behind his back. His demeanor gave everything away. Not only did he *not* believe his own words, knowing damn well whatever he was going to say would be met with resistance and, admittedly, some shouting on my end, maybe even from Emily, as well, but he looked perplexed on how he might resolve or end our upcoming "discussion."

My father was a man of great wealth and one of the leading men in his industry. He had power. Respect. Adoration from millions. Yet, standing before me, he was nothing more than a man about to divulge something his children wouldn't like or even adhere to, possibly causing a rift in the relationship. I hadn't meant to be so dramatic, but I was confident I was going to be pissed off beyond reason.

My dad faced me, but kept whatever distance remained between us intact. My mom continued to sit on the sofa next to Emily.

"It's come to my attention that due to an incident last night, I've got to put my foot down." His words couldn't be more unclear.

"What incident?" I racked my brain, cursing myself for drinking so much that I couldn't recall most of the evening. Bits and pieces filtered in, but not enough to create a full memory.

"Weren't you there? Or were you too intoxicated to remember?" I would've liked to say that my dad talking to me in such a way was a rarity, but as of late, it had become the norm. He was worried about me, had said as much on numerous occasions, but I assumed it was just him playing the parenting role. Saying the necessary things when I acted up and brought negative attention to the family. He loved me, but I couldn't bring myself to change.

With my head held high, I responded with false bravado, "I wasn't drunk." I lied, of course, and from his raised brow, I knew he knew I hadn't told the truth. "What incident are you talking about?"

He suddenly lost all his calm reserve and crushed the space between us. "I'm talking about Kurt."

"What about Kurt?" I had no idea where he was going with this.

"I don't trust him. And I don't like you hanging around him."

"Well, seeing as how I'm a grown woman, I can hang out with whomever I want."

"Not when you make decisions that take you further down the wrong path, Cara." A fire lit behind his green eyes, his anger bubbling to the surface with each word.

My hand took up residence on my hip. "What are you talking about?" *Damn you, alcohol.*

"Drugs. I'm talking about Kurt giving you drugs." Like a fucking lightning bolt to my brain, I recalled Kurt handing me a small baggie. I'd texted him to bring me some coke, knowing I'd need it to lighten my mood. A mood that had been soured before

I'd even left the house.

"How do you know about that?" I gasped, not even trying to deny it. I looked at Emily but realized she hadn't been the one to tell our parents. She'd never rat me out like that. The only other person it could be was either Ford or Owen, and my bet was on Ford.

Memories started to flood in.

Ford making a beeline for Kurt and me when we were sitting at the bar.

Him and Owen practically dragging Kurt out of the club.

Me being angry with Ford for stepping over the line and intruding on something he had no business doing.

"At least you're not going to stand there and lie to my face." There were a few extra stress lines around my father's eyes lately, and I had no doubt I was the cause of them.

"It's like drinking. I'm not addicted to anything. I'm just having a good time when I go out."

"That's the problem, sweetheart," my mom interrupted, rising from the couch and coming to stand in front of me. Next to my dad. A united front. "You're not just having a good time. You're headed toward rock bottom, yet you don't want to see it." She reached forward and squeezed my hand. "Why are you so hellbent on destroying your life?"

I scoffed, pulling away from her. "I'm hardly destroying my life." My tone mocked hers, yet my eyes started to well with tears. Was the glassiness due to anger they were confronting me on business that wasn't theirs? Or was it because I knew they loved me, and deep down I hated hurting them?

"This little talk is over," my father shouted. "You're no longer allowed to see Kurt. In fact, neither one of you are to date anyone until the threat against our family has been taken care of." He looked back and forth between me and Emily, who was still seated.

"You can't be serious." He didn't answer. "Dad. Tell me you're not really going to try and tell me who I can hang out with. I'm twenty-five years old."

"Not yet you're not. And if you keep going at this rate, you won't make it to your birthday." He clutched my mom's hand in his.

"Stop being so dramatic," I chided, furious with this whole song and dance.

"I mean it. No dating." He pointed his finger first at Emily, then at me, holding his stance a few seconds longer. "And even when this threat is put to bed, Cara, you're not to see Kurt."

There were so many things I wanted to yell at my dad, but none of them were respectful. In fact, they were downright mean, but as angry as I was, I wouldn't stoop that low. I turned toward Emily, trying to gauge where her head was at. She wasn't dating anyone, and as far as I knew, there wasn't anyone on the horizon. Unless, of course, she wanted to be with Owen. Even I knew that possibility was bleak, especially considering the situation.

"Are you going to jump in here? Help me out?"

"I... uh...." She took a second to gather her thoughts. "It's not the worst thing."

"What isn't? Being told what to do like I'm a child, or not being able to see Kurt?"

"You don't even really like him," she blurted, walking toward us. "What's the big deal?"

"What's the big deal?" I parroted, staring at everyone in disbelief. Had they all gone stark mad? Was I being punked? I couldn't fathom the possibility of agreeing, and because curiosity had always been my downfall, I dove in head first. "And if I don't?"

My dad frowned. "If you don't what?"

"Stop seeing Kurt, or whomever else I want?" I retreated a step, although based on my father's expression it should have been more than one. His nostrils flared, but he managed to keep his composure.

I loved to rile people. When I pushed the envelope, took things a step too far and the person exploded or internally combusted, a part of me felt… complete. It made me feel empowered, in a sick and twisted way. The drinking and the drugs worked against the control I wanted over my life, but the substances provided me with something greater. Numbness. An escape from the past that continued to haunt me.

A therapist I'd seen years ago, someone the court mandated after a weekend filled with too much fun, told me the reason I loved to push people was that it took the focus off me. If I was fixated on others, and how to get a reaction out of them, I didn't have to look inward and find out why I acted the way I did.

I never saw that quack again.

"I didn't want to have to do this, but you've left me no choice." For a split second, I wished to take back my question because I knew I was going to regret asking it. "If you don't do what I'm asking, what I'm telling you to do for your own good, then you'll be cut off."

He'd never threatened such a thing before, so I wasn't entirely sure what he meant. I got the gist, but I needed the whole scope to know what I was dealing with and how to proceed.

"What do you mean?"

"You know what I mean. Cut off. No more shopping. No more trips." He leaned in. "No credit cards. No access to my money." Before I could go off on a rant, he clarified the rest.

"You will still have a roof over your head and your vehicle, although you won't be driving it right now, but other than that… zilch."

My head spun with the ramifications. Part of me wanted to scream at him that I didn't need his money, that I could get by on my own, but the reality was that I couldn't. I'd depended on him my entire life, on both my parents. I'd never pushed myself to pursue a goal. I wanted to create my own clothing line, but there was never a pressing need to do so, so I remained lax about it.

But apparently, things had changed.

"And don't even think about trying to convince your sister to give you hers because she's on board with it all."

"How do you know she's on board? You've only just told us." I glanced back and forth between him and Emily. "Right?" My sister averted her eyes for a moment too long. "When did he talk to you about this? How long have you known?" My imagination ran wild. Had they been in cahoots for days? Weeks? Was last night the last straw? The catapult for putting everything into place? Crazy demands and all?

"Just this morning," she mumbled, continuing to keep her eyes distant from mine.

I dipped a toe into unfamiliar waters, and before I drowned myself unnecessarily, I stood tall and closed my mouth. There was no way I'd give him the satisfaction of agreeing to his outlandish demands. But I didn't want to lose the benefits of my lifestyle either. So, until I decided what to do, I supposed it was best to remain quiet, something that was rather difficult for me.

I left the house without another word, my steps heavy with purpose as I rushed toward the guest house, hellbent on confronting the one person who was behind my father's outlandish demands.

CHAPTER
SEVENTEEN

Ford

"Do you think he's upset you told him?" Owen asked.

"He didn't sound thrilled with the late-night phone call, and he probably didn't want to hear it, but I'm sure he's not shocked by the news." My brother sat across from me, some home improvement show playing in the background while we talked about what happened the previous night.

There was no way I was going to stand by and be a voyeur while his daughter's actions put everyone at risk. She may have seen it as her personal business, but when she interacted with that shady motherfucker, she invited my input. Anyone who would give her coke was not to be trusted in my book. Sure, maybe my experience with our sister had tainted me, but all thoughts of Julia fell to the wayside as I tried to rationalize my actions.

I didn't tell Walter everything, though, leaving out the specifics, but I hinted around enough that he knew she was doing more than drinking. I'd made the suggestion he restrict both of his daughter's social interactions, code for dating, until the mysterious threat was abolished once and for all. Then they could go back to their lives, but not until then. If he happened to fire me, then how they chose to live their lives wouldn't concern me. I wouldn't lose sleep over it.

As I brought my drink to my lips, the French doors to the guest house crashed open. Startled, splashes of water hit my jeans and parts of the cushion underneath me.

"Fuck." I wiped away the droplets from my lap before glancing up at the person filling the doorway. Cara looked like some sort of wild woman. Sections of her hair had fallen loose from the high bun she shoved her tendrils into, her shirt lopsided like she'd been tugging on it. Her face was flush and flushing redder the longer she locked me in the depths of her icy stare.

It was an odd thought, but her anger intrigued me. Not that I hadn't been on the opposite side of her fury before, because I had, but there was something about the way she squinted her eyes and clenched her delicate hands into fists that made me smile. Internally, of course. Otherwise, I'd have no doubt she'd pick up the first thing she could and hurl it at my head. And there was a heavy lamp sitting on the table to her left.

I knew why she stood in front of us, working hard to control her breathing. All I needed was for her to start talking.

"What did you tell my father?" she shouted, stepping inside without an invite. I supposed she didn't need one. In the span of two seconds, Owen shifted in his seat, made eye contact with me, then rose from the sofa.

"I'll be upstairs." *Wuss.* The bastard left me alone with the raging woman. But because he hadn't been the one to inform her father about her "activities," part of me didn't blame him for dodging the eye of the impending storm.

"Relax. I didn't give him specifics." I stood and walked past her toward the kitchen. She followed behind me, almost bumping into me when I turned around too quickly.

"Relax? Are you serious?" She pushed back a tendril of hair that had fallen over her eye. "You told him enough, which by the way, wasn't your place." I swore her cheeks were more flushed than a moment ago. "He told Emily and me we couldn't date anyone until he finds out where the threats are coming from." I must've given her a look because her chest expanded, and her lips parted wide. "It was you," she accused.

"What was me?" I played stupid.

"You were the one who suggested we not date anyone." It wasn't a question. Her eyes tapered into thinner slits. "Don't bother denying it."

I found it pointless to lie, so I didn't. "I'm only trying to do my job." Leaning back against the counter, I shoved my hands into my pants pockets, releasing a deep breath because I was bored with the back and forth. What was done was done, and Walter had proven to be a smart man. A concerned father who'd made the right decision when he implemented my suggestion. "I also advised him that it was in your best interest to cancel your trip to California, but he said he didn't want to do that. Not yet, at least."

"How do you know about our trip?"

"It's my responsibility to know everything concerning you."

Her frustration barreled off her while she tried to hold steadfast onto whatever reserve she still had left. She took to pacing in front of me. To see her disoriented was new. Cara was someone who seemed sure of herself, even though I suspected some of her bravado was false. She put up a good front, though.

Tense silence passed between us.

"Are you done?"

Her steps froze while her head snapped in my direction and her eyes widened.

"You were hired to do a job. That's it. Watch me from afar." She barely took a breath. "Make sure no one kidnaps me."

109

She looked at me with such intensity, if I were a lesser man, I would've been quaking in my shoes. "Keep your distance and your nose out of my business."

She turned on her heel and stormed out, complaining the entire time.

As I watched her walk away, I couldn't help but think that while I wanted to throttle her during her rant, the image of kissing her seemed more appealing. That it might've been a quicker way to shut her up.

CHAPTER EIGHTEEN

Cara

Utter confusion engulfed me. I couldn't narrow down any of my emotions because they were all over the place. I was embarrassed and upset my parents found out about the previous night, even though Ford said he didn't spill the specific details. But my dad knew. He knew that I wasn't just drinking, and while I stood by my decision to live my life the way I wanted to, I couldn't help the pang of guilt that ate me up inside when I looked into my parents' eyes. Disappointment. Worry. Maybe even a touch of fear.

While I should at least consider their concerns, I wasn't about to give in when threatened. And that was exactly what my dad had done. Threatened me and my lifestyle. It was because of him that I'd grown accustomed to a certain standard of living. So to threaten to rip all of that away unless I conceded to his sudden demands was ludicrous.

I could admit that I'd been sheltered most of my childhood, parts of my adulthood mixing into that sentiment in the ways that I wasn't subjected to hardships. But there was a part of my past that had changed me, shaped the person I grew up to be. Not wanting to dwell on something I couldn't change, however, I focused on the task at hand, which was to get as far away from my house as possible.

When I was in the guest house confronting Ford about what he'd done, I spotted the keys to my Porsche on the table near the door, the same keys I swiped when I'd stormed out.

A small window of opportunity presented itself. I knew it was only a matter of time before Ford realized the keys were missing, so I rushed into the house, ran up the stairs and down the hall toward my bedroom. I passed Emily's closed door and couldn't help but think how deeply her betrayal had cut.

Siding with my parents? How could she? I realized we weren't as close as we'd once been, but life had gotten in the way. We'd taken up different interests, me with partying and living to have fun, and she with all her do-good deeds. We'd drifted away from each other, but I never would've chosen to go against her. I would've had her back, no matter what.

Once I'd quickly changed my outfit, I fired off a quick text to Kurt and told him I was on my way over. After he replied with a simple *OK,* I grabbed my purse and tossed my cell on the bed.

Adrenaline pumped through my veins, my heart beating hard against my chest as I barreled down the steps and out the front door, heading straight for the SUV. Still no sign of Ford or anyone else, for that matter.

I barely locked my seat belt into place before I sped down the curved driveway. The tires hadn't squealed, but I was sure someone heard the engine turn over, and although there was no way for anyone to get in touch with me, I had no doubt a certain someone was going to be scrambling to try and figure out where I'd gone.

Even if Emily offered up information as to where she thought I might've gone, she didn't know where Kurt lived. He'd recently moved into his own place, and not many people had the address. Under normal circumstances, I would've gone to see Naomi, but my sister knew where she lived.

I'd bought myself a few hours of solace, time enough to try and figure out how to handle the situation with my dad.

In no time at all, I turned left off the main road and started up the long driveway to Kurt's house. Nothing but trees shaded both sides of the graveled pathway, the illusion of privacy fleeting beyond the millions of leaves shielding his property.

The farther I traveled up his driveway, the more it dawned on me that all Emily would have to do was get in touch with my best friend, seeing as how Kurt was her cousin. Chances were good he'd given her his address.

Okay, so maybe my plan of escape wasn't perfect, but it would still buy me some time away.

As I drew closer, the trees subsided, and I was presented with wide open space, the gravel kicking up beneath my tires as I drove toward the front of his house. Kurt stood in his doorway, his hair slicked back from an apparent shower and his robe in danger of popping open any second. Good thing he didn't have any close neighbors to speak of.

After throwing the vehicle in park, I shut off the engine and took several seconds to try and calm my heart. The entire ride over I thought about nothing other than how upset my family would be at me for taking off or how pissed Ford would be that he'd have to chase me. And although the latter thought should've amused me more, I had a split second of regret for my actions.

I truly didn't feel I was in any danger. Celebrities received hundreds, if not thousands, of threats a year, and nothing ever happened. Much like the threats we'd received in the past. No follow through.

My behavior could be miscued for immaturity, but I was rebellious by nature. Impetuous. Mix in hotheaded and it wasn't a recipe for any kind of rationality.

"Hey, babe," Kurt greeted, taking me into his arms as soon as I'd approached. "I meant to call you about last night, but I didn't know what to say. I think I'm still trying to process why those assholes got involved." He ushered me inside and guided me toward the living room.

I'd mentioned that my dad had hired security to watch over me and Emily but never got into any details with him. I'd told Naomi, but if she relayed that to him, he never disclosed.

Kurt's house was quaint. Not as big as ours, but spacious enough he had room for everything he needed and then some. He'd never given me an official tour of the place and I didn't ask for one. I couldn't care less about the newest surround-sound system he'd had installed or the eighty-five-inch 4k 3D flat-screen hanging on the wall. I had even less interest in the hot tub that was delivered last week or the four-person shower he'd often boasted about. All my concerns zeroed in on whether he could make me forget about my life for a couple hours. Sex or drugs would do the trick. Maybe both.

"I'm sorry about all that." I walked ahead of him and sat in the oversized chair in the middle of the room, tucking my legs underneath me and nestling in to get comfy. I wanted to elaborate but couldn't think of anything else to say. Truth was, I didn't want to rehash last night. All I wanted to do was forget.

As if reading my mind, Kurt poured something out on to the table in front of me. When he moved to the side, I saw a small mound of coke. While he busied himself cutting up the powder into thin lines, I couldn't help but replay my parents' words in my head. *You're not just having a good time. Why are you so hellbent on destroying your life?* They'd both forgotten what it was like to be young and have your whole life ahead of you. To live free and to soak up each opportunity and just have fun. My internal debate zinged back and forth as I accepted the rolled-up twenty and crouched over the substance that would take me out of my own head for a while.

After I inhaled the first line, I barely took a breath before the second one vanished. My face went numb soon afterward.

One breath.

Two.

Three.

Then another.

A hundred more breaths passed through my lungs before the blissful euphoria coursed through me, and with it came a surge of energy, a plethora of words falling from my lips before my brain could filter any of them.

"I hope you're not upset about what happened last night." *Apparently, I'm going to rehash last night after all.* "I can't control what he does or what his brother does, for that matter. I wasn't even asked before my dad hired them. But why would he be concerned about how I'd feel? It's not like he ripped away my privacy or anything." I briefly made eye contact with Kurt only to see that he was listening attentively. I pointed toward the rest of the white powder. "Aren't you going to have some?"

"I had some right before you got here." He moved closer. "But don't worry, I have more if you want."

I moved to lean my head against the back of the chair, continuing to babble on about last night and how we were having such a good time before the shit hit the fan, when Kurt pressed his lips to my neck, his tongue flicking out to taste my skin. I didn't have a problem fucking him. I rather enjoyed it, but I wanted to relish in my bliss for an uninterrupted moment.

He lifted the hem of my shirt, and before I could open my mouth to tell him to wait, his fingers squeezed my nipple. Hard.

"Ow." I clutched his hand to my chest so he couldn't do that again. "Not yet," I warned, releasing him and shoving him back so I could stand. But he wasn't having any of it.

"Why?" He rested his hands on my waist, anchoring me to my seat. I wasn't afraid of Kurt, so I wasn't alarmed when he refused to back away. "I thought you liked it rough." He flashed a smile.

"Just not right now. All right?" I waited for him to release me, which he did, but only after studying me for what seemed like forever. The way his eyes searched my face made me think he was going to say something deep or ask how I was or what I was thinking about since I'd texted him out of the blue and showed up at his house soon after. But nothing of the sort happened.

"Fine." He backed up. "Do you want some more?"

I shook my head. While my endorphins were on overdrive, all I wanted to do was continue talking and try and burn off some of my heightened energy, but I never got the chance.

The front door to Kurt's house burst open, the sound alone making me jump up from my chair and run toward the noise. The opposite of what any other rational human being would probably do. *Apparently, I'm invincible.*

CHAPTER
NINETEEN

Ford

The saying "fit to be tied" described precisely what I'd been feeling as soon as I realized Cara had stolen her keys and took off. And even though she'd left her phone behind I'd still been able to find her. We'd installed trackers on the vehicles, a detail we didn't tell Emily or Cara. Either way, she wasn't gonna get far from the house before I started out after her.

I knew whose house it was I pulled up in front of as soon as I saw the black Mercedes sedan out front. I walked around the back to look at the license plate, just to be sure. What she saw in that guy I'd never know. That was a bit of a lie. Cara was pissed her father laid down the law, and that I'd been the one to tip him off to her behavior. No doubt she wanted to rebel as much as possible, and I had an inkling she'd come to see this douchebag not only because he was now *forbidden,* but to take him up on his offer from last night. The *offer* I'd thrown behind the bar before she could partake.

I moved through the foyer of the house with speed and accuracy, sidestepping Cara when she approached, ignoring her screams, berating me for busting in, and headed straight for Kurt. I was silent the entire time, my shades in place to shield my eyes and the threat laced behind them.

"What the fuck, man?" Kurt bellowed, backing up repeatedly until his back hit the wall. I followed his line of sight when he glanced over at the table. Lines of coke. A rolled-up bill laying next to them. Smudges of the substance, indicating someone had indulged. As I crushed the short distance remaining between us, I saw that he'd certainly used that shit. But had she?

In hindsight, I should've ignored him, focusing on retrieving Cara and nothing else. But something inside me wanted to make Kurt pay, the need to protect Cara from the likes of him overwhelming me. I couldn't make sense of it, and I didn't have the time to try and understand my irrational thoughts, so I acted instead.

Gripping Kurt by his robe, I slammed him against the wall he'd just been pinned to.

"I thought I already warned you to stay away from her." The growl in my voice made me uneasy. I could only imagine what it did to him. The guy was simple to read. With widened eyes, his dilated pupils focused on me, but it was the slight tremble in his chin that told me he was petrified. I towered over him and outweighed him by at least forty pounds. Even though he was scared and unsure of what else I was going to do, he looked over at Cara, who was still yelling behind me, and attempted to put on a front.

"You need to let go of me right now," he threatened, his false bravado starting to waver when I tightened my grip.

"Or what?"

He never answered, instead taking a breath and narrowing his smarmy, coked-out fucking eyes. It took most of my restraint not to pluck them out of his head. "Who do you think you are? Busting into my house and threatening *me*?" He shouted the last word. "Cara's not yours. She's mine. And you can't keep me away from her."

Cara had ceased screaming, and for as much as I wanted to turn around and see if she was still there, I knew the cause of her sudden silence was the declaration this asshat just made. Laying claim to her like she was a piece of property. And from the likes of him? I found it disgusting and not even in the realm of okay in my book.

Deciding enough was enough, and realizing I had to have a little talk with Miss Dessoye, sooner rather than later, I pulled Kurt close, only to slam him back against the wall. I smiled when I heard the breath leave his lungs.

"I won't tell you again. And if you choose to ignore me, I'll let your father in on your little secret." I took out my phone and snapped a picture of the coke on the table. Then one of him. "He thinks you're clean and sober. What do you think he'll do if he finds out you're not?" I never gave him time to answer. "He'll follow through with cutting you off, and this time for good."

"How... how do you know anything about me?" he stuttered, and it was then I caught a glimpse of the real him. A guy who portrayed one version of himself to the world, someone who appeared to have it all, but he was really a guy who didn't have the first clue about himself.

I'd retrieved Kurt's last name, Mansfield, from Emily on the ride home the night before and had given it to Owen, instructing him to find out as much as he could. With a bit of digging, calling on the special skills of Cal, one of the other guys in our firm, Owen was able to obtain some pertinent information about him.

For starters, he'd been in and out of rehab several times over the past few years, his father footing the bill each time. But dear ol' dad, who was the CEO of a well-known tech firm, had a gambling problem, and threatened to cut his son off if he re-lapsed again. I supposed he needed all the money he could get for his own addiction.

A glimmer of fear pulsed behind Kurt's blown-up pupils, and it was enough to let me know he'd listen this time. He lived off his father's money and spent his time partying as much of it away as he could. No way he was gonna risk that.

"Stay away or else." I released him before turning to face Cara. Surprisingly, she was still there. Most likely intrigued by my encounter with her little boyfriend. Or should I say ex-boyfriend? Or whatever the hell he was to her. No matter, he wasn't allowed anywhere near her. Both by my threat and by the threat of her father. Even if she did try and contact Kurt, my gut told me she wasn't worth more to him than him keeping up his lifestyle.

I walked toward her with purpose. Silence ensued. A good ol' fashioned standoff. But because I wanted to get the hell out of there as soon as humanly possible, I spoke first. "Are you ready?" My question had so many meanings. Are you ready to leave this house? Are you ready to stop rebelling against everyone close to you? Are you ready to grow up? Are you ready to stop pissing me off?

"Hmph," was the only sound she made before she disap-peared through the broken door. The sashay of her hips did nothing to suppress the disappointment I held toward her and what she'd done here today. If I had any question whether she'd snorted that shit, all I had to do was look into her eyes. The same as Kurt's. Blown. The blush of her skin was another indicator. As well as the speed with which she raced down the driveway, barreling toward the driver-side door.

Once I'd realized Cara had taken off, I'd grabbed Owen and we'd left the house. I'd almost forgotten about Emily until I'd seen her through the kitchen window. Once my brother had filled her in on what happened, together, we were on our way to find her sister within minutes.

My brother and Emily were waiting for us in Emily's car. My quickened long strides had me standing next to Cara in seconds, snatching the keys from her hand.

"I don't think so."

She reached to take them back but failed. "I can drive myself back." She tried once more to retrieve the keys, but when she saw I wasn't giving in, she gave up. But instead of getting in the Porsche, she took off down the driveway, rushing like she'd just set the place on fire.

"Hey!" I shouted, but she kept going, so I hopped in the vehicle and took off after her. She was fast, but she wasn't faster than the expensive hunk of steel I navigated behind her. I rolled down the window. "Get in." Nothing. She ignored me and kept speed walking. "I mean it, Cara. Get. In." More insolence. "If you don't get in right now, I'll be forced to tell your father what happened and insist you cancel your little birthday trip to California." That got her attention.

"You wouldn't." Although she didn't phrase her response as a question, it most certainly was.

"You know I will." I drummed my fingers against the steering wheel.

"Why? Why do you keep sticking your nose where it doesn't belong?" I opened my mouth to answer, but she shook her head, showing me the palm of her hand. "Never mind. I don't care why." Her right foot propelled her forward and I cleared my throat.

"Don't call my bluff," I threatened. I could almost see the wheels turning in her head, working through every possible

S. NELSON

scenario until she'd mentally exhausted herself in the span of a few seconds.

She pulled on the door handle of the rear door, but it was locked. My eyes were glued to her while she waited for me to let her in, and had she not slammed her hand against the doorframe, I would've kept watching her.

"Open. The. Door." She was angry, but instead of continuing with the odd struggle for power, I clicked the locks and she jumped in. Truth be told, I was shocked she didn't ride back with Emily and Owen.

She stared out the window, no doubt to avoid my eyes in the mirror each time I looked back at her. Several times, I heard her sniff, then witnessed her pinching her nostrils.

I often wondered if I'd had more conversations with my sister if things would've turned out differently. If I'd been more attentive, taken her calls more, or put aside my need to earn more money and had checked in on her more often, would she be alive today? Expressing those thoughts to Owen, over and over after her death, earned me a stern talking to, reminding me it wasn't our fault. That we didn't know she had a serious problem. But I called bullshit every time he spewed those words. We should've known. Julia was our baby sister and because of our neglect, she was dead.

Or to be more accurate, her death happened because of an argument I had with her. But the last thing I wanted to do right then was rehash old memories because I needed to focus on the issue at hand. The woman sitting behind me. Someone who refused to take accountability for her actions because she was self-centered. And immature, to boot.

Before I could stop myself, my mouth opened, and words flowed freely. Too freely.

"You're selfish," I blurted. So many other words could've been spoken, but those two were the ones forced from my throat.

"Excuse me." It was the first time she looked forward, her eyes catching mine in the mirror.

"You heard me. You're not thinking about anyone but yourself. It's the definition of selfish." As usual, my sunglasses shielded my eyes, which worked to my advantage because I was harder to read that way.

"What business is it of yours to even be concern—" She turned her attention back toward the window. "You know what? I'm not going to give you the satisfaction of answering you. What I do is my business. Not yours. How I act and who it affects is of no concern to you. I don't understand why you care so much anyway. You're hired to watch over me and nothing more. You shouldn't be talking to me otherwise." She swung her eyes back toward the front of the vehicle, toward me. "And for your information, I need to be a little selfish. Who the hell else is going to take care of me? Huh? My parents won't be there to always help me out, and my sister has her own life, one she obviously doesn't want to include me in seeing as she's sided with them over me." She rambled on for another twenty seconds before finally saying, "So if I'm selfish, there's a good reason for it."

I couldn't help myself. "So much for you not answering me." The corner of my lip curved, and she gasped, most likely angry she'd done what she hadn't wanted to, which was engage me.

"Smug bastard."

"I've been called worse."

The rest of the drive back was in silence.

CHAPTER
TWENTY

Cara

The chime of the doorbell drove me down the stairs and toward the front door, needing to explain everything to my best friend like never before. The past two days had passed by in a blur, mainly because all I did was sleep and lose myself by binge-watching Netflix shows.

I opened the door to find Naomi on the porch, but she wasn't alone. Ford stood right next to her. In fact, he blocked her entrance into the house. I cleared my throat, and he half turned in my direction, but not enough to fully look at me.

"All visitors have to be cleared beforehand." The gruff of his tone prickled my awareness he was so close, but his voice, paired with the rigidness of his posture, reminded me I was beyond infuriated with him, and as such, I wouldn't pay him or his absurd rules any mind.

"That'll never happen." I reached around him and grabbed Naomi's hand, pulling her into the house behind me. Normally, we'd sit in the living room or hang out by the pool, but I wanted some privacy, if that was at all possible with Ford watching my every move.

"What's his problem?" she asked, flopping on top of my bed to get comfortable. "He's hot as shit, but he seems very moody." Naomi twirled the strands of her red hair around her finger a few times before she jumped up, sitting Indian-style and looking like she had the biggest secret.

"What?"

She hesitated. "I'm not sure I should tell you." Her bottom lip disappeared between her teeth before she shook her head. "Forget I said anything. I don't want you to be upset."

"Upset about what?" She shook her head again, keeping her lips sealed. "What is it?" I prompted, curious to hear what she didn't want to say.

"It's about Kurt."

"What about him?" My mind went crazy, thinking of all the possible things she could have to tell me about him. Had he told anyone what happened at his house with Ford the other day? Had he made threats toward him?

"Are you sure you want to know?"

"Oh my God, Naomi. Out with it." I sat in the chair in the corner, the same one Ford had pulled next to my bed and had passed out in.

"He was hanging all over some skank at the club last night."

"So."

"So?" She leaned across the bed and stared at me, reading my expression for my true feelings. But there they were, out in the open for her to see.

"Yeah. So. I don't care who he sleeps with."

"Wait, I'm confused. Aren't you two a thing?"

"Not anymore. Ford saw to that." If I were honest, having Ford warn Kurt to stay away from me, and hearing that Kurt had already moved on to someone else didn't upset me. It was the fact that Ford had overstepped and humiliated me in the process that I had issues with. I wasn't in love with Kurt, far from it. He was just a guy to pass the time. But I had thought he liked me more, although having someone like Ford threaten him probably squashed whatever feelings he did have toward me.

Naomi swung her legs over the edge of the bed. "What do you mean?"

Before I got into the story, the one I'd been dying to tell her about, I needed something to take the edge off. "Do you have any candy?" I was referring to cocaine, and by the way she glared at me, I knew she wasn't happy I'd asked.

"I stopped doing that shit, and you should, too. It's no good for you."

My bestie had met a guy a couple of months back, and ever since then, she'd changed a few things about herself. Nothing for the worse, only better. And while I was happy that she was happy, I wasn't like her. I liked the way I was. I enjoyed my lifestyle. I had no plans of altering my life any time soon. Well, more than the required amount since the inclusion of our security.

"Do you have anything?"

"I think I have a Valium. Do you want that?"

"Please." She scrounged around in her purse until she found it. I had no idea how old it was, and I didn't care. After I swallowed it, I joined her on the bed, the both of us relaxing and lying side by side.

After a short bout of silence, she reached over and squeezed my hand. "So, what happened?"

I released a breath and started from the beginning. Some of it she knew and some she didn't, mainly what happened at Kurt's house.

"After I found out that Ford was the one who ratted me out to my father, putting the thought in his head that I shouldn't date anyone, especially Kurt, I was furious. So I took off to his house."

"To the one person you were forbidden to see. Typical Cara," Naomi chided, flashing me a quick grin.

"I suppose." I smiled back. She was right, of course. Tell me not to do something, and I'd go out of my way to do it. "Anyway, I was only there a short while before Ford barged in. Literally. He broke the front door."

"Holy shit!"

"Yeah, holy shit is right. At first, I thought he was just going to make me come with him, but then he saw Kurt and attacked him."

"What did he do?" Naomi turned on her side, and I mimicked her posture so we faced each other. Growing up, many people often thought Naomi was my sister. While I couldn't see the resemblance, we did share the same shade of blue eyes and similar shaped nose, hers dusted with freckles.

"He slammed him against the wall and threatened him to stay away from me." I broke eye contact for a moment before looking back at her. She knew I partied, coke my recent drug of choice but unease unfurled in my stomach about telling her this part of the story. Probably because she'd just reminded me of her disapproval. "He saw the coke on the table and told him that he'd tell his father all about it if he ever came near me again."

"How does he know his father?"

"I don't think he does, but he knew enough details to put the fear into him. To make him believe his dad would find out if he didn't listen. And I have no doubt Ford would do exactly as he threatened, if need be."

Naomi rolled onto her back and stared at my ceiling.

"What?" No response except for a slight tilt of her lips. "What?" I repeated, hitting her thigh with the back of my hand. "Tell me."

"I don't know anything about Ford other than he's gorgeous, tall, mysterious, and moody."

"Sounds to me like you know a lot about him," I joked, mirroring her expression. Her description of Ford was accurate, but she didn't know about all the other stuff. Like the way he watched me. He seemed uninterested, like having to look out for me was a bore, but then there were a few times I caught a glimpse of something else on his face. Most of the time he had on those damn glasses, but the few times I looked into his eyes, I thought I caught a glimpse of something else there. Curiosity? Interest? I couldn't be sure because it always disappeared before I could dissect it.

My best friend also didn't know about the times he'd overstepped his security detail. Showing up in my bathroom while I was bathing, although I'd essentially done the same to him, catching him walking into his bedroom in nothing but a towel. She was present when he'd embarrassed me when I'd thrown the pool party, so she had some idea of what I was dealing with. I'd filled her in here and there, but most times I'd been so frustrated with him—and always having him around—that I glossed over the topic, wanting to discuss anything else.

"I'm just saying if it were me, I wouldn't be complaining about having to look at him every day." Her smile widened, and all I could do was shake my head.

"He is nice to look at." I couldn't believe I admitted that, but it was to Naomi. She wouldn't hold it against me. "It doesn't mean I like him. Not one bit. In fact, I'm counting down the days until this is all over with and he's gone for good."

"But until then...." She bit her bottom lip and gyrated her hips, mimicking sex.

"I don't think so."

"Tell me you've never thought about him while you flicked the bean." She laughed when my mouth fell open. Not because I was embarrassed to talk about sex, because I most certainly wasn't, but the thought of masturbating with the image of Ford in my head... was so wrong.

"There hasn't been much of that these days."

"So, you're not denying it, then."

"I'm saying that there are cameras in every room of the house, minus the bathrooms. So, it's not like I can do it before bed like I used to."

Naomi's nose crinkled. "That sucks." I nodded. "You'll just have to take longer showers." She leaned over and kissed my cheek before hopping off the bed and heading toward the bathroom.

My eyes zoned in on the camera above the window and were fixated there until Naomi reemerged. I tried to think of ways to get back at Ford for everything he'd done, to get under his skin in some way, and I believed, thanks to my bestie, that I found a way.

CHAPTER
TWENTY-ONE

Ford

Minus the incident with Cara's friend Naomi earlier, I made sure to lay low these last couple of days, simply because I didn't have it in me to get into any more altercations with Cara. The woman drained me, and I berated myself for letting her get to me. When I discussed my issues with Owen, he told me I was all worked up because I liked her. Like... *liked* her. He earned a punch for saying that stupid shit. He rubbed his arm and grinned, leaving me to brood by myself.

After finishing up an episode of some crime show, I decided to call it a night. I'd finished my last set of rounds an hour ago, avoiding Cara who was hunkered down on the couch watching TV. I'd barely paid her any attention as I walked through the entire house.

As it was almost midnight, my brother had already turned in. I double-checked the locks to make sure the place was secure before heading into the spare room, which had been converted into a makeshift surveillance room. I checked each camera to ensure everything was quiet when I came across the one set up in Cara's bedroom.

I'd been respectful, always looking away whenever I saw her emerge from her bathroom in a towel or her loosely wrapped robe. She knew I could see her. Hell, she'd even accused me of watching her, which I never did. Not for long, anyway.

But for some reason, my eyes stayed glued to the screen. She wasn't doing anything different than she had before, with the exception that every move she made loosened the belt of her robe. But she never retightened it, like she normally did. Instead, she let the silk material part, exposing the fullness of her tits before the flat of her belly appeared. Then her robe widened even more until it had completely come undone.

She was naked. No panties. Completely bare.

She flitted about her room with no concern that I could possibly be watching her. I did catch her looking into the camera every so often, so I questioned whether she was doing this on purpose or not. But why after all this time would she taunt me? How would she know I'd even watch? How would she know it wouldn't be Owen checking the cameras before turning in?

The thought of my brother seeing Cara naked instantly irked me, but I tamped down my odd reaction before it got the best of me.

I shouldn't care, but I did.

I should look away.

I should leave the room and go to bed.

She'll never know, so what's the harm?

But I'd know, and I wasn't some kind of creeper. At least, I'd never been before.

Cara moved about the room, disappearing into her closet only to reappear moments later. She opened and closed each of her dresser drawers but never pulled anything out. Then she turned on her bedside light and turned off the overhead. I could still clearly see her as she crawled on top of her bed then laid on her back, her robe still wide open.

I wanted to look away. I berated myself for not walking away ten minutes ago, but I couldn't move. All I could do was watch her, curious to see what she was going to do, and why the hell she kept looking over at the camera.

If I removed all the interactions I'd had with Cara, take away all the times she'd been rude toward me, baited me, yelled at me… take all of that out of the equation, I was left with a beautiful woman whom I was very much attracted to. I could never act on it, however, even if I wanted to, which I didn't because I didn't like her. I worried about her well-being and was concerned she was living her life recklessly with no regard for anyone but herself, but that was as far as it went.

All the rooms were equipped with audio. Normally, we turned the sound off, unless there were guests in the house. We had to be aware of any and all conversations. And after what Cara pulled the other day, I made sure to leave the audio on in her room when she talked with Naomi. I had to know if she was planning any future escapes. Thankfully, she wasn't. Not any she voiced out loud, at least.

My ears had pricked when they mentioned my name, of course, but it wasn't anything I didn't already know. She admitted to her friend that I was nice to look at. I knew she found me attractive, but that was most likely where it ended for her—as it did for me where she was concerned. Then she mentioned something about not being able to masturbate as often as she used to because of the cameras.

As if on cue to drive me crazy from the recollection of their conversation, Cara rooted through her nightstand. Then it happened. She pulled something out and laid it on the bed. Before I could zoom in on what it was, I heard a faint buzzing sound. Immediately, I knew exactly what she had next to her.

Before I could convince myself to stop watching, realizing I'd taken it too far as it was, she widened her legs and placed her vibrator over her pussy. Her back arched a little at first contact, and I cursed myself because I knew I couldn't, or wouldn't, look away. A soft moan fell from her lips, so soft I would've missed it had I not been paying such close attention.

Since I'd been ready for bed, the only thing I wore was my boxer briefs. A thin piece of fabric separating my dick from my hand, and at the rate Cara was going, it wouldn't be long before I grabbed myself and started stroking. But that would be wrong, so I dueled with the need to join her in self-pleasure and to keep my hands off myself. For the time being, the latter won.

I was mesmerized by the way she teased herself with the toy, gliding it over her clit, then down to her entrance where she inserted the tip before pulling it out and dragging it back up to her clit. As she repeated the movement, her moans increased and her body twitched a little more each time.

My cock thickened, straining to burst free, but I refrained. Barely. Heavy breaths racked my body while I continued to keep my restraint intact, but the more seconds that ticked by, the harder it was becoming. Every fucking pun intended.

"Ford." I looked around my room, but when I heard it again, I knew who'd said it. Cara. She was moaning my name. At first, it was faint, but it got louder the more her body rocked against her toy. Was she playing with me? Fucking with me? Was this some sort of game for her? Hoping I'd be watching? If so, what was her plan? What did she think she'd gain from her brazenness?

Or was this for real? Was she really thinking about me as she fucked herself? The latter thought was more enticing, but also more dangerous.

From the rhythm of her body, it appeared she was close to coming. I gripped the arms of my chair so damn tightly I swore I was going to leave an imprint of my fingers.

With Cara's right hand busy with the vibrator, her left one trailed up and over her belly until she reached her tits. She squeezed one after the other, pinching her nipples as she drew closer to orgasm. Her pelvis thrust upward, harsh and abrupt every few seconds. Faster and faster.

So many movements, all leading up to her explosion. I grabbed my dick and struggled with pulling myself free and joining her. But I couldn't. It just didn't feel right. Not that watching her entire display was the right thing to do, but to add in my own pleasure was going too far.

I heard her call my name again, followed by, *"I'm gonna come."* One last thrust. One last circling of her clit. One last deep penetration of the vibrator and her body seized up, her thighs clamping together. She must've been holding her breath because a whoosh of air rushed from her mouth, followed by a satisfied groan.

After she'd composed herself, she rose from the bed and disappeared inside her bathroom. She was only gone for a couple of minutes, but the entire time I wondered what she was doing in there. When she reentered, her robe was closed. She walked toward her dresser and pulled out a tank top and some pajama shorts, changing there in the middle of the room. But I supposed it didn't matter since I'd already seen all of her in the most intimate way.

Pushing away from the screens, I decided to finally call it a night, although I doubted I'd be getting any sleep. Every move she'd made replayed in my head, and I couldn't stop thinking about her little show. A half hour later, no closer to passing out,

I hopped in the shower and prayed the cool water would tamper my raging hard-on. But it didn't work so I was left to my own devices. With my head resting against the cool tiles, I stroked myself to the image of Cara fucking herself. It didn't take long before I came, the remnants of my guilt at being her voyeur washing away with the water.

CHAPTER
TWENTY-TWO

Cara

I woke up with a spark of excitement. Today was one day closer to our birthday trip to California. I could hardly wait, despite a certain someone essentially being glued to my side, even while in another state.

Naomi was almost as eager as me, but I wasn't so sure my sister felt the same. There had been a rift between us since the day I discovered she'd sided with my parents. But because I didn't want anything to spoil our impending birthday celebration, I decided to seek her out and have a little chat. See where her head was at and all that jazz.

I didn't have to look far. She was laying out by the pool, reclining in one of the loungers with her nose in a book. We were different in so many ways, her obsession with books one such example. I was all for a hot, steamy romance novel, as was Emily, but she broadened her reading horizons with all sorts of genres. Mystery. Paranormal. True Crime. History. Biographies of some people whom I considered the most boring of subjects. Her last read was on Eleanor Roosevelt. But to each their own, right?

Changing into my swimsuit, I joined my sister on the patio. Owen wasn't present, but I was sure he was somewhere nearby, as was his brother.

Images of Ford bombarded me as I sat next to Emily, and the last thing I wanted to think about right then was him. Or what I'd done last night. I wondered if he'd watched, and if so, what had he been thinking. Or to be more blunt, what had he been doing? There was no guarantee he'd seen me at all, but then the opposite could also be true.

"Hi," I greeted, tapping the top of her book to get her attention. She'd been so enthralled she hadn't noticed me sit down. She rested her book on her chest and smiled.

"Hi."

We looked at each other for a moment, neither of us quite sure what to say. I wanted to pepper her with questions, to demand answers about why she'd chosen their side instead of mine, but I knew better. Whenever I came at Emily like that, she shut down and didn't say much. She'd let me rant until I tired of the one-sided conversation, and leave. And because I never felt I was wrong, I refused to apologize. Eventually, we'd move on. But I wanted to have a real conversation this time.

"I wanted to ask you about what went down. With Mom and Dad?"

"What about it?" Her blasé tone annoyed me, but I didn't want to get too heated too quickly. So I let it slide.

"Why didn't you give me a heads-up? You let them blindside me."

"I just found out an hour before they showed up at the house." Her fingers played with the edges of her book, her dislike for any type of confrontation showing.

"It was an hour more than I had," I shot back, making sure to keep my rising temper at bay. I wanted to talk to her, and if I started acting like my usual self, I knew I wouldn't get far.

Emily turned on her side to fully face me. "What do you

want to know, Cara? Why I agreed with Mom and Dad for not letting you see Kurt anymore? Because the only answer I can give you is that he's an ass and is no good for you. Besides that, he's a bad influence."

"A bad influence? What are we, twelve?" My sarcasm did nothing to deter her from continuing, her to-the-point approach surprising me.

"You can make fun all you want, but you know damn well what I'm talking about. I understand that you want to have fun. You're still young, not married, and don't have kids. I get it. But at some point, you have to grow up and make a plan for your life. A goal of some sort. Partying, trying any kind of drug out there just to prove you're cool or something is just stupid."

"I don't try every kind of drug," I corrected, scrambling to come up with any kind of defense. But I fell short.

"I'm sorry. I'm not siding with you on this. Although, Dad restricting us from dating altogether is a bit extreme. That I'll give you. But it's not like we can do anything about it. Besides, it won't last forever." She turned on her back and opened her book, but before she started reading again, she looked over at me. "I love you." She allowed several seconds to pass. "I just don't want you to hurt yourself, that's all."

"I wish everyone would stop fucking worrying about me. I know what I'm doing. I'm. Fine," I emphasized. I didn't know what else to say. I hid behind my words, my false bravado, but the reality was I was upset and disappointed, and I wasn't convinced all my emotions should be directed toward my sister or the rest of my family, for that matter. Some of it should be pointed at myself, but I didn't want to deal with figuring out why, so instead, I got up from the lounger and started to walk away.

"I'm going to be out here for a bit if you wanna jump in." It was her attempt at smoothing over the uneasiness between us. I appreciated it and accepted.

"You're not coming in?"

"I did already." She must have gone in a bit ago because her suit was dry. "I wanna finish my book." *A Room of One's Own* by Virginia Woolf.

"Interesting read?" I asked, placing my right foot into the water to test the temperature. Perfect.

"Very." She smiled wide before pulling the book back up in front of her.

For the next ten minutes, I swam continuous laps before hopping on one of the floaties, relaxing and soaking up the heat from the sun. I untied my bikini top and let the material shield my nipples. I also lowered my bottoms as much as possible while still being covered. Although, there wasn't much to lower because my bathing suit was already skimpy. But if I could avoid tan lines as much as possible, I tried to.

With my eyes closed, I attempted to focus on something fun and exciting rather than all the other shit floating around inside my head. My trip. But my enthusiasm was short-lived when I heard his voice.

Ford.

Something about his presence put me on alert, the tension in my muscles returning with vigor. None of our encounters had been pleasant, and there was no hope in sight for one to happen anytime soon.

"Cara." My name sounded like acid on this tongue. Or was my assumption ill placed?

"What?" My tone held no pleasantry, praying he'd get the hint that he was interrupting my relaxation time. I chose to keep my eyes closed, and if he considered it rude, I couldn't care less.

"Are you almost finished?"

"With what?"

"The pool."

"Why?"

A brief silence ensued before he said, "I want to get some exercise in and wanted to use it."

He wanted to use the pool? I wasn't sure why that came as a shock to me, seeing as how he'd used it numerous times before, but it was weird that he was asking me about it.

Then it dawned on me that he was most likely half dressed, and when that image barreled in, my eyes popped open. And sure enough, he stood by the edge of the deep end, staring down at me as I floated by. A pair of knee-length board shorts was all he wore. I'd seen him shirtless before, but nothing like this. The way the sunlight bled all over him made him look exquisite. He was cut in all the right places—toned and muscular, but not too much. Just enough to make any woman drool. His skin was kissed by the sun, and I couldn't keep from wondering if *he* had any tan lines to speak of. The waistband of his shorts hid part of a scar on his lower right side and I wondered what the story was behind it, and why I hadn't noticed it when I walked in on him in his room. That was before I remembered I'd been enthralled with seeing his eyes for the first time.

"You don't need me to get out for you to use it. It's big enough for the both of us." The implication that I wanted him in the pool with me wasn't what I wanted, but I wasn't going to cut my time short because he wanted to get in some exercise. "It's huge." Our pool wasn't Olympic size, but it was bigger than the normal in-ground.

I watched for his reaction, but he gave me nothing. Not a raise of his brow or a shake of his head. I did, however, hear him mumbling something before he dove in, and I'd be lying if I said my eyes weren't glued to him the entire time he swam to the shallow end, then back toward me. He was quick. Powerful. I attempted to ignore him, but I couldn't seem to help myself. And the one time I glanced over at Emily, she smiled and wiggled her brows. I wanted to smile right along with her, but I didn't want to give her the wrong impression, the impression that I liked him in any way.

But that didn't mean I couldn't appreciate how hot he was. Mix in a sudden need to goad him, and I decided to ask him something I'd been wondering since I opened my eyes this morning.

I allowed him the time he needed to do his laps. Thirty minutes of him swimming back and forth, never seeming to tire. Thirty minutes of me sneaking peeks at him when he wasn't looking, watching the way he glided through the water like it was his second home, the way his muscles twitched with each stroke. Thirty minutes of my body becoming heated, and it had nothing at all to do with the sun beating down on me.

Ford slowed during his last two laps, resting on the ledge of the pool after he finished. He dunked his head under the water and pushed his hair back when he surfaced. He then placed his arms on the concrete and pulled himself up and out of the pool. The corded muscles of his back moved in unison, and I hated to take my eyes off him. And as he walked by me, toweling himself off, I asked my question.

"Ford."

He ran the towel over his hair, parts of it sticking up and making him look sexier. "Yeah?"

"I was wondering something." My tone was pleasant, enough to make him take a step closer so he could hear me.

"What's that?"

"You watch anything good last night?" I studied him, waiting to see if he'd inadvertently let me know he'd seen my little show. And there it was. The slightest widening of his eyes. It was so quick I would've missed it had I not been staring at him.

But his response was even quicker. "Not particularly. Nothing I haven't seen before." *Touché.*

"Are you looking for a good movie to watch?" Emily interrupted, unaware of what was going on. "Because I saw a great documentary on—"

"Oh my God, Emily. *Any* documentary is not my idea of a good time."

"Your loss," she responded, seemingly content to get back to her book.

Instead of bantering with my sister, I watched Ford walk toward the guest house, the confidence in his gait eliciting an ache deep within that confused the hell out of me.

CHAPTER
TWENTY-THREE

Ford

The water washed over me as I rested my head against the tile, much like I'd done less than twenty-four hours ago. Only this time my dick wasn't clenched in my hand. Although, if I kept thinking about Cara's question, her way of letting me know she'd known what she was doing, hoping I was watching, I might have stroked myself.

Who did she think she was playing with? I wasn't some schmuck who'd fall all over myself or her, for that matter, dying to get her attention. She chose to put on that little show. I just happened to be going over the cameras at that exact time. *Then stayed to watch the entire fucking thing.*

Lost to my thoughts, I never heard my brother enter the bathroom. "Hey," he shouted, pulling back part of the shower curtain.

"What the fuck? Get the hell out of here." *Christ!* He scared the shit out of me.

"Hurry up. Walter's on his way over. They got another note."

"You couldn't tell me that from the doorway?" He laughed before closing the door, leaving me to finish washing up. Once I dried off, I was dressed and ready in five minutes flat.

As I walked through the house, I couldn't help but recap what had happened earlier. When I'd walked out on the patio, I'd seen Emily sitting in one of the loungers reading a book. She wore a bathing suit, a one-piece. She was beautiful and had a great body, but I didn't look at her like that. Besides, my brother would be pissed off if I let my eyes linger too long on her, not that he should care, seeing as how she was our client and all. But I knew better.

Then as I walked toward the deep end, that was when I saw Cara in the pool. I blamed the sun for shining too brightly for the reason why I hadn't seen her sooner, or maybe I was too busy praying I wouldn't run into her anytime soon. Unrealistic, I knew, but I did it just the same.

She was practically naked, but that was to be expected. During the small amount of time I'd known Cara, I realized she loved to push the envelope in any way she could. As soon as I saw her exposed skin, my thoughts had drifted to last night, and I struggled to push them to the side, focusing instead on doing what I came outside to do. Use the damn pool. Then she invited me in with her. Well, not *with* her, per se.

While I'd caught her watching me as I swam, I never gave her any indication I was aware of her attentions. Not that I hadn't glanced at her every now and again, but I'd never admit as much.

I heard Owen and Walter conversing in the kitchen of the main house and hoped I hadn't kept them waiting too long. Whenever my mind wandered, I lost track of time.

"Hi, Ford," Walter greeted, extending his hand as soon as I was close enough to reciprocate. "How are you? I hope my daughter isn't giving you too much trouble." His strained smile indicated he knew she was. I never told him about Cara's escape to Kurt's house and what she'd done while there, deciding it was best to keep that one under wraps. But if she tried it again, all bets were off, and whatever consequences landed at both of our feet, we'd have no choice but to deal with them.

"Everything is fine," I answered, hoping he believed my lie. He dipped his head slightly before walking into the living room to join his wife and daughters. The three of them were seated on the larger sofa, their eyes quickly finding those of the patriarch.

"Show them," Diana instructed. "They need to see it."

Of course, we needed to see the newest note, but it must've been more unnerving than the other two to have her this upset. Not that she hadn't been before, because she was, but this time was different. I could feel it in my bones.

Owen and I took our seats on the free sofa, leaning forward with unease. Walter pulled the note from inside his jacket pocket and handed it to me.

"We've already had it tested for fingerprints, and like the others, there aren't any."

I was more comfortable handling it knowing I wasn't ruining the chance of finding who'd sent it. Carefully, opening the paper, I read the contents.

'The farther away they are, the easier it'll be to make you pay.'

It didn't take a genius to know that whoever sent this note knew something about the impending trip the women had planned to California. Question was, was the threat enough to make Walter put the brakes on their birthday celebration trip?

"They know," Diana offered, her chin quivering in fear. "How do they know? Who is it?" She spoke quietly but loud enough for all of us to make out her words.

"I'll find out, sweetheart." He pulled her close and kissed her temple before rising to stand by the corner of the couch. His attention zoned in on Cara and Emily, who were locked on his stare, waiting for what was coming next. Cara's shoulders tensed while Emily seemingly remained unfazed by it all. She was more agreeable, so I doubted whatever Walter said would anger her like it would her twin.

Walter paced, running his fingers through his hair in frustration. He stopped every few steps, looked at me and Owen, then his children, before continuing. It went on for several moments before he paused and finally spoke.

"I think it's best you cancel your trip to California." As soon as the last word left his mouth, I homed in on Cara, waiting for the explosion. She was seconds away from losing it, not a care in the world for the tiny bits of deluge that would soon cover her family.

She stood abruptly, and just when I thought she'd dive into a rant about how it was unfair of him to suggest such a thing, she took a breath and raised her head, her posture straightening with poise. She opened and closed her mouth several times but never spoke. She appeared to be at a loss for words, which was uncanny, given she'd never had the issue before, not while I'd been in her presence, at least.

Cara turned toward her mother. "I'll be on my best behavior. I promise." She didn't include Emily with her plea because we all knew her sister wouldn't be a problem. "Besides, these guys"—she pointed toward me and Owen—"won't let anything happen to us. We're in good hands."

Walter contemplated her plea, even though it'd been directed toward Diana. Their parents exchanged a coded look. "I don't like it," Walter finally spoke. "You'll be too far away from us if anything happens. It'll be the perfect opportunity for whoever sent this note to follow through with their threat." He shook his head. "No, I'm not comfortable with any of it."

I glanced at Cara from the corner of my eye. Hers were filling with unshed tears, her cheeks flushing pink in the moments that followed. Her sister, however, hunkered down on the couch, sneaking peeks at her parents then at Owen, looking like she wanted to say something, but never did. She also didn't seem as if she was upset. Maybe she was thankful she didn't have to let her sister down by canceling their birthday celebration. Emily didn't strike me as someone who enjoyed partying, and with her father insisting they cancel their trip, she might even be relieved. It was all just a guess, of course.

"Please don't punish me," she whispered. "I know I haven't been the best daughter, and I know I've embarrassed you more times than I can count."

"Cara, this has nothing to do with—"

"We promise to listen to everything Ford and Owen say." The reluctance in her voice screamed she was lying, but I suspected her parents hadn't picked up on it. I had no doubt Emily would be on board with our directive, but I knew, as surely as I stood there, Cara would put up a fight. "If they think wherever we are is unsafe, we'll leave. No questions asked."

"I don't think it's such a good idea." Her father shook his head softly, his pensive demeanor conveying he was conflicted about whether he should give in. In the end, it was Diana who pushed him toward the final decision.

"While I don't want either of you to be so far away from us right now, I believe Ford and Owen can keep you safe from harm." She pinned us with her stare. "You are not to let them out of your sight, not for one second." Her husband parted his lips to speak, but she just grabbed his hand and nodded. Another coded message.

"Fine," Walter reluctantly agreed. "But you're taking the

private jet, and you're not staying anywhere other than our place in Modesto."

Cara's lips turned upward in a genuine smile, Emily mirroring her reaction, although there was something behind her expression that told me she'd rather be staying home.

"We planned on both of those things, so it all worked out." Cara gave her parents a hug before disappearing upstairs. I was left to wonder if she would try and stay true to her word to her parents. Would she give me a hard time, or would she follow instructions if a situation arose that we felt wasn't safe?

Only time would tell.

CHAPTER
TWENTY-FOUR

Cara

The day had finally arrived. July twenty-fourth, the day before mine and Emily's birthday. Twenty-five on the twenty-fifth. It only happened once in a lifetime. Was I going to celebrate a little bit extra because of it? No doubt. Any excuse to have a great time. I only hoped no one got in my way of doing so.

I'd promised my parents that if Ford and Owen truly felt we were in danger at any point during our trip that we'd leave wherever we were, no questions asked. But the more I thought about it, the less I believed we were in harm's way, and I refused to cower under ridiculous threats I was confident were bullshit.

Whoever had sent those notes to my dad probably just wanted to freak him out. Maybe it was an actor he'd refused to hire. Or it could be a delusional fan, looking for their fifteen minutes of fame and nothing else, barring they left enough evidence to trace the notes back to them. Hell, it could be a simple prank from someone close to him. That would be warped and perverse, but it was a possibility.

My dad had arranged the flight on the smaller of his private jets. The one we were taking sat twelve comfortably, and since there were only seven of us, it was plenty spacious. Emily was bringing Karen Tulson, her best friend since grade school, and

Naomi was bringing her new boyfriend, Benji Masten. Their relationship was fairly new, and I'd only met the guy a handful of times, but he seemed to really like my BFF, so he was okay in my book.

I counted down the minutes until we were able to board the jet and take off. I needed this little getaway so badly. After everything that had happened in the past few weeks, I craved some time to unwind and focus on one thing and one thing only. Celebrating my birthday. Our birthday.

My sister, my parents, or even Ford would tell you I *celebrated* something on an almost daily basis, but this was different. A quarter of a century birthday only came around once. Naomi told me earlier she had a surprise for me once we landed in California. I tried to make her tell me, reminding her how I hated surprises, but the woman was a goddamn vault.

The flight time was just under five-and-a-half hours. Enough time to get the pre-party in full swing, although the atmosphere wouldn't be as carefree and fun with Ford on board.

Ever since he'd been hired, I felt trapped. God forbid I did anything without my shadow breathing down my neck, and I had no doubt his eyes, even while shielded behind those shades, would be watching every move I made. But there was only so much trouble I could get into thirty-thousand feet in the air.

Emily didn't mind Owen's presence at all. Whenever I'd asked her about him, she'd smile and tell me how nice he was, or that she was attracted to him, but that was as far as it went. I suspected she wasn't completely honest with me, though. She never used to keep things from me, but I supposed once I started hiding certain aspects of my life, I'd shoved a wedge between us.

Not to get me wrong, I loved my sister like no other. She was my twin. I'd even go so far as to say she was my better half.

We had an unbreakable bond, one that just happened to have some cracks. My hope was that we could become as close as we once were... before.

Not wanting to dwell on the past, or the seemingly impossible hopes for the future, I was pleased to have the distraction of the flight attendant passing out glasses of champagne. Everyone took one except Ford and Owen.

"You don't need to sit so close. No one is going to kidnap me on the plane." Ford sat directly across from me, ignoring all the other available seats on the jet. He didn't banter back, instead dividing his attention between the window and his phone. I had no idea what he was looking at, and I doubted he'd tell me if I asked.

He remained quiet among all the chatter, his shades securely in place. He appeared to use them as a shield, something he could hide behind so he didn't have to interact. Or he was creeping behind them, watching everyone without them being aware. But I *was* aware. I was all too aware of his presence, whether his focus was on me or not. Most times, it was the former.

I snatched an extra glass off the attendant's tray and presented it to Ford. "Take it," I instructed, leaning forward until I breached his personal space. He turned his head away from the window and toward me.

"No, thanks."

"Come on. I won't tell."

"I don't drink on the job." He leaned farther into his seat and crossed his arms over his chest. I couldn't help but stare at the way the fabric of his shirt stretched over his flexed biceps.

"You're always on the job. Don't tell me you haven't had one single sip of alcohol this entire time."

He didn't answer me; instead, he directed his attention back to the outside world. Rude. I was only trying to be nice, and look where that got me. I swore, if I didn't know better, I'd say Ford deliberately went out of his way to ignore me, or incite me in some way. Maybe it was the second glass of champagne talking. Alcohol sometimes made me more sensitive to my surroundings, even though all I usually wanted was to be numb, even when I was trying to have a good time.

"You're impossible," I mumbled, but before I could leave my seat to join the others, Owen plopped down next to Ford, bumping his shoulder with his own.

"What's up?" he asked Ford.

I watched the interaction between the brothers with slight fascination. I'd only seen them chat a couple of times prior, but it'd been all business. This time, however, Owen seemed to be enjoying himself, all while remaining professional. His older brother should take some pointers.

"Just counting down the minutes until we land." Ford's attention remained out the window.

Owen leaned in and talked quieter, but because I sat so close, I heard every word. "You need to lighten up, brother. Get rid of that chip on your shoulder for the next few days."

Ford shifted in his seat. "Don't lecture *me* on how to act."

"What's that supposed to mean?"

I suddenly felt like I was intruding on a personal conversation, which in reality, I was indeed doing.

"You know exactly what I mean." Ford finally looked at his brother, but not before glancing my way beforehand. "You better get your head out of your ass and stop fucking around. You were hired to do a job. Nothing else." His words were low and clipped, and had I not had the same suspicion about Owen and Emily, his words would've gone right over my head.

Owen's response was to look over at me and flash me a strained smile. He left his seat and walked toward the back of the plane where my sister was seated next to Karen. I watched him the entire way, witnessing the scowl on his face as he sat across from Emily. Because of the noise of the other's, I couldn't quite hear what she'd asked him. Whatever it was, he just shook his head, pulled out his phone, and diverted his focus to his screen.

Deciding to take a chance and see if Ford would talk to me about something we both suspected, I changed seats and sat right next to him.

"What are you doing?" he asked, shifting and leaning closer to the window.

The champagne provided me with a bit of liquid courage, or maybe it was seeing Ford in such a sour mood that prompted me to take that seat.

"Don't worry. I won't bite." My tone was light and casual, lacking the typical snippiness of many of our prior and short conversations. "Would you please take off your sunglasses?"

"Why?" He continued to lean away from me, an action which I found delightful. He'd just proved I made him uneasy, much like he did to me.

"Because I'd like to have a conversation with you where I can see your face."

"You can see my face just fine," he retorted, taking a deep breath while continuing to keep his distance.

"You know what I mean." Five drawn-out seconds passed before he lifted his hand to his face and removed his shades, placing them in his lap, his agreeability surprising me.

"Happy?"

"Yes." I wasn't sure if it was the soft tone in which I used to answer, or the fact my hand was so close to his on the armrest, but he turned to look at me. His eyes roved over my face, his brows creating a deep crease in between. He seemed confused by the interaction. I couldn't say I blamed him.

"Well?"

"Well, what?" My frown mirrored his, but my body language was different. Where his was standoffish, mine was to be perceived as engaging. I'd gotten nowhere with him acting like myself, so I decided to kill him with kindness, so to speak. Or, at the very least, not be so damn bitchy.

"What did you want to talk to me about?" Oh yeah, I wanted to have a conversation. Initially, I planned to ask him about his thoughts on Owen and Emily, but the more I became mesmerized with his eyes and all the secrets he hid behind them, the more I wanted to talk about him.

"I figured it was time for us to get to know each other a little better." I took a small sip of my drink, intently studying him.

"I know everything I need to. But thanks." His response was curt.

"You think you know me, but you don't. Most people don't," I offered, shocked with my comeback. I drained the rest of my champagne and snapped my fingers at the flight attendant.

"Typical," Ford grumbled.

"What is?"

"Your attitude."

Baffled, I urged him to continue, surprised he hadn't stood and sat somewhere else. "Do tell." Normally, I would've blown him off and drank myself into a stupor, but my inner voice told me to stay put and make him talk to me. Or attempt as best I could. I doubted anyone could *make* Ford do anything.

"You're fully aware of how you act. You don't need me to break it down for you." The corners of his mouth curved up, but he wasn't smiling. His expression was more of a snarky grin. I pushed him to talk, and now it seemed he wasn't going to hold back. He shifted his body to face me and leaned uncomfortably close, his eyes searching mine for something. Anything I assumed. "What happened to you?" Gone was my fascination with getting him to open up about himself, his question knocking the air from my lungs.

"Wh-what do you mean?" No one had caused me to stutter in ages. My tongue poked into the side of my cheek, and I drew a long breath before responding. "Nothing happened to me," I barked, drawing the attention of my sister, who turned in her seat to look at me. She mouthed, "You okay?" to which I nodded.

"Well, something did," Ford countered. "Otherwise, you'd act more like Emily." Comparing me to my sister was a common occurrence. My parents had been doing it for years, and I'd learned to accept it. But something about the way Ford said it insulted me, like he was implying I wasn't entitled to have my own personality apart from my sister.

"Just because we're twins doesn't mean we're the same person." My reply sounded defensive, but he'd flustered me to the point I couldn't think straight. I didn't know if it was that damn piercing gaze of his or his accusatory tone that had me unnerved.

It wasn't until Ford looked away that my heartbeat slowed, the thumping of my pulse regulating back to normal. Even though I'd been the one to push him into conversation, it was he who ended it with his simple probing question. A question that hit deeper than I could've ever anticipated.

CHAPTER
TWENTY-FIVE

Ford

As I hoped, Cara left me alone for the rest of the flight, entertaining herself with the other members of her party. She avoided any and all eye contact with me, although she couldn't tell when I was looking at her because I'd thrown my shades back on. Even though we were in the air, and I knew there was no threat to her well-being, other than herself, of course, I kept a close eye on her.

Two black Lincoln Navigators waited for us when we landed, and after loading the luggage into the backs, we took off for the house we were going to be staying at. One of Walter's many homes, nestled on ten acres of land in the city of Modesto, tucked away from everything else, perfect for limiting distractions. The drive took forty-five minutes, and although Owen and I had minced words back on the plane, I was thankful he rode with me. Which meant Emily sat next to Cara in the back. The rest of the party had taken the second vehicle, following close behind.

Exiting the interstate, it was another ten minutes until I turned down a long dirt driveway. The estate was well hidden, which was undoubtedly on purpose. As we drew near, the house came into view, the setting sun lighting the horizon on fire and casting a glow over the enormous home, which turned out to be a log cabin. The biggest log cabin I'd ever seen, but not the typical house I'd suspected, although it was grand just the same.

Everywhere I looked, I saw huge windows running from floor to ceiling. In hindsight, probably not the safest home, but who could've anticipated the threat against their family? Walter had given me the security code and told me while it was simple to operate, it was top of the line. Because it was settled in the middle of nowhere, multiple cameras had already been installed. Not as many as back in the New York house, but sufficient enough for us to do our jobs properly.

The rocks of the driveway kicked up beneath the tires until I finally came to a stop near the front porch. Exhausted, all I wanted to do was hit the hay, but a quick glance at my watch told me it was only eight thirty in the evening. Which meant there was a good chance the women were going to want to go out. I only prayed they were as tired, but as the other SUV pulled up behind us, and the occupants jumped out, they chatted about where they all wanted to go once they'd changed and freshened up.

"Cheer up, man." Owen slapped me on the back. "We're in California."

"We've been here plenty before."

"Yeah, but not for some time." He helped Emily with her luggage and walked up the steps to the front porch. Extracting a key from his back pocket, he opened the door but not before telling everyone else to wait outside until I completed the initial walkthrough. Owen stayed behind with the others, just to be safe. I was thorough but quick, wanting to get this over with as soon as possible so I could rinse off and relax a little before we headed back out. To where, I could only imagine, but I didn't want to think about that right then.

As soon as I stepped inside, my eyes widened at the state of the place. Gorgeous. I wasn't one who was impressed easily because I'd been inside many a fine home, but something about the place eased some of my anxiety.

To the left was a wide, wooden staircase, wrought iron swirling between the top and bottom of the banister. Above opened to a balcony, looking down on the living area below. An enormous stone fireplace took up the majority of the far wall ahead of us, two big brown leather sofas positioned in front of it for a nice, cozy feeling.

The open concept led to a state-of-the-art kitchen with marble countertops and a stone backsplash, all the appliances stainless steel. There was another sitting area on the other side of the room, as well as a custom-built sauna toward the back of the house.

Venturing outside to finish my check, I saw there was a fire pit set deep in the stone patio, ten seats placed around it in a circle. Under any other circumstance, I would've loved to light a fire and relax out there well into the evening, but I was on duty. A little farther out was a large pool, with lounge chairs surrounding it.

Once I was satisfied, I reentered the house and made my way back toward the front porch, signaling to my brother that everything was all clear.

"It's about time," Cara snarked before wheeling her luggage behind her. I was used to her by now, so whatever attitude she wanted to shade me with wasn't going to get under my skin. Not anymore. I'd made a deal with myself on the plane ride over that I wasn't going to be as stressed out as I had been. I was going to continue to do my job to the best of my ability, but I wasn't going to allow Cara to rile me the way she had since the day I met her. She was who she was, and I wasn't going to change her. Not that

I wanted to. I'd admit that I'd overstepped my bounds on a couple of instances, but I'd been reacting because of my guilt, something Owen had brought to my attention before. I didn't want to hear him, but he was right.

Cara wasn't Julia.

Sometime later, while almost everyone was in the main living area, talking and having a drink, there was a knock on the front door. Owen and I locked eyes before rushing toward the door, simultaneously pulling our guns from the holsters tucked underneath our jackets.

Whipping open the large wooden door, we came face to face with a small, white-haired man, his eyes bulging at seeing our guns pointed in his face. As far as we were aware, there weren't going to be any visitors that evening, so our actions were a precaution.

"Who are you?" I asked, the bass in my voice clipping all three words.

"I... I...."

"Spit it out," Owen barked.

"I'm the chef," he finally said, a bead of sweat forming on his brow. Looking behind him, I saw a truck parked to the side of our vehicles. Rocco's Catering.

Before we could ask him another question, Naomi pushed between us, unfazed by seeing our guns drawn.

"This is my surprise for Cara," she said, shaking her head in disbelief. I knew she was aware of why her best friend had a security detail, so for her to be surprised we'd acted in such a way baffled me. Although, it only drove home once again how much of a lack of concern they possessed for the whole issue. "Put those damn things away." She glared at the both of us until we lowered our weapons.

"Do you have anyone else with you?" I asked, peering around him to see if someone was next to him on the porch.

"Just my assistant. She's in the van." I hadn't noticed his French accent before then, although, to be fair, we hadn't given him much of a chance to talk.

"I'll go check," my brother offered. "Make sure everything's clear before they come inside." I nodded and stepped onto the porch, essentially pushing the old guy back.

"What's going on?" Cara had been upstairs and had no idea what was going on.

"This is the surprise I was telling you about," Naomi answered, her disapproval written all over her face when she looked back to me. *Great, now I have to deal with two women glaring at me for the rest of the night.*

Cara's demeanor switched in the span of a millisecond as soon as she realized who stood outside the door. She hugged her friend before ushering the old man inside. They bustled past me, but not before she chastised me for doing my damn job.

"Don't you know who he is?" I didn't have a chance to answer before she said, "Michel Rocco. He's one of the most famous French chefs around. God, Ford. Get a clue."

Don't let her get to you. Don't let her rile you. Ignore her. It's not worth getting pissed off about. Instead of answering, realizing if I spoke right then I'd most likely say something inappropriate, I chose to remain silent, following the three of them into the kitchen.

"You can set up in here," Cara offered before telling the man how excited she was to eat everything on his menu that evening. She smiled and carried on a conversation with the guy, and for a brief moment, I was jealous of the ol' bastard. Not because of who he was, because I hadn't a clue, but because Cara had never looked at or spoken to me in such a manner. As if she liked me. Hell, I didn't *need* her to like me. On the contrary, it made my job easier because she didn't, sort of. But was it too much to ask for indifference rather than all-out contempt?

Once Owen deemed the van was free from threat and that the woman assisting the chef was harmless, he allowed her to enter, even helping them bring in some of the items they needed to cook. He was a better man than me.

I hung back, making sure to keep out of everyone's way. I had no desire to eat any of the recipes the guy whipped up, most of it I couldn't even pronounce. Although, in my defense, it was French cuisine and I preferred meat and potatoes.

It took two hours to complete all seven courses, and the only thing to come out of it for me was the fact that everyone was stuffed and too tired to move afterward. Which meant there would be no clubbing that evening.

Thank Christ for that. I'd take any reprieve I could get.

CHAPTER
TWENTY-SIX

Cara

"I think I gained ten pounds," I complained, gingerly rubbing my belly while sprawled out on the couch.

"I don't think I'll ever need to eat again." Karen laughed, mimicking me while occupying the opposite sofa, sharing it with my sister who had her head leaned against the back of it, moaning from overindulgence. Much like the rest of us.

Naomi and Benji were in the kitchen making drinks for everyone, and while I was stuffed, I always had room for a cocktail, or two, or three.

"Here we go." Naomi walked back into the room, Benji hot on her heels. He was a cute guy, not my type, but cute all the same. His light brown hair was cut short, the type of texture that if he let it grow would look like a puffball, it looked to be that curly.

The way he gazed at her when he thought no one was looking was touching, and it made me wonder if anyone would look at me in such a way. Before I got too sentimental, I accepted my drink and took a large sip before realizing how strong it was. Not that I couldn't handle it, it just took me by surprise.

"Damn, woman." I coughed, covering my mouth to keep the rest of it from spraying out. "You could've warned me."

"Sorry." The wicked grin on her face told me she knew exactly how strong she made the drink.

"Do you want me to add more club soda?" Benji offered, his hand outstretched to take my glass in case I agreed. Naomi's specialty was an Old Fashioned, and normally she made them with the perfect mix of bourbon, Angostura bitters, sugar, and club soda. Only this time, she didn't flick her wrist back quick enough when pouring the bourbon.

"No, I suppose I'll make do." My mock martyr comment had Naomi smiling.

"Oh, however will you manage?" She patted my leg to make room for her and Benji after she passed out the rest of the drinks.

"I have no idea," I jested, taking another sip. After the fourth, I deemed it was the best drink I'd had in a long time.

A half hour passed with chitchat about how scrumptious the dinner was and how I'd never expected such an awesome surprise. Then we talked about some possible clubs we'd like to hit the next night, taking full advantage of being in California to celebrate.

We were going to meet up with a few of our friends who lived out here, so if there was somewhere we wanted to go but couldn't get on the VIP list, which would be a rarity for us given everyone in the free world knew who our father was, I was sure they'd have an alternative place for us to party.

I was busy trying to devise a plan if, or I should say when, Ford stepped in and pulled his usual shit of destroying my fun. He was a buzzkill, I'd be damned if I allowed him to ruin our birthday. The only problem was, I had no idea how I would stop him when the time came.

If I was drunk, which I planned on being, my defenses would be down, and in that case, one would think it would be good to have Ford around. But I wasn't that person. I'd been taking care of myself for years, and I didn't need someone else to do it for me.

Before I got all riled up over something that hadn't even happened, I finished off the rest of my drink, looking around the room to locate the man in question.

He stood next to Owen in the corner of the room. Of course, they'd be the ones looking more like guard dogs than security guys. They were talking softly, and I could only imagine what the topic was that held their interest. Were they pissed off they had to leave the state? Were they putting together a game plan for their entire stay, improvising with their new surroundings? Were they talking business at all or about something personal?

Neither one of them ate the dinner that was prepared, disappearing from the dining area altogether. Owen looked like he was starving, licking his lips every time he happened to walk into the kitchen while I was throwing a thousand-and-one questions at Chef Rocco.

I had a feeling Owen would've joined us, but Ford had something to do with his absence. Part of me understood that they shouldn't become too comfortable with their clients, but the other part of me wondered if there was another reason he chose to keep his distance, seemingly imposing his need for separation on to his younger brother, as well. Although watching Owen and Emily together as I had from time to time, I realized Owen wasn't as gung-ho to stay away from the woman he was hired to protect.

I often wondered if Ford was as standoffish with all his clients. Had he spoken his mind and acted toward them as he did with me? Had he walked in on other women naked in the tub or overstepped his bounds and ratted them out to whoever hired him?

I doubted I'd get answers anytime soon, so I sat up on the couch and cradled my empty glass in my hand.

"Do you want another?" Naomi was next to me before I could answer, taking the glass from me and walking into the kitchen. "I don't know why I asked. Of course, you do." Had I not been feeling nice, I would've read too far into her comment.

"How about we take this outside?" Benji asked, jumping up to help Naomi with the drinks when she reappeared. "It's a gorgeous night outside, and I believe I saw a fire pit out back."

"I love that idea," she said, leaning in for a quick kiss. They were a cute couple, and I hoped for her sake that this one worked out. Naomi didn't seem to have much luck, always picking the wrong guys. Although, I didn't have any room to talk. My list was a mile long of guys who were bad for me. But in my defense, I never wanted a relationship with any of them. I only wanted to have some fun. Some of them wanted more, but I cut that shit off before they got too attached and ended up annoying me. Kurt had been on his way to joining that list, so I should be relieved Ford threatened him to stay away from me. I couldn't get on board with the way he handled the situation, though.

"I'll grab us something in case it gets cooler." Emily disappeared upstairs, returning with a handful of fleece blankets, the pile of thickness securely tucked under her chin as she walked toward the door, Karen following closely behind. And since nature had come knocking, I used the powder room off the kitchen before joining everyone else outside.

The fire had already been lit by the time I took my seat next to my sister, settling into the comfy Adirondack chair for a night of laughs and memories.

Looking around, I noticed Ford and Owen hung back behind the rest of us, and it annoyed me beyond measure. Maybe it was the alcohol talking, or maybe it wasn't, but I turned in my seat to face them both, my choice of words getting right to the point.

"If you don't sit down, you'll have to go inside."

"We're fine where we are." Ford shoved his hands in his pants pockets, widening his stance and letting me know he had no intention of moving. Owen, however, lowered his head to stare at the ground quickly before making eye contact with Emily, then me. He wanted to sit but wouldn't go against Ford. A united front of sorts.

"No, you're not." I twisted back around. "You're making everyone uncomfortable leering at the back of us."

"You don't have to be so rude," Emily chastised, smacking me on the leg.

"I'm not. I just don't want them standing behind us the entire time. It's weird." I had no doubt Ford would ignore me and stay right where he was, but when Emily turned to look at Owen, I saw the look she gave him, and for a moment, I was jealous of their unspoken connection. Her eyes shifted from him to two of the empty chairs, then back again, drawing her mouth into a straight line before biting her bottom lip. She wanted him to sit with us, but didn't want to outwardly support my harsh direction.

Surprisingly, they decided to sit, walking toward the empty seats, making sure to leave two spaces between them and Benji and one between them and Karen. They sat with us but still separate, which was fine with me, as long as they weren't standing guard.

Because the sky had darkened long ago, Ford had removed his shades and placed them on top of his head. An unexpected move for someone who always seemed to want to stay hidden as best he could. But I supposed he wouldn't be able to see any-thing with them in the dark, the only immediate light from the fire roaring in front of us.

Sometime later, Naomi informed the group that we'd run out of bourbon and asked anyone if they wanted some wine. Almost everyone declined, except for me. I wasn't done drinking and quirked my brow at the ones who were.

"We're celebrating people, come on." I laughed and ac-cepted one of the wine glasses in Naomi's hands.

"Better be careful mixing alcohol like that." Ford crossed his one leg over the other, his ankle resting on the opposing knee. Even though we were mostly shrouded in the dark, and he sat on the opposite side of the circle, I knew his eyes were on me. Watching. Waiting.

"I'll be just fine. I'm a pro." My response was meant to be lighthearted, but I couldn't say the same for his.

"Apparently."

"What is your problem?" I challenged. Emily and the oth-ers shifted in their seats, most of them aware of the dynamic between Ford and me. "I'm just having a good time, but that's not acceptable enough for you. Just because you've got a stick up your ass, don't ruin it for the rest of us." In my frustration, I gulped down half of my wine, all while keeping my eyes on him. His only reaction to my outburst was to smirk.

"Okay..." Karen interrupted, taking some of the atten-tion away from me and Ford. "How did you two get into this business?"

Owen was the one who answered. "After eight years in the military, we decided to open up our own security firm. We re-ceived all the necessary training while in the Marines, threat assessment, surveillance detection, etc. and figured we'd put it to good use afterward. Never mind that I was an expert marksman." He smiled and shrugged. "If ever that talent was called upon." He looked to Ford to see if he was going to jump in. He didn't.

"Did you ever have to shoot anyone?" Benji seemed genuinely interested, leaning forward in his chair.

"Only once."

"Did you kill them?" Karen piped in, equally intrigued with the conversation.

"Yes." His answer was short, but the effects of having to say that one word caused him to drop his chin to his chest and hunch his shoulders.

Emily stepped in and changed the subject. "Do you have any other siblings?" Her question surprised me because I would've thought as close as she and Owen had seemed to become, she'd know something like that. Maybe my assumption about the two of them was wrong. Before I could lean into her and ask, the oddest thing happened.

Owen answered 'yes' while Ford answered 'no' simultaneously.

The night just got more interesting.

CHAPTER
TWENTY-SEVEN

Ford

I never expected anyone to include us in the conversation. Hindsight was always a bitch, though, and had I known we wouldn't have been there strictly as observers, I would've retreated toward the house, keeping a close eye on them but from a considerable distance, essentially adhering to what Cara wanted us to do in the first place.

Everything was fine until Emily asked her question, an inquiry that confused me because I thought Owen would've told her all about Julia. Unless talking hadn't been high on their agenda of things to do while together.

It was the first time in a long time anyone asked that type of question, and because I didn't know how to answer, I blurted 'no' while my brother blurted 'yes,' probably just as confused as what to say as I'd been. Our differing answers wasn't what angered me; it was the fact that because we had opposing responses, we'd piqued the interest of everyone present, especially Cara. And she was the last person I wanted prying into my personal business.

My muscles tensed in preparation for the next question. As I waited, I focused on the sound of the crickets chirping in the dark, the sizzling sound of the wood drawing my attention to the flame dancing in the middle of our circle, praying someone would broach another subject, and fast.

I swore an hour passed but it was mere minutes, the tension intensifying until I finally chose to break it.

"I'm heading in." We'd done our checks inside and outside the house, and nothing seemed suspicious, but I'd be sure to keep a close eye on Cara until she retired for the evening, something I could do from a distance this one time. Owen attempted to stand, but I stopped him with a hand on his shoulder. "No, you stay."

Under normal circumstances, I wouldn't leave my post, but because all was quiet and my brother could handle himself if anything happened to arise, and I'd be close by, I turned and walked back toward the house. Every step closer eased the stiffness in my body, knowing I wouldn't have to say anything I wasn't ready to, divulge personal information to people I hardly knew, Cara included. Although, I knew her better than the others.

My body prickled with awareness as I turned the door handle and entered the spaciousness of the house. Someone was close behind, and it took me no time at all to figure out who. The hairs on the back of my neck stood at attention, a sign *she* was there. I seemed to be on constant edge whenever Cara was around, that night was no different. I had to be prepared, for what I couldn't say but I knew my guard had to be up and reinforced.

"Why did you leave so soon?" she asked, hot on my heels as I walked through the rooms. She wasn't drunk, but she was close. Her steps were heavy, filled with determination to bother the shit out of me, I just knew it. "Did we say something to make you leave?" Her tone taunted me, and I wondered if she meant to do so. Regardless, I ignored her, busying myself with checking the downstairs before ascending the steps to investigate the second floor.

After checking the first bedroom, I walked back into the hallway, but instead of having the space I needed to proceed, I bumped right into her, knocking her back. I gripped her shoulders to steady her, the heat from her skin warming my palms.

"What are you doing?" I towered over her, but my dominant stance didn't intimidate. Instead, she leaned closer.

"Why don't you want to talk to us?" The alcohol on her breath was potent, and I was sure the number of drinks she'd consumed altered her perception of what was appropriate. Or at the very least, decent social skills, like being able to pick up on one's resistance to engage.

I should've paid attention to my own definition of proper social skills because my hands were still on her. I never released her when I steadied her; instead, my fingers dug into her flesh, holding her in place.

Cara looked into my eyes and just when I thought she was going to divulge something meaningful, possibly intimate, she closed her lids. Her breaths were quick and choppy, her lips parting in anticipation for what appeared to be a kiss. She leaned even closer until her chest touched mine.

I cleared my throat, and it was then that her eyes popped open in surprise.

I had no idea what the woman was thinking. Did she think that after all the time we'd spent together, which had been hostile, that all of a sudden, during an off-putting encounter in an abandoned hallway, that I'd disregard all rational thought and common sense, hold her close and ravage her? Or had she not thought it out as intricately as I had? Maybe she was feeling nice, found an opportunity, and wanted me to partake. I could stand there all day questioning her thoughts and motives, but it would get me nowhere.

Because my thoughts took me there, I couldn't help but wonder what could've happened between us had our entire situation been different. Sure, the physical attraction was there, but nothing else existed. She didn't know me, and what I knew of her, I didn't like. I didn't understand her behavior or why she acted like she did, and fortunately, I didn't need to. I was hired to protect her, nothing else. And I didn't gravitate toward women who couldn't stand to be around me.

She remained motionless, spurring me to end the encounter. "What are you playing at?" No use in beating around the proverbial bush. "Do you think that all of a sudden I'd want to kiss you? After the way you've treated me? Talked to me?"

Her lips parted wider, but the only thing to escape were a few strangled gasps. She jerked her head back and widened her eyes.

"What are you talking about? You're the one who's clutching on to me, not the other way around." I released her immediately, realizing I should've done so earlier.

Instead of arguing, or debating who was in the right, or the wrong, I stepped to the side. I was seconds away from walking away when she reached forward, completely ignoring the ever-present tension between us and acting like I hadn't just said what I did, changing the subject altogether.

"What is that?" She was referring to the pendant I wore around my neck. Usually, I kept it hidden under my clothes, but she saw the top of it, and in her typical disregard for personal space, she thought she had the right to touch it. Yes, I was oversensitive when it came to the last gift I'd received from my sister, but I didn't care. I guarded it like the most precious object because that was what it was to me.

I closed my hand around it, so she didn't have access,

physically or visually. "Don't," I warned, curling my lip to show her how serious I was. She ignored me, of course, attempting to remove my hand so she could touch it, to which I backed farther away, shaking my head the entire time. I didn't want our encounter to turn volatile, but I sure as hell wouldn't hold my tongue if she persisted to push me.

"Why won't you let me see it?" Cara cocked her head to the side and frowned.

"It's none of your business."

"It just looks like a necklace." She tapped her finger against her bottom lip. "Or is there a camera in there? Are you recording every interaction we have? Because that's kind of creepy. Even for you, Ford." I wished I had a comeback that would wipe that smug grin off her face. But the only weapon in my arsenal was the truth.

"There's no camera."

"Then let me see it."

"No."

She crossed her arms over her chest and pursed her lips. "Why?"

"I don't have to explain why."

"When you're being this secretive about it, yes, you do. In fact, I feel that my safety is being compromised with how odd you're acting right now. Maybe I should call my dad." Her idle threats didn't rattle me. What did, however, was the fact that she had little regard for other people's privacy, thinking she had the right to intrude whenever she wanted. A byproduct of growing up entitled, I supposed.

Even in the midst of her threat, no matter how inconsequential, I was thrown back into the memory of my beautiful baby sister. The pendant I wore was in the shape of a shield, a cross etched in the middle of it. Julia had had the back engraved with a quote I once told her I liked. *Fear not, for I am with you.* It was a blip in one of our many conversations, but she'd remembered my fondness for the quote. I wasn't a religious man, but something about it spoke to me. What I didn't realize was how ominous her gift would become, because two months after she gave it to me, she died.

Even though I've never taken it off, and a plethora of emotions rained down on me like a tidal wave whenever I touched it, from sadness to regret to anger and desperation, I liked to think that whenever I clutched it tightly, Julia was somehow there with me. *Fear not, for I am with you.*

As if sensing I needed help, Owen appeared at the top of the steps. I hadn't heard him approach and berated myself for allowing Cara, and my need to keep my personal life private, to distract me from my awareness of my surroundings.

"You okay?" His question was directed at me and not at Cara. He'd witnessed many of our interactions and knew how much of a pain in the ass she was, and that I wouldn't physically overstep. So, if Cara and I were squaring off, odds were that I was the one needing to be rescued from the encounter.

"Yeah. Just doing the rounds." Luckily, my brother's presence had broken whatever state of delusion Cara found herself locked in because she glared at me, her typical expression aimed in my direction, and disappeared down the hall and into one of the bedrooms, ending the oddest encounter between us yet.

CHAPTER
TWENTY-EIGHT

Cara

As I lay in bed the following morning, I thought about the interaction between me and Ford last night in the hallway. But in order to figure out why he'd been so standoffish with me, something that wasn't out of character for him, I first had to figure out why I followed him inside the house in the first place. Actually, I knew why. It was because something personal had been broached when Emily asked both him and Owen if they had any other siblings. The conflicting answers made me want to pry into their business, more so because any piece of personal information about Ford intrigued me. It shouldn't. Nothing about his life should interest me, but the man was so secretive, and I had to be honest, Emily wasn't the only one who loved a good mystery.

I'd seen the necklace he wore around his neck before but never cared to ask about it. Not until that night. Not until I thought his defenses were down enough where he'd give up some information about himself.

Settling under the covers, praying that sleep would steal me sooner than later, my mind drifted to the one comment he'd made. The one that took me by surprise. The one that was beyond any scope of truth. The one that was so preposterous, he'd stunned me into silence.

"Do you think that all of a sudden I'd want to kiss you? After the way you've treated me? Talked to me?"

He made it seem like I was sending him the signal that I wanted his mouth on me. Indicating that all I'd been dreaming about for days was the taste of his kiss, wondering if he'd be as delicious as I thought he'd be. How I would feel in his arms as he let go and showered me with all the passion I knew he held deep within him.

Wow! Where the hell did that all come from?

It all boiled down to one question, above all others. Had I wanted him to kiss me in the hallway? I couldn't answer that one way or the other. The man infuriated me like no other, yet I was crazy attracted to him.

He was gorgeous. And those damn eyes of his... I could stare into them for hours on end. Ford was rude and condescending at times, but he was also complicated and secretive, attributes that hooked me quite easily.

What was the saying? There's a thin line between love and hate? Well, was there also a thin line between lust and fury?

So, again, did I want him to kiss me? I was gonna go with abso-fucking-lutely.

"Happy birthday!" I jumped on Emily's bed while she was still trying to rouse herself enough to get up and start the day. I retired for the evening after my encounter with Ford, so I wasn't sure what time Emily turned in. She wasn't hungover because she didn't particularly care all that much for alcohol, so I knew she hadn't drunk much, but there were bags under her eyes all the same.

"Happy birthday to you. But you're up way too early," she complained, rolling over and taking the covers with her. I snatched them off her before hopping off the bed.

"Come on, sleepy head. We have to plan our night."

"Who are you, and where is my sister?" Emily tossed one of her many pillows at me, hitting me in the chest before it hit the ground. She smiled before throwing her arm over her eyes.

I was in an unusually good mood, especially for it being so early in the morning. Typically, my ass didn't get out of bed until at least ten, and here it was only seven thirty. Tossing and turning the previous night did nothing to deter my surge of energy, and it was all me. No enhancements.

"What time did you get to bed?" If she thought I was going to leave her alone, she was mistaken. I plopped down in the chair by the dresser.

"A couple of hours after you followed Ford inside." She moved her arm enough for me to see her wiggle her brows.

"What's that look for?" I knew exactly what it meant.

She ignored my question. "What did you do?" She dropped her arm altogether and sat up, resting against the mahogany headboard, her eyes pinning mine to try and detect any trace of bullshit I was about to spew her way.

"I didn't do anything."

"Then what did he do?"

"What does that mean? He didn't do anything."

"So are you telling me that you followed him into the house, where you two were all alone, and nothing happened?" Did Emily know something I didn't?

"That's exactly what I'm telling you. After he abruptly left the group, I happened to have to go to the bathroom. It was just coincidence that I followed after him."

"Uh-huh." She chuckled. I threw the pillow back at her, and it hit her right in the forehead. "Ouch."

"It's made of goose feathers. It didn't hurt one bit." She smiled. "Anyway, I passed him in the hallway and asked him why he left. He never told me, so I let it go and went to bed." Okay, so I omitted a few things.

"Really? Because Owen told me he walked in on you both, and it looked like something was about to happen." She pushed away the covers and dangled her legs over the edge of her bed. "And he said it wasn't the first time either."

My posture stiffened. "Owen doesn't know what the hell he's talking about."

"Oooo… I knew it!" Emily hopped off the mattress and closed in on me. "I knew something was going on."

I stood as well. "What are you talking about? There's nothing going on. We don't even like each other." She parted her lips to respond, but I never let her utter a word. "Besides, don't divert the attention away from you and Owen."

Emily briefly closed her eyes and drew in a breath. "There is nothing going on between us. We're just friends."

"You shouldn't be friends with your bodyguard."

"But you should irritate him and treat him like shit?"

"What?" I didn't know how to respond to that one.

"You heard me." All of a sudden, we'd gone from jesting tones to accusatory ones.

"I thought you said you thought there was something going on between us. Now you spit out that I'm mean to him. Make up your mind, Emily."

We both remained silent, waiting for the wave of frustration to pass.

Emily retreated to the bed, sitting on the edge as she had

moments before, looking down at her lap. "There isn't anything going on between Owen and me, other than I like him. And I think he likes me." She picked her head up to look at me. "We talk all the time. He makes me laugh."

"You know that's not a good idea, right?" Emily had always been the responsible twin, the one with the good head on her shoulders. I barely remembered a time when she'd been in trouble. Not in school. Not with my parents and certainly not with the law. No, that was my job. I was the one who didn't care about rules. The one who constantly threw caution to the wind and never dealt with the consequences of my actions.

"I know it's not ideal, but they won't be our bodyguards forever. Only until the threat is handled." She lowered her head back down and broke eye contact and there was something about the way she angled her body away from me that I found odd. But I didn't delve into it because there simply was no merit behind my suspicion.

I sat next to her, taking her hand in mine. "Listen, do what you want. Far be it for me to tell you not to do something just because you shouldn't. Hell, I do shit on purpose." We both laughed. "If you both like each other, then fuck everything else and go for it." I bumped my shoulder into hers. "Besides, he's hot as hell."

"So is Ford."

"Ford's an ass."

"And you're—"

"I'm what?" I tilted my head, and she squeezed my hand.

"I love you so much, but you're not the easiest person to get along with sometimes. I'm used to it, but he doesn't know you like I do. He doesn't see all the good things you have to offer." My eyes became glassy. "You're smart and funny and once upon a time you were driven. You wanted to start your own clothing line. You wouldn't shut up about it, keeping me up into the early morning hours just talking about how you were going to have boutiques all over the world and jotting down a list of models who you'd hire to walk in your shows."

I bit my lip and pulled my hand from hers. "I was a kid then."

"It wasn't that long ago, Cara. What happened?"

I angled my body away from her and plastered on a fake smile. "Life happened. Now, let's talk about something more important. Like where we're going tonight."

She knew when I'd moved on to other topics of conversation there was no going back. We'd had our moment and I'd cherish it, but I wasn't about to ruin the entire day by going down memory lane, especially when painful memories were hiding behind every corner.

CHAPTER
TWENTY-NINE

Cara

I hadn't seen much of Ford during the day, except when I ran into him in the hallway, almost exactly where we'd been standing the night before. We glanced at each other but never uttered a word. I contemplated apologizing for my behavior when we'd interacted, but I couldn't bring myself to do it. Call it pride or arrogance or thinking I really didn't do anything wrong, but I simply passed by without so much as a hello.

Pushing all thoughts of the man to the back of my mind, I focused on the night ahead. We were busy getting ready for a night of fun and maybe even a bit of debauchery when my phone rang.

Stephanie Adler. One of my oldest friends but someone whom I'd become distant from over the years, ever since we turned fourteen. Soon after she moved to California with her family. And while I had been sad to see her go, it was for the best, for reasons I never spoke about. Not to anyone.

"What's up, woman?"

"Happy birthday."

"Thank you." While we kept in touch through social media, I hadn't talked to her in over a year. We texted occasionally but rarely spoke on the phone. I chalked it up to life.

"Please wish Emily a happy birthday for me."

"I will, but you'll see her later tonight so you can tell her in person." I put the phone on speaker and set it on top of the vanity. I needed both of my hands free to style my hair.

"That's why I'm calling. I can't make it tonight."

"Really?" I failed to keep the disappointment from my voice, pausing midway through dragging my hair through the curling iron, quickly finishing when I realized I'd stopped.

"My mom isn't feeling well, so I'm flying home to check on her."

"Is it serious?"

"I don't think so, but I didn't like how she sounded. If my dad wasn't out of the country, I wouldn't worry so much because he'd be with her, but I don't like her being by herself. It's only been a year since she received a clean bill of health." She paused for a moment, her voice stuttering when she spoke again. "I just worry about her, you know?"

"I totally understand. No worries. Go be with your mom. Tell her I said hello."

"I will."

"I'm bummed I won't see you. We'll have to get together soon." I made sure to keep focused on our conversation. Otherwise my mind would wander into the past and that was the last place I wanted to go. Talking with Stephanie brought up all sorts of mixed emotions, but I only wanted to focus on the positive right then.

"Funny you say that, because I'm hosting a charity auction next month and wanted to know if you could come. You and Emily both." Before I could accept or decline, she said, "Please say yes. I'd love to see you."

There were numerous questions swirling around my brain,

but the only one I asked was, "Will your parents be there?"

"The charity is to raise money for breast cancer, so my mom will definitely be attending, but I believe my father will be out of the country again. His job is keeping him busy these days." The last she'd told me, her father was the CEO of some international bank.

"Sounds like fun. Send me the information, and I'll check my schedule." I knew damn well my schedule was free, but I didn't like to commit to anything right off the bat.

Back in the day, Stephanie and I had been the best of friends, taking turns hanging out at each other's house. My parents joked that they had three daughters, not two.

Then one day… everything changed. I stopped going over there, making up excuses that I was busier with school, a legitimate reason because I'd picked up a few AP classes. That was also the time I'd begun hanging out with Naomi. The whole point was moot, however, because halfway through the school year, her family up and moved to California. Her parents moved back to New York sometime after Steph graduated high school, but she chose to stay behind to attend Berkeley. We'd obviously kept in touch these past years, but I missed the friendship we had once upon a time.

A knock at my door tore me away from all the what-ifs that forever plagued me.

"Come in," I called, focusing on styling the rest of my locks. I kept my eyes on my reflection and not on who entered my room. After all, it could only be one of six people, but even though the pool of people was low, I didn't expect Owen to walk in.

"Can I talk to you for a sec?" He leaned against the frame, clasping his hands in front of him while he seemed to contemplate whether he should enter. He eyed me with wariness, and I couldn't decipher if he was going to ask me something about Emily or decide to talk about his brother. What he wanted to say about Ford was anyone's guess, but curiosity made me swivel in my chair.

"Sure."

He remained still, glancing around my room before resting his eyes back on me. I was sure it was the job that had him assessing his surroundings so diligently, but they'd already completed their rounds so he was here on more of a personal mission.

"I wanted to wish you a happy birthday."

"Thank you, but I doubt that's why you came up here." I flashed him a smirk before crossing my legs, being sure to cinch my robe tightly afterward. While Owen was an attractive man, I wasn't interested in him because I knew Emily was, and that meant he was off limits. For all the immoral, questionable, and downright atrocious things I may have done during my life, I'd never crossed the line and gone after any of Emily's boyfriends or showed interest in anyone she liked.

"It's not the whole reason, no." He tilted his head from side to side, parting his lips to speak only to close them. He struggled to find his words, which only intrigued me more.

"Oh, this should be good." I leaned back in my seat and pursed my lips. "Out with it, Owen."

"I wanted to talk to you about Ford."

"What about him?"

"He's still upset about last night, and when he internalizes everything instead of letting it out, like he's doing right now, he festers, then erupts at what seems like a small thing." He took a breath and pushed away from the doorframe but didn't enter.

"I know you're excited about celebrating your birthday tonight. So is Emily. But I was hoping you'd consider keeping the antics to a minimum."

"Antics?"

"You know. Doing things to rile Ford."

"First off, your brother and I have clashed since day one, and trust me, he has no problem telling me what he thinks." I stood and walked toward the edge of the bed where my outfit was laid out. "Secondly, I have no idea what you're going on about. What exactly is he still upset about from last night? When I ran into him in the hallway, I asked why he'd come inside. That was harmless, if you ask me." Of course, I left out all the other details of our conversation.

"May I come in?"

I nodded, taking a seat on the edge of the bed. Whatever he needed to tell me wasn't something to be taken lightly. If that were the case, he would've stayed near the door.

"Ford would kill me if he knew I told you this. But I think it'll help explain his behavior not only last night, but in general. You see, the man you know isn't the real Ford." He stroked his jawline before pinching his chin.

"What do you mean?"

"The broody, temperamental guy you've come to know over the past few weeks didn't always exist. Sure, he's always been a pain in the ass, opinionated, and unpredictable, but he was also full of life. Fun. Forever the optimist."

"What the hell happened to him, then?"

"Our sister, Julia."

"So, there are other Masseys?" I smiled, but it disappeared as soon as Owen shook his head, making me tilt mine and perch forward.

"No. Which is why we both answered Emily's question the way we did." He gazed at the ceiling before locking eyes with me, his posture straightening during the brief silence. "Julia was our younger sister. Ten years younger than Ford, eight younger than me. And because there was such a big age difference, we tended to be a bit overprotective. Ford more so than me."

"That's not surprising." I could only imagine the torment Ford put that put girl through.

"He chased away any guy who came sniffing around, intent on making sure she remained a virgin until she was at least thirty." Owen smiled. "They got into some heated arguments, but because Ford was, well, Ford, she'd appease him and move on. She was smart enough to know that she'd never win, often complaining to me and asking if I could get him to back off. But I never could. Ford was a stubborn bastard."

"Was?"

Owen laughed, resting his hands on the arms of the chair, tapping his fingers against the fabric. "Is." The quiet stretched between us, but it wasn't uncomfortable. Owen's lips curled up as he stared out the window, most likely lost in memories. And while he was occupied with the past, my mind raced with images of Ford and what he was like before. Which brought me back to our conversation. What happened that changed Ford from the man he used to be? I assumed their sister passed away. Although there could've been a falling out between them. While I hoped it was the latter, instinct told me differently.

"What happened with Julia?" His quick breaths told me I'd startled him.

"She died seven months ago." Even though I'd been prepared to hear those words, he still managed to shock me. Pain shadowed his face at having to answer, and I couldn't imagine how raw her loss was for him. For both of them. I couldn't fathom what I'd do if I lost Emily.

"Julia had a problem. When she turned sixteen, she started acting out. Partying. Ditching school. Even running away from home a couple of times. It wasn't long before she started doing drugs, and while we all tried our best to help her, sometimes using tough love, we failed." Owen lowered his head and took a deep breath. His next words tumbled from his lips, his intake of air ragged and distorting the sound of his voice. I had to lean closer to hear him. "She was high when she crossed lanes into oncoming traffic, killing herself on impact." He rubbed the heel of his palm against his chest, his eyes glassing over as he looked over at me.

"I'm so sorry, Owen." I didn't know what else to say, and I found myself entangled in an awkward moment of silence, both of us fidgeting in our seats.

"So, that's why Ford has gone a little overboard with you."

"I don't understand."

"You know…" He hesitated a moment before continuing. "What you've done while we've been here.…"

My posture became rigid. I sat up straighter and crossed my arms over my chest. "I'm still not sure what you mean."

"It doesn't matter." Owen shook his head. "You're grown and can do whatever you want. It's just that when Ford interferes, crosses the professional line, it's because your behavior reminds him of Julia."

"But I'm not her."

"I know that, and Ford knows that, but I think because he couldn't get through to her, couldn't save her, he's focusing more energy on trying to do that for you."

"I don't need saving. I'm fine." I uncrossed my arms and stood up, indicating we were done. Owen stood as well.

"I hope I haven't upset you, Cara. I'm just worried about Ford, and figured that if you knew a little bit about why he acts the way he does, you'd...."

"I'd what?"

"I don't know. Maybe take it easy on him?"

"You know your brother isn't the most pleasant person, right?'

He smiled. "I do. Although, like I said, he wasn't always like this."

"I understand he has a job to do, but you need to tell him to calm down. We're here to celebrate our birthday, and I want to have a good time. Like you said, I'm grown. I can make my own decisions. As long as I'm not getting behind the wheel of a car drunk or high, he shouldn't interfere."

Owen flinched, and it was then I recalled my words.

I closed my eyes for several seconds and exhaled. "Sorry."

"It's all right." His lips formed a thin line before he disappeared from my room.

Thanks to our brief conversation, I understood a little more about his brother and why he acted the way he did. I had compassion for what they went through. I did. But I wouldn't hold my tongue if I felt Ford overstepped on this trip or even when we got back home.

As I busied myself with finishing to get ready, I couldn't help but wonder if it was wrong to be thankful someone else struggled with heartbreaking circumstances? To possibly share a connection that I wasn't alone in trying to wrap my head around the what-ifs and the why mes?

CHAPTER
THIRTY

Ford

Who the hell names their club No. 4? Why not No. 1? It was an odd thought but the only one I permitted myself to focus on as we drove up in front of the first club of the evening.

In total, the ride had taken just over an hour, traffic a nightmare almost the entire time. Asshole drivers swerving across the six-lane highway, most of them too busy on their phones to pay attention properly. I swore it was like no one had heard of Bluetooth. *Your vehicle will read your text messages for you people.* And besides, nothing was that important that they had to read it while driving.

I pulled up behind Owen, throwing the Navigator into Park, barely having enough time to exit the vehicle before Cara hopped out. Tossing the key to the valet, I briskly walked behind her, my eyes trained on every movement she made.

She'd chosen to wear a red strapless dress that evening, one that barely covered her. It fell mid-thigh and didn't leave much to the imagination. Truth was, I couldn't care less what she wore. However, the skimpier her clothes, the more I had to deal with unwanted attention from the fuckers who'd be gawking at her, the ones who'd bravely approach. Or should I say stupidly approach her?

"Goddammit," I mumbled, my long strides placing me right next to her in seconds. When I met my brother's stare, he smirked, which only served to sour my mood.

As we approached the front of the building, it was clear to see the club was popular, the line curling around the corner a dead giveaway. As we drew closer, I overheard people gasping then mumbling. They recognized Cara and Emily. So, not only was I going to be on high alert because we were going to be surrounded by a multitude of strangers, but I also had to deal with possible admirers of the women. And let's face it, people were crazy, and some would do whatever it took to meet someone in the public eye.

Cara didn't have to give her name to the bouncer out front. He glanced from her to Emily to the rest our party, squinting at Owen and me before removing the classic red velvet rope to allow us inside.

"It'll be fine, man. Don't stress so much." Owen slapped my back. "Nothing is gonna happen. Besides, I doubt we'll even be here long enough for anything to pop off."

"You're not helping." We'd only just arrived, and the fact we were going to be club hopping, as Cara had mentioned earlier on the ride here, already exhausted me. I was hoping they'd settle in and decide to spend the majority of their celebration in one place, eliminating multiple spots to God only knew where.

"You want a drink?"

"No. And you better not have one either." Owen shook his head in what I could only assume was amusement.

"I know, you ass. I meant do you want some water or club soda or something like that."

"Not right now." I should've known my brother wouldn't be so careless as to drink on the job. Although, truth was, we'd been on the job since the first day we'd arrived at the Dessoye residence, only partaking in a single shot to calm the nerves after the women had settled in for the evening.

Owen and I found a place to stand and keep watch over everyone in the party, particularly Cara and Emily. They were our responsibility, but because their friends were present, as well, we had to make sure nothing went down that would inadvertently affect them.

The first hour passed without incident, everyone drinking in moderation and enjoying themselves. Well, everyone except me, of course. I swore people probably viewed me as some sort of statue, but I had to give off the perception of a serious guy, which I was, most of the time. Besides, this was my job, and there was no room for error. One slip could be catastrophic. I had to constantly be on my game, something I envied about Owen. Even while taking his post seriously, he looked like he was enjoying himself.

I glanced around the club, observing all the other patrons. With so many people crammed into one space, I was surprised there wasn't a fire-code violation. I had no idea why people wanted to spend their night bumping into others, spilling their drinks, and getting all sweaty in the process. I had other ideas of how to get all worked up, and it had nothing to do with grinding on unsuspecting strangers to the beat of the newest pop song.

As if she could read my suddenly dirty thoughts, my eyes caught Cara's, and while she was in full conversation with Benji, laughing at something he said, his girlfriend and her best friend smiling right along with them, she locked her stare on me, her grin momentarily faltering.

She waved the bartender closer, leaning over the bar to speak into his ear. The hem of her dress rose higher, and I swore if she moved any closer toward him, everyone would be able to see the bottom of her ass cheeks. I studied the interaction between the two of them and didn't like the smug look on that bastard's face. He leered at her when she pulled back, his eyes devouring her like he had a shot at fucking her. Which he most certainly did not, not while I was around.

A sudden heat traveled through my body when he reached over the bar and pulled her back toward him, planting a kiss on her cheek as if it was the most normal thing to do to a patron. Then a thought dawned on me. Did he know her? Had she been here before? She lived in New York, but I highly doubted this was her first trip to the West Coast, especially since her parents owned a house here. She could very well be acquainted with the bartender. Hell, she could have slept with him, for all I knew. While his occupation didn't seem like the type of person Cara would go for, I'd come to discover there was no rhythm or reason when it pertained to that woman.

I completely forgot Owen was standing next to me, too involved with paying attention to the blatant flirtatious behavior between Cara and that man-bun-wearing shithead. So, his voice startled me.

"What's the matter?" he asked, following my line of sight. I grunted in response, having no patience for words. "Stop being so paranoid, Ford. She's fine. They all are." He leaned against the wall, completely oblivious that I wasn't worried about her well-being. Or rather, I was concerned about her welfare, but not because I thought someone was going to swoop in and snatch her up, but because I thought there was a great possibility that she'd try and leave with either that bartender douchebag or someone else entirely.

Cara was young, gorgeous, and came from money. She

wasn't tied down to anyone, so she most certainly could hook up with whomever she wanted. I knew that. I truly believed in her right to do it. But something wasn't sitting easy with me, and I couldn't pinpoint what it was. While my rational thoughts should've prevailed, all I could focus on was getting her away from that guy and shielding her from anyone else who might take it upon themselves to walk up to her and start flirting.

Was I overprotective? Was I just trying to prevent a situation before I had to jump into action and get involved?

"Wait. Are you jealous she's talking to that guy?" Owen's voice annoyed me more than ever before, and it had nothing to do with his tone, but rather his question. An absurd one at that.

"Not a fucking chance." My harsh reply gave everything away, making me come to grips with the fact that I was indeed jealous. Although, I couldn't fathom why.

"Oh my God. Yes, you are. I knew it."

I curled my hands into tight fists, keeping them at my sides so as not to grip my brother and slam him against the wall. "Shut the fuck up. You don't know what you're talking about. Just because you're—"

"If you comment again about me and Emily, I swear I'm gonna hit you." Owen's posture straightened. I'd touched a nerve, much like he'd just done to me. "Besides, I'm not the one looking like I'm about to rush over there and beat the shit out of someone." *He got me there.*

"I don't like how close he's getting to her. It's not safe."

"She's fine."

"She's my responsibility," I countered, bending my leg and resting my foot against the wall behind me. Otherwise, I feared I'd give in to my baser instinct and erase the space between

Cara and me and cause a scene. Much like I'd done with Kurt not too long ago. And I remembered how well that went.

"You like her. There's nothing wrong with that. So, to be jealous she's flirting with another guy is totally understandable." Owen taunted me, and I couldn't figure out for the life of me why he had a death wish so fierce he never relented. "Maybe when this assignment is over you can hook up with her. You know, take her on a date and shit." My brother loved to push my buttons, and if he didn't shut his mouth, the only scene I'd be making was wiping the floor with him.

I gritted my teeth. "You know damn well I don't like her like that. I just don't feel like getting physical tonight."

"Getting physical is exactly what you need. Maybe you'll calm down a bit if you get some."

I craned my neck toward him and snarled. He was used to my reactions, so he never flinched. Anyone else would've pissed their pants had they witnessed my clenched fists, flared nostrils, and the pulsing vein in my forehead.

"Oh, calm down. You know I'm just fuckin' with you." He laughed, but I didn't find anything he said funny. "Listen, there's something I should probably tell you." My eyes were pinned back on Cara. The bartender tended to other patrons, but he'd placed several shots on the bar for her, Emily, and their friends before he continued with his duties.

A few words left Owen's mouth, but I didn't hear any of them. Instead, my feet propelled me forward, knocking into several people on my way toward the bar. Some guy had come up behind Cara and wrapped his arms around her waist, holstering her from her feet. The look of surprise on her face had me shoving my way past the remaining people until I was standing right next to her.

Without so much as a warning, I reached around her and grabbed the fucker by his neck, my grip intensifying in a matter of seconds. The guy released Cara, and with my free hand, I moved her to the side before she had time to contemplate what just happened.

"Wh... what the hell?" he cried out, trying to push away from me, but I held on tightly. I twisted his right arm behind his back and shoved him against the bar, bending him until his face hit the wood.

"Don't you know it's rude to touch people you don't know?" There were so many other things I wanted to shout at him, but that was the one my brain chose to filter through my mouth.

"What are you talking about? I *do* know Cara." He was still kissing the wood of the bar when Owen joined me, flanking him on the other side.

"Knowing who she is and knowing her are two different things." I had no idea why I continued to hold a conversation with him. I should be tossing him out on his ass.

Someone yanked on my arm. When I turned my head, I saw it was the woman in question, pulling on the sleeve of my jacket in a frenzy.

"Are you out of your mind?" she shouted, standing so close I could hear every word above the obnoxious drum of the music. "Nick is a friend of mine." Her eyes widened and her face flushed, and all I could think about while looking at her was if she looked the same in the throes of passion. *Where the hell did that come from?*

"You know him?" My question hit her ears right before Owen backed up a step and placed a hand on my arm, the one still holding Nick's hostage behind his back.

"Yes. Now let him go." Cara tugged on my sleeve once more, harder when I refused to budge. "Ford," she threatened. "So help me God, if you don't let him go, I'll scream bloody murder." A small part of me wanted to call her bluff. Besides, what was the worst that could happen if she followed through? We get kicked out of the place? Might be worth it.

"Let him go," Owen demanded, reaching forward and trying to help Nick stand up, all while he was still being restrained by me.

Looking from my brother to Cara then back again, I released Nick and stepped away, glaring at the fucker just in case he got any ideas about swinging at me.

Taking a better look at him, I concluded that he seemed familiar, but I didn't know where I knew him from. He'd never been to the house in New York, not since we'd been employed. And I didn't remember seeing him out anywhere I'd accompanied Cara.

"Maybe you should take a walk. Cool down." My brother leaned in close, but I retreated, not wanting to move an inch until I received the full story on our newest guest. Owen gave up on me and walked toward Emily, taking his place behind her.

"You owe my friend an apology." The feisty woman in front of me held her ground. She swayed a bit but held her own. "You had no right to do what you did, and you know it."

"I had every right. I don't know him. He could've been some lunatic. All I saw was him walk up behind you and pick you up off your feet." I stared straight ahead so as not to look directly into her face.

"Well, he's not."

"It's okay, Cara. I'm fine," Nick interrupted, rotating his arm to assuage the ache. I'd been put into that hold a few times in my life, and it hurt like a bitch when applied with full force. I'd only used half on him.

I turned my stare on our newest guest, sizing him up in a matter of seconds. Dark brown hair. Tall. Thin, but not lanky. Good-looking. Almost too much so. He was borderline pretty. He didn't look like much of a threat up close, but I wasn't about to apologize for doing my fucking job.

"It's not okay." Cara turned her back to me, wrapped her arms around his shoulders, and planted a kiss on his lips, acting like we were all just hanging out. Like nothing had happened. She'd been drinking for a while, and the effects of the alcohol had taken their toll. Her speech was a little slurred, and she wasn't as steady on her feet.

I wasn't sure if it was the residual adrenaline pumping through my veins, my sour mood, or a mixture of both, but I did something, in hindsight, I probably shouldn't've.

Instead, I should've listened to Owen and walked away.

"I need to talk to you," I barked, grabbing Cara's hand and gently but forcefully pulling her behind me toward the hallway, away from everyone's prying eyes. She hurried to keep pace with my long strides, and as soon as we cleared the crowd, I slowed my steps. She didn't utter a single word in protest, but I couldn't be sure her reaction wasn't because of her inebriated state, her shocked state, or both.

Abruptly turning to face her once I knew we were alone, a feat in and of itself in a place this crowded, I took a single step closer to her. The height difference was exaggerated in such close proximity, an advantage I'd use to my benefit. I needed her to be unsettled, to back off, and behave herself. For both of our sakes.

We studied the other's face for what seemed like forever.

Her skin had pinked. Her chest rose then deflated quickly, and I swore if I placed my hand on her chest, I'd feel the thump of a heartbeat.

"Out with it." She placed her hands on her hips, her right one slipping off her dress before she hoisted it back in place.

"I don't mean to be—"

"Yes, you do. You mean to be whatever it is you're going to say." She shoved her finger into my chest, her nail poking me, irritating me. "A bully? An overbearing pain in the ass? Someone who can't help himself?" My only reaction was to grit my teeth. I didn't want to give her the satisfaction, yet again, of her knowing she was getting under my skin. "What, Ford? Say it. I'll be quiet now and let you finish your lie."

Cara stumbled to the side. Before I could instinctually grab her to steady her, she braced herself against the wall next to us.

"I was hired to do a job, one you continually seem to make harder each day. Your father said no dating. Sound advice and you're going to abide, especially while we're out here. Besides, you told him you'd listen to me."

"I know what I told him." She cocked her head and pursed her lips, staring intently at me while it appeared she contemplated what to say next. "So, no dating means no fucking, then?" Her choice of words was no surprise.

"Exactly. No guys. Period."

"But you're a guy."

I shook my head, her comeback coming out of left field and confusing the hell out of me.

"So?"

"So, you said no dating. But you're a guy. One who's always around me. Watching me."

She's drunk and making no sense.

"I'm hired to protect you, so yeah, I have to watch you. And by the way, don't flatter yourself."

"It's my birthday, Ford." She laughed and leaned against the wall, tracing the same finger she poked me with moments ago down my chest.

She was all over the place, but once I realized she wasn't going to lay into me for attacking her friend, I relaxed and released some of the tension in my muscles.

"I know it is." I looked around, and the only other people I saw were a few women exiting a nearby ladies' room. I thought perhaps Emily or Owen, or both of them together, would've come searching for us.

Cara pushed off the wall and into me, grabbing my jacket with both hands. "So where is my birthday kiss?"

Before my brain could compute her question, before I had time to react and step away, she rose up and planted her lips over mine.

CHAPTER
THIRTY-ONE

Cara

In the back of my mind, I realized that I wasn't making any sense and that my moods were switching on a dime. Ford had pissed me off, as usual, yet I found myself openly flirting with him in a darkened hallway. Just the two of us. And to make matters worse, I threw all rational thought to the side, ignored my inner voice telling me what I was about to do was a horrible idea, and kissed him before he even realized what I was doing.

I'd be lying if I said I hadn't thought about locking lips with him, but I never imagined it would happen, especially with me being the one to come on to him and make the first move.

Having alcohol as an excuse was perfect, though. It allowed me to act brazenly, casting aside all caution and having a devil-may-care attitude. It was why I'd done most of the things I had in my life. Without liquor or drugs, I probably would've shriveled up and become a recluse. Okay, maybe not that dramatic of a difference, but close.

My lips continued to cover Ford's, his breath minty and fresh while mine could knock over a horse with how much I'd had to drink, I was sure. Self-consciousness or self-awareness didn't exist in that moment, however. All that mattered was the man in front of me and what would happen next.

I hated how scrambled my thoughts were, bouncing from thinking this is a great idea to wondering what the fuck I was doing. The entire time our mouths were fused together, Ford never made a move to break the connection. Was he surprised? Or was this something he wanted, as well? Had he thought about me in that way before?

With my hands still gripping his jacket, I stepped into him, my chest pressing against his. He was warm. Even through his clothes I could feel the heat of his body and wondered how his naked skin would feel on mine. Would he burn me up?

Instead of pushing me away, he placed his hands on my upper arms, squeezed, and lifted me up and into him. As if I wasn't close enough already. The second his tongue passed his lips and touched mine, I was a goner.

All the past interactions with him were a blur. I couldn't remember why I'd ever given him a hard time or bitched and complained that he was always around. I couldn't even remember why I didn't like him. Because in that unbearably intimate moment between us, all I could think about was what I would have to do to convince him to keep kissing me.

The moment I opened my mouth to accept him, he growled, the sound guttural and animalistic. His breath fanned my face as his tongue swirled with mine, the force of his kiss literally making me weak in the knees, damning me for all other men. I'd never in my life had such a visceral reaction to kissing someone before, and believe me, there had been plenty of people to make that comparison.

Ford swung me around and pushed me against the wall, his hold on me never wavering. Not for a second. Not until I released his jacket and snaked my hands around his neck, gripping the back of his head and anchoring him to me. I never wanted the moment to end, but sadly I didn't have a say in the matter.

His fingers dug into my arms right before his mouth abandoned mine, pushing away from me, and dropping his arms as if I'd burned him.

"That never should've happened." His eyes darkened, and even in the ill-lit hallway, I saw the regret laced behind them. Was kissing me the worst thing in the world? Talk about a kick to my ego.

Ford towered over me, and right then, I'd never felt smaller. Instead of giving into the frustration and humiliation of him being the one to spur the regret bullshit, I pushed everything else aside and played it off as no big deal.

Although before I could spin my lies, he took another step back and ran his hands through his hair before linking his fingers and resting them on top of his head while he released an elongated breath.

"Don't go freaking out," I warned. The more I watched him, the more I wanted to have been the one to end the kiss and tell him what a mistake it was. Hell, I might've even slapped him for good measure. But since I was the one who initiated it, I doubted that would've gone over well.

"That can never happen again. Ever," he reiterated. He retreated another step. "I mean it, Cara. Ever."

Okay. Enough is enough.

"Get over yourself, Ford. It was one kiss. It didn't mean anything." My tone belied the hurt I felt, but in order not to show any vulnerability, I needed to appear aloof.

He lowered his arms and shoved his hands in his pants' pockets. The dim light in the hallway hit him at just the right angle, showcasing his full lips and chiseled jawline. And when he turned his head slightly to the side, his eyes lit up. Earlier, I'd demanded that he leave the shades at home, reminding him that he needed to blend in, and having him shielded in sunglasses inside the club would make him stick out like a sore thumb. Not that he didn't do that already, but he certainly didn't need to add to the distraction.

"We need to go."

"I'm not leaving. I'm not done yet. Besides, I have a few more friends meeting us in a bit."

"I don't mean the club. I mean we need to get back out there with everyone else before they start to think something." He scratched his cheek. It hit me that he was uncomfortable.

"You don't strike me as someone who gives a shit what anyone thinks." I folded my arms over my chest, and had I not been staring at him, I would've missed him catching a glimpse of my tits.

"I don't."

"That's not what it sounds like to me." I knew the mindless back and forth irritated him.

"I meant what I said before," he said, switching the subject entirely. "No hooking up with anyone. So whatever flirtation you have with that guy ends there."

I closed my eyes and drew air into my lungs. "You have no idea who he is?"

"I don't care who he is." The muscles in his jaw clenched, and I could've been mistaken, but Ford could almost pass for someone who was jealous.

Deciding I didn't want his assumptions to linger, only because he'd continue to dampen the rest of the evening with his broodiness, I revealed something about Nick that would hopefully make him back off.

"Nick's gay. But I'm surprised you don't already know that."

"Why would I know that?"

"Everyone knows it. He's only one of the most famous male models in the industry. He's the *it* guy right now. And he's very open about his sexuality."

"Yeah? Well, I don't follow that type of stuff." He swung his arm out, wasting no time.

I led him back into the heart of the club, joining everyone else at the bar, right where we'd left them. Emily looked at me as soon as I approached. I winked, silently telling her everything was okay. I thought for sure someone would've made mention of us being gone so long, but in reality, while it seemed like an hour, we were only gone for ten minutes. Not enough time to cause any sort of suspicion.

Soon after the encounter in the hallway, I found I was feeling rather nice. I wasn't falling down drunk, but I did stumble from time to time. At some point, Emily shoved a glass of water my way and watched until I'd drained the entire contents. She was always looking out for me, and it was times like tonight I truly appreciated my sister. I should probably tell her that more often.

As I'd mentioned to Ford earlier, a few more of our friends showed up at the club, shouting with happiness as they drew near. I hadn't seen Calvin or Neely for close to two years, one year and three hundred sixty-four days too long. I loved these two because they knew how to let loose and have a good time. My kind of good time.

Calvin sauntered over first, drawing me into a tight embrace as he twirled me around. Good thing I knew how to hold my liquor, or the jolt of being lifted into the air and spun in a circle would've made me sick.

"Happy birthday, love." Calvin gave me a kiss on the mouth,

and for some reason, my eyes diverted to Ford to see if he'd seen. Of course, he had. He was always watching. I swore the corner of his lip curled upward, but then again, maybe my mind was playing tricks on me.

There were no romantic feelings between Calvin and me. He was more like a brother than anything. Although, one night, many moons ago, he'd confessed that he'd had a crush on me when we'd first met, which was seven years prior. I'd reciprocated those initial feelings, but who could blame me? He looked like the stereotypical surfer guy. Blond shoulder-length hair, eternal tan, cut physique. Nothing romantic happened between us, though.

"Thank you. I'm so happy you're here." I moved to give Neely a hug next. "You look fantastic. What's your secret?" Her skin was sun-kissed, as was Calvin's, but Neely had more of a glow about her. An exuberance. Her black hair was cut into a stylish bob, her bangs making me envious because I couldn't pull them off myself.

"Pregnancy will do that to you." Calvin frowned.

"What? You're pregnant?"

"Shhh. I'm not telling anyone yet." She smacked Calvin on the arm. "I'm only ten weeks along and don't want to jinx it."

I watched the glances they shared, their own silent code. "I gather you don't approve of the baby daddy?" I smiled because I knew Neely hated that terminology.

"Eww, Cara. Just no." She laughed but stopped when Calvin opened his mouth, sensing he was going to go into a tirade, which he often did when he had a strong opinion about something, or in this case, someone.

"Call me crazy, but I don't think that a guy who surfs all day long then hangs out with his buddies is gonna wanna be responsible for a baby. I have no idea what he does for money, and Neely won't tell me anything. She just tells me to mind my own business and be happy for her. Well, I can't do th—"

Neely covered his mouth. "Did you have to ask his opinion?" She kept her hand in place and shot him a warning look. He narrowed his eyes, but when Neely took her hand away, he didn't say another word about the guy.

"Are you dating this guy, or was it just a hookup?"

Calvin parted his lips but shut them as soon as Neely smacked him in the stomach.

"Initially, it was just a one-nighter, but we ran into each other again, and again. And well, now we're kind of dating."

"Does he know you're pregnant?"

"No, he doesn't," Calvin answered for her. "And I don't think she should tell him either." He put his arm around her waist and pulled her close. "I told her I'd be the baby daddy if she wanted."

Calvin and I chuckled at the disgusted look on her face. "No one will be referred to as baby daddy."

I had an inkling that Calvin had feelings for Neely, but he'd never said anything to warrant my hunch. It was just the way he looked at her, like she was the only woman in the room.

"Who's a baby daddy?" Emily asked, reaching first for Neely then Calvin to give them a hug.

"I'll tell you later." She looked confused but quickly forgot all about it as soon as the three of them started chatting.

CHAPTER
THIRTY-TWO

Cara

The next two hours flew by. I tried my hardest to enjoy myself, but that was hard to do with Mr. Grumpy Ass watching me like a hawk. Every time Calvin put his arm around my shoulders or Nick kissed my cheek, I swore Ford was gonna flip out. He acted more like a jealous boyfriend than anything. He physically kept his distance, which was a smart move on his part because the more liquid courage that flowed through me, the more I'd be apt to say whatever came to mind. No filter in place. Although, anyone who knew me would say I didn't have a filter to begin with. But I did. I could only imagine people's reactions if I said every little thing my brain concocted.

"Bathroom?" I looked at all the women in our circle. Karen and Naomi shook their heads while Emily and Neely stood to follow me. I moved to hop off my stool and stumbled, my left ankle giving out as soon as my foot made contact with the floor. Ford was on me in seconds. He'd been holding up the wall twenty feet away, so I had no idea how he'd reached me so quickly. But he saved me from falling on my ass, so I was thankful, although as soon as I was steady, I shoved his hands away and glared at him. Admittedly, I was still a little sore about his rejection earlier, but I'd be damned if I let him know he'd hurt my ego.

He moved to the side to allow us to pass, but followed closely behind. I had no doubt he'd be keeping guard outside the ladies' room until we emerged. Shit, if he could get away with waiting inside the restroom, he would.

"I'm having so much fun," Emily sang on her way toward one of the stalls. It was a rarity that my sister let her hair down and enjoyed herself. She was always so busy with her volunteer projects to stop and take time for herself.

"Someone's feeling good." I occupied the stall next to her, Neely disappearing into the only other empty one.

"I really am." The flush of the toilet drowned out the rest of what she was saying, but her tone told me she was still wearing that goofy smile of hers. I could admit I was jealous of Emily's carefreeness tonight. *Was that even a word?* I shrugged, not caring either way. She didn't have someone practically breathing down her neck, watching and judging every move she made. Owen was laidback. Engaging. Dare I even say fun? I saw them laughing together and wished I could have that kind of repertoire with his brother.

"I can't believe we're twenty-five already." I finished up and exited the stall. And that was the moment when I came face to face with the one bitch I couldn't stand.

Heather Dumont.

"Is it someone's birthday?" she asked, grinning like she was privy to the juiciest secret. Or lie. She was good for spreading lies about me.

"What are you doing here?" I sidestepped her and turned on the faucet to wash my hands, watching her in the reflection of the mirror above the vanity.

"I just had to come and check out the place I've heard so much about." She looked at her image and re-applied her lipstick.

"It's okay." She shrugged then fussed with her long auburn hair before blowing me a kiss in the mirror. "I'm only in town for the night. Have to head back to Paris tomorrow morning." I remained silent, which only prompted her to keep annoying me. "Have to finish shooting."

"French porn?" Emily asked, flipping on the faucet next to me. I choked on my laughter, not expecting my sister to say anything, least of all that. Emily wasn't confrontational, so her jab said everything. She couldn't stand Heather almost as much as me.

"That's Cara's specialty," she shot back, turning and leaning up against the sink so she had a good view of us.

"Fuck you, Heather. You know damn well you're the one who started that rumor about me." And she had. We'd been at the same party two years back, and because my father hadn't hired her for one of his films, which ended up being a huge blockbuster hit, she took it out on me. Okay, I might've provoked her after she started a fight with one of my friends for accidentally bumping into her and spilling her drink. Anyway, she told people I'd been involved in an orgy and that the entire tryst was taped. It wasn't true of course. The most adventurous I'd ever gotten was with two guys, and it certainly wasn't filmed. And I couldn't prove it, but I knew she was the one who'd leaked the last set of photos that warranted a conversation between me and my parents. Ones where I'd fallen down drunk after a night of partying.

A few years prior, Heather was considered the new America's sweetheart. She looked like the girl next door but with sex appeal. Unfortunately for her, her reputation on and off set caught up with her, and now she was lucky if she was offered one role a year.

The toilet flushing interrupted the building tension in the small space, but not for long. Neely walked out of the stall and used the sink to my left.

"Who's this?" Her question was genuine. Neely hardly watched television or went to the movies. Hell, I don't think she ever read a gossip magazine. She was too busy painting and trying to land a gallery who would showcase her work.

Neely having no idea who Heather was turned out to be the perfect insult. Heather's mouth fell open, looking like someone had just smacked her. Something I was going to do if she didn't get her skinny ass away from me and soon.

"You're kidding, right?" She was flabbergasted.

Neely cocked her head to the side, looked at me then Heather then back to me. Emily snickered beside me, which only made me smile bigger.

"She's not, and it seems this is just the start of people not knowing who you are. You better soak up whatever notoriety you have left before it vanishes." I pushed past her and walked out of the restroom, Neely and Emily following me into the hallway.

I stopped abruptly when Ford appeared out of nowhere and blocked my path. "I was five seconds away from coming in there."

"As you can see, I'm fine."

I moved around him but not fast enough because he blocked me once more. "You need to start taking this seriously." *Here we go again.*

I dropped my shoulders and sighed, my sister and Neely walking past us to join the others. I needed another drink to try and get back the good feeling I had before entering the bathroom. I parted my lips to tell him it was only a trip to the ladies' room and that he was overreacting, as usual, when Heather walked up next to us.

"Who do we have here?" she cooed, batting her eyelashes at Ford. Her flirtation burrowed under my skin and my annoyance with her spiked to a whole other level.

"Cara's security," was all Ford answered, but it was enough to bait her curiosity.

"Security?" Her one-word question screamed so many things. Confusion. Interest. Jealousy? "Why would Cara need security?" She looked me over from head to toe, then back again, curling her lips in disgust.

Ford didn't answer that time, and I'd never been so grateful for his aloofness. Or was that him being professional?

"Hmm... I think I need some security of my own." She ran her finger down his arm, and she would've continued blatantly coming on to him had he not interrupted her.

He took a step back, enough of a space that her hand fell away. "I don't have any openings." If she was offended or disappointed, she didn't show it. Instead, she continued pestering him.

"Can you take my number for when you do?" He probably had no idea who she was or that we were enemies, although I doubted he'd care either way. Owen walked over to us before Ford could deny or accept her request, handing Heather his business card. He overheard her solicitation.

"You can call that number, and we'll see who is available to assist you." Owen smiled, and naïve him thought he was drumming up new clientele. Little did he know, she was a handful. Worse than me.

"I want *him*, though." She pointed at Ford and licked her lips.

"I'm sorry, but he's not available."

"Then I'll wait." She walked away before Owen could say anything else.

"Well, that was odd," he said, scratching the top of his head. He leaned against the wall but straightened back up when Emily came over to join us.

"Everything okay?"

"Yeah. That bitch was trying to get her hooks into Ford." I tried to keep the jealousy from my tone, but I didn't think I pulled it off.

"Did I miss something?" Owen asked, taking a step closer to my sister before leaning into her and whispering something into her ear. She smiled, and it was the last straw. Not the fact that she was happy, but that I wasn't. Not completely.

I needed to leave and go somewhere else. Somewhere Heather wouldn't be. I headed back out to where our friends were and found them right where I left them, laughing and enjoying themselves.

"Hey, where the hell were you?" Nick put his arm around my waist and drew me closer, planting a kiss on my temple. I didn't bother looking to see if my shadow was watching because right then, with my souring mood, I couldn't care less.

"Bitch Dumont is here." I snuggled closer, needing the support of a friend.

"Yeah, I saw that. You okay?" Nick knew all about the shit between me and Heather, so thankfully I didn't have to vomit out all the details.

"I just want to get out of here."

"Unfortunately, I can't go."

"What?" I pouted. "Why?"

"I have an early morning shoot, and I need my beauty rest."

I could never stay mad at Nick. He was the kindest person I knew. A true sweetheart. Too bad he batted for the other team. Otherwise, I think we might've been good together. Even as the thought entered my delusional brain, I knew it was a lie. I wasn't good with anyone. Even if I gave a guy a chance, I'd somehow purposely sabotage it. My one-time, court-appointed therapist said I kept myself at a distance from people, for fear of getting hurt. *Did I mention I never saw that quack again?*

"I understand."

"We can't go either." Calvin and Neely were standing close and had overheard us. "Neely isn't feeling well so I'm gonna escort her home."

I reached out and grabbed her hand. "Are you okay? It's not the—" I pointed to her belly.

"No, it's not that. Well, it kinda is. Morning sickness my ass," she mumbled, forcing a smile when Calvin kissed her cheek.

So, our party had just been reduced by three, but there were still the original five, seven if you counted Ford and Owen, which I most certainly was not.

After everyone said their goodbyes, we waited outside for the valet to bring the vehicles around. Ford was off to the side talking to his brother, seemingly preoccupied, but I had no doubt his attention would be back on me in seconds. I only had a small window of opportunity to act if I wanted to salvage what was left of our celebratory evening.

I nonchalantly made my way toward Emily and whispered in her ear. "Let's get out of here."

"We are. That's why we're standing here." All of a sudden, her eyes widened. "Don't even think about it. You know you'll get in trouble."

"Trouble? I'll get a talking to, but that's it and you know it."

She wasn't biting. "Live a little. It's our birthday and we deserve to have some fun. Besides, do you honestly think we're in any real danger? Because nothing ever happened before," I reminded her. "This is just Dad being overprotective. Unnecessarily so, if you ask me. If I thought we were in jeopardy of being snatched up, I'd be attached to Ford twenty-four hours a day.

"I know. And I *am* having fun." And she was, which I was happy about, but I wanted to let loose without prying eyes watching my every move.

"But we could have more. Unchaperoned."

My eyes pleaded with Emily, and I didn't know if it was because some of her sensibility or inhibitions had been washed away with the alcohol she'd consumed, or she wanted the same thing I did, but she finally agreed.

"Fine. But we can't lose them for the rest of the night. You know it's not safe for us, especially so far away from home. I want to have fun, but I don't feel like ending up in the back of some windowless van.

Raising my shoulders, I bit my bottom lip to try and contain my excitement, finding it hard to remember the last time Emily and I did something reckless together. It'd been years.

Casually walking toward Naomi, Karen, and Benji, I informed them of our plan. There was another club I wanted to visit that was forty-five minutes north of where we were. After giving my best friend the details, I suggested we hop in two different vehicles, making it less obvious what we were doing.

When I glanced over at Ford and Owen, I saw my guy looking at me. I played it cool, and since there wasn't anyone else outside with the rest of us, he must've deemed it safe because he turned back toward Owen and they continued with their conversation.

Now, all I had to do was figure out how to pull this off. First things first, shut off my phone, but I'd have to wait until we were on the go before doing so. Otherwise Ford would get the alert.

Secondly, we had to figure out how to get to our new destination. We couldn't hop into one of the Navigators because they had tracking devices on them, I was sure of it. Knowing my father, and Ford, if they didn't come with them, they were installed before they arrived to pick us up at the airport.

But there were Uber drivers dropping people off. I had to convince one of them to take us without scheduling a pick up. Good thing I had a wad of money on me.

As luck would have it, two Uber vehicles pulled up right behind one another. As soon as the people exited, I approached the driver, and because of where our security were standing, I was hidden from Ford's sight. I knew I only had seconds to make our plans come to life before he noticed I was gone, so I went into a full-on rant, pulling a couple fifty-dollar bills from my clutch.

"I know I didn't reserve a ride, but I need to get out of here and fast." I flashed the driver the money. "Can you please take us?" His eyes lit up right away.

"Get in."

Emily and I hopped in the back seat, and when I turned around, I saw the other three entering the car behind us. I faced forward, and that's when I saw Ford and Owen rushing toward us.

"You need to get us out of here. Now!" I shouted, slapping the back of his seat. He didn't waste any time before he stepped on the gas full throttle, squealing the tires away from the entrance of the club.

I pulled out my phone and turned it off before putting the device back into my clutch.

"You need to do the same." I looked at Emily and watched her as she powered down her cell. She fidgeted in her seat several times, turning around to see if we were being followed. And we were, by our friends. "We'll be fine. We won't be out of their sight for too long. But hopefully long enough to have a bit more fun." I wiggled my brows, and surprisingly, Emily laughed and seemed to relax for the remainder of our trip.

CHAPTER
THIRTY-THREE

Ford

"What the fuck?" I shouted, slamming the palm of my hand against the steering wheel several times. The moment I took my eyes off her, she'd hopped in a stranger's car and took off. I had no idea how she managed to convince Emily to partake in something so goddamn reckless. I thought she had better common sense. Apparently, I was wrong. If I didn't end up hospitalized after this job was finished, I'd be one shocked sonofabitch.

"Calm down, man. We'll find them." We decided to drive together, leaving the other SUV back at the club with instruction we'd be back to retrieve it.

"How are you not pissed off?" I kept my eyes pinned to the road ahead, careful not to drive like a lunatic, especially since we had no idea where we were going. We'd seen the direction the cars went but didn't know if they took any of the numerous exits off the highway or kept traveling north.

"I *am* pissed. But getting all worked up isn't going to help. We need to focus." Owen appeared relaxed. The only sign he was indeed angry was the tightening of his hands.

"Check your phone again," I demanded, looking behind me before changing lanes, the slow ass in front of me only going eighty miles an hour.

"Don't get us killed."

"Just worry about getting that signal, and I'll worry about the driving." He was the worst back-seat driver and right then I had no patience for his comments whatsoever.

"Still nothing."

I'd once told Cara we could track their phones even if they turned them off. I'd lied. We needed one of their devices to be on in order to do our jobs effectively.

I crossed another lane of traffic, debating whether to call Walter and inform him of his daughters' actions. I never filled him in on the last time Cara took off, but this might be a different story altogether. It was both of them, and apparently neither one was being sensible, not that I expected Cara to be.

The woman was infuriating to the nth degree. I was sure she was having a good laugh about it right then.

Cara only ever worried about having a good time, all other consequences be damned. So what that it was their birthday? She wouldn't have many more to celebrate if she kept acting the way she had been.

"I think I have something. No... never mind. Shit!" Owen refreshed the app numerous times, trying to locate a signal on either of the women's phones. "Come on, Emily. Turn your fucking phone back on," he muttered, typing out a code before refreshing once more.

"I've been driving for almost thirty minutes and don't know if we're even going in the right direction. If we don't find them soon, we're going to have to call Walter." It wasn't ideal, especially seeing as how he entrusted us with his daughters' lives, but if something happened to them, he should know ahead of time that something went wrong.

"I know." Owen's acknowledgment did nothing to assuage

my growing anger, but at least we were both in the same boat. Both had taken off on us. I believed I'd be more upset if it had just been Cara. I took a small amount of solace that Emily had ditched my brother, as well.

Ten minutes passed and still nothing. That was until Owen's phone lit up, indicating it'd picked up the signal we were waiting for.

"Is that it?" I shouted, turning to look at him before back at the road. "Did you find them?" Seconds passed but I swore it was an hour. "Owen! Is that them?"

"Christ, hold on." One breath. Two. "Yup. Got 'em. It's Emily's phone. She turned it back on. Take the next exit. Looks like we gotta backtrack a bit, so step on it." Him giving me permission to go faster was all I needed to hear. The force of the Navigator's pickup slammed him back in his seat. "We need to get there in one piece," he added, checking the security of his seat belt when I chose to accelerate once more.

CHAPTER
THIRTY-FOUR

Ford

Close to an hour later, we pulled off the highway and onto a dirt road, with nothing else around for miles. What kind of club would be all the way out here?

"How's that signal?"

"Good. Strong. They should be just up ahead."

As I continued to drive, I thought about everything I wanted to say to Cara and to Emily alike, but more to Cara since I'd bet money she was behind the whole escape. And our conversation would go one of three ways. She'd ignore me altogether and continue to piss me off, or she'd rant about the fact I worked for her, even though technically I worked for her father, and that I should do as she asked and not the other way around. Or, she'd be more drunk by the time we got to them and come on to me again.

I couldn't help where my mind wandered without provocation.

That kiss.

I tried not to think about it after it happened, but the memory of her pressed against me, with our mouths fused together, and my tongue playing with hers... it was getting me hard. Not an ideal situation.

I chalked the whole thing up to me being horny. I would've never kissed her back otherwise. A stretch of time had passed since I'd gotten laid, and in order to stop fixating on Cara's mouth and what she'd done to me, I needed to bury myself inside of someone else.

"There," Owen pointed out, disrupting the erratic flow of my crazy thoughts.

I followed his line of sight, which of course was straight ahead, and saw what he did. The sign out front read Indulge, and I held a sneaking suspicion this wasn't like No. 4. The parking lot was full, so whatever place this was, it was a popular one.

As we approached the entrance, we passed by a row of motorcycles, and I didn't think anything of it until we stepped over the threshold and saw exactly what type of club it was, the type I had a hunch it might be.

They ditched us to go to a strip joint?

"Well, I didn't expect this." Owen tilted his head to the side and looked at our surroundings. The place was packed, every table and booth occupied. The bar was full, as well. There wasn't an empty seat in the place.

Everywhere we looked we saw strippers, all in various stages of undress. The ones on stage were naked or on their way to becoming so, whereas the ones making their rounds around the club were barely clothed. I'd been in some dive strip joints before, and this wasn't one of them. All the women looked healthy, if that made sense. And each one was beautiful, some even classy looking, which was an odd comparison for a woman who took her clothes off for a living.

"They're here somewhere. Let's split up so we can get the hell out of here as soon as possible. I don't like the looks on some of these guys, and I don't feel like beatin' the shit out of someone right now. But I will if I have to."

"You got it." He walked toward the other end of the club while I started searching where I was, walking past each table and looking at every individual. While our main concern was Cara and Emily, if we found Karen, Naomi, or Benji, we'd find the other two.

The longer it took me to find them, the angrier I became. I felt more like a goddamn babysitter than personal security. Concluding that they weren't in the main room of the club, at least the section I'd searched, I ventured into the hallway. I was stopped as soon as I entered, an overly large security guard blocking me from continuing.

"Can I help you?" The guy was big, standing almost toe to toe with me, but outweighing me by at least thirty pounds of pure muscle. His bald head gleamed from the overhead light, making him appear more menacing. This place didn't fuck around when it came to safety, and I had to respect that, seeing as how I was in the business. But whatever thoughts I had about the guy or the place weren't going to deter me from going back there to search for Cara and Emily.

"Nope. Just looking for someone." I tried to move past him, but he stopped me by placing his hand on my shoulder. "You need to stop touching me," I warned, but he kept his hand in place. Heat rose within me, but I forced a slow breath out through my nostrils trying like hell to tamp down the raging beast inside. Not only did I have to deal with the bullshit of the women taking off on us, putting themselves in danger and embarrassing the shit out of me and Owen, but now I had to deal with this muscled asshole who refused to stop touching me. My last nerve was plucked, and if something didn't happen soon, and in my favor, I feared I was going to blow. Once and for all.

"I'll stop touching you when you turn your ass around and go sit back down. You can't come back here unless one of the dancers brings you." The twitch in his eye told me he wasn't playing around and would do anything he needed to in order to do his assigned job.

"I'm not a customer. I'm looking for someone who took off on me, and I need to find her to get her out of here."

"Chasing your girlfriend?" The corners of his mouth curled, and I swore I was ten seconds away from smashing my fist into his face.

"No, not my girlfriend. A client."

"Oh, so you're a pimp?" His grin intensified and my fist tightened.

"No," I repeated, that time clenching my other fist and releasing an audible breath. When he didn't budge, I blurted, "Just let me check the rooms quick. You can even accompany me if you like."

"No."

Just as I made a move to go around him, although I knew it would be futile, I caught a glimpse of Cara coming out of one of the rooms, one of the strippers trailing behind her and laughing. It wasn't until she walked up behind the bouncer that she saw me, her smile morphing into a frown.

"Took you long enough," she mocked, winking at me before walking back into the center of the club. I followed. I seemed to always be following her, and it pissed me off more right then than ever before. Her insolence and don't-give-a-shit attitude pushed me over the edge, and before I could get ahold of my rising temper, I grabbed her wrist and halted her from taking another step.

There were so many things I wanted to say to her on the ride there, but the question that came out of my mouth wasn't one of them.

"What were you doing in that back room?" Clearly, she'd been getting a lap dance. Hey, to each their own, but I didn't have a clue she was also interested in women.

Instead of demanding I release her, she turned around and stepped into me, placing her hand on my chest. "Wouldn't you love to know?" Her words slurred and her eyes glassed over. I hoped she hadn't taken anything from anyone here.

"There you are," my brother yelled, briskly walking up to us with Emily right next to him. In fact, the rest of them were with him, as well. Thankfully, no one had been harmed, and we could finally get the hell out of there.

Naked women, booze, and horny men were not a great combination. I needed to remove everyone as quickly as possible before anything unexpected popped off. Drunk people didn't need a reason to start shit, and I wasn't about to stick around and be a part of it if anything went down.

"Let's go."

"I'm not ready yet," Cara challenged, no regard to what Owen and I had just been through, going out of our minds trying to find them. Never mind how upset we both were. I glanced over at my brother and caught a glimpse of Emily trying to talk to him, but he ignored her, instead looking straight ahead. His posture was rigid, his shoulders tense.

I wanted to throw Cara over my shoulder and carry her out of that club kicking and screaming. Maybe I'd even smack her ass a few times in the process. I was a firm believer in a nice swat when brats misbehaved. Of course, I pushed down my baser instincts and stood there, not so patiently waiting for her to come to her senses.

"Maybe we should go." Emily walked up next to her sister and grabbed her hand. "We had our fun. Now, let's just go back to the house and relax."

Cara yanked her hand away. "I said I'm not ready yet. Maybe I want to try my hand at the pole."

"Cara, stop it. You're drunk. There's no way you're getting on that stage and making a fool of yourself. I won't let that happen." Emily had certainly come out of her shell, and I was happy there was someone else there ready and willing to try and talk some sense into her.

"I'm not that drunk," she countered.

"You can barely speak without slurring your words," I barked, lowering my voice once I'd caught the attention of one of the other bouncers, who then signaled to someone else, a guy in a leather vest. They conversed among themselves before pointing at our group directly afterward.

"Fuckin' great. This is all we need. You happy now?"

"I'm fine." Cara laughed, as if the entire situation amused her. Well, it certainly wasn't funny to me, and if I had to work night and day to figure out who the hell was sending those threats to Walter just to get this damn job over with, I'd do just that. The woman standing before me had fried my last nerve.

"Do we have a problem here?" the guy in the leather vest asked, looking like both the guy next door but also someone who could kick the shit out of you without much effort. His hands were wrapped, an indication he most surely was some sort of fighter.

"Yes, we do." Cara approached the guy and smiled. He didn't look at her with awareness of who she was or even with sexual interest. "I want to stay and have some fun, but he wants to drag me out of here."

The guy made eye contact with me. "Is that so?"

"You don't know what you're getting mixed up in. Trust me. Don't believe a word she's saying."

He turned his attention back to Cara. "Is he bothering you?"

The world stopped spinning for a second, and during that time, Cara turned to look at me, bit her bottom lip, schooled her mischievous expression, then looked back at the guy.

"Yes, he is."

"Okay," he said, "let's go." He swung his arm toward the door. I didn't budge. "If you don't leave right now, I'm gonna force you out, and I doubt you want me to embarrass you in front of your friends."

"They're not my friends and you need to mind your business."

"This shit is my business. Don't you know where you are?" Out of my peripheral, I saw movement to my right, two other guys in leather vests moving toward us.

What were the chances these guys were just buddies who happened to be wearing the same outer attire?

What were the chances those weren't their bikes out front?

And what were the chances that we found ourselves in the middle of a biker strip club?

The last thing I wanted was to get into some kind of fucking brawl with a bunch of bikers, just because Cara was a stubborn pain in the ass who didn't know what was good for her. But it appeared as if that was exactly what was going to happen because I wasn't going anywhere without her.

Owen was next to me, Emily still standing next to Cara, while Naomi, Benji, and Karen were behind us, watching as everything unfolded.

"Listen, all we want to do is leave without an incident,"

Owen spoke up. "We're responsible for these two," he said, pointing to Emily and Cara. "So, we can't leave without them."

"I don't care. Apparently, she doesn't want to go with you." He looked from Owen to me then back to my brother.

"Jagger," one of the other guys shouted, weaving through the crowd before walking up next to him. "We got a problem?"

"Nope. Just informing these guys they have to leave."

The one in front of us, Jagger, continued speaking but I never heard what he said, too busy staring at his friend in disbelief.

It'd been quite a few years, but there was no mistaking who I was looking at.

It was him.

My brother had recognized him right away, as well. "What are *you* doing here?" Owen asked, throwing his hands out to his sides.

CHAPTER
THIRTY-FIVE

Cara

My eyes were glued to the men who'd walked up to us, and while I thought the situation had turned in my favor, I quickly noticed that it'd shifted away from me. Who the hell were these guys?

When I'd given the address to our driver, it was to a club I'd visited several times but years ago. Apparently, they were no longer in business, which we could tell as soon as we drove up, but not wanting to take another ride, we decided to check out the club that had taken its place. Truth was, the parade of motorcycles out front cinched the deal. I'd always been a sucker for a man who could ride one.

At first, Emily didn't want to go in, but when our friends pulled up alongside us, she agreed to give it a shot. I told her if we didn't like it after one drink, we'd go someplace else.

We were inside for close to a half hour before Ford and Owen came busting in, and although we hadn't lost them for long, I reveled in the time I had without someone cramping my style and watching me like a hawk.

I accepted a private dance from a stripper named Diamond. She was beautiful, and I appreciated a work of art. Besides, I was drunk and wanted to throw caution to the wind and have a good time. Nothing happened in the room, other than her showing me her skills. I tipped her accordingly but allowed Ford to think I messed around with her. The way he looked at me didn't sit well, so I refused to give him any information. He could think whatever he wanted of me, had been doing so since the first time I met him.

"What are *you* doing here?" Owen asked the large man standing in front of him. He was about an inch taller than Ford and very good-looking. Not mysterious, brooding, pain-in-the-ass good-looking like Ford, but in his own way. His clothes were in sync with his friends'. Dark jeans, T-shirt, leather vest, and shit-kickin' boots. When the one they referred to as Jagger turned around, I saw the emblem on the back of the vest. A skull with a sword through it and the words *Knights Corruption*. My suspicions had been dead on. I guessed from the chromes of steel out front that there were some guys from a biker club inside.

The guy engaged in conversation with Owen shook his head before approaching, offering his hand before pulling him in for one of those guy hugs. When they broke apart, they were both smiling.

"Me? What the hell are you two doing here?" He embraced Ford next, and the look on Ford's face threw me. His stoic expression morphed into a genuine smile, erasing the tension he seemed to carry around constantly.

Ford was gorgeous, and that was him being moody and difficult and stubborn and... the list could go on and on. But mix in a smile, and he was out-of-this-world hot.

My thoughts immediately drifted to our kiss and how I hadn't wanted it to end. I'd still be devouring him in that hallway had he not stopped it.

"We're here on a job," Ford answered, shifting his attention to me for a moment, which was when his smile fell, his expression switching back to annoyed.

"Oh, she's not your ol' lady?"

"Uh… not a chance."

I ignored his dig and focused instead on the guy's question. Or part of it.

"You really use that term? For a girlfriend?"

"And wife. Sure do."

His glance was back on Ford. "You sure you're not with her? I'm a pretty good judge of character, and it seems like there's some tension between you."

I walked up to the guy and touched his vest. He looked down at my hand, then at me. "You bet your ass there's tension. Your friend here is—"

"Cousin."

"What?"

"Ford and Owen are our cousins."

"Our?"

That was when another guy came into view. There was a height difference between the two, but they shared the same shade of dark hair. While the taller one had a shorter cut, the other's fell to the top of his shoulders, neatly tucked behind his ears. Good genes ran in that family.

"This is Hawke, and I'm Tripp. And you are?" I liked him, his self-assured grin putting me at ease.

"Cara. And this is my sister Emily." I looked for the rest of our party, but they'd left us and were standing near the bar.

"Are we all done with the pleasantries now?" Ford's tone was gruff. No nonsense as usual.

"Tripp?" He'd been watching Ford closely, but when I called his name, he looked at me, his eyes crinkling.

"Yeah?"

"Maybe you could convince your cousin to lay off and let us have some fun. It's our birthday, after all." I pulled Emily closer and kissed her cheek.

"Is that so?" Hawke walked around us and inched his way in between, throwing his arms over our shoulders, set to guide us toward the bar.

"Not a chance. Hands off. I don't need you encouraging them. They've had plenty to drink already." Ford removed Hawke's arms from around us and moved us to the side.

"I think *you* need a drink." Hawke tucked an errant strand of hair back behind his ear.

I pointed at the only broody bastard in our group. "He needs more than a drink."

"We're on duty. No drinking." Ford kept his eyes pinned to his cousin and away from me. I knew he heard me but chose to ignore me.

"How about some pussy then?" I blurted, smiling when Tripp and Hawke stared at me with wide eyes.

"Are you offerin' him yours, sweetheart?" Tripp laughed as he smacked his cousin on the back.

Contemplating my answer because I wanted to shout "hell no" but also "yes" at the same time, I leaned into my sister, needing her to physically keep me from falling. The club spun for a few seconds before stopping. Long enough for me to continue participating in the banter.

Deciding not to answer at all, I went in another direction. "How about I buy him a private dance?" I reached into my clutch and pulled out a hundred-dollar bill. "Will this do?"

"Put your money away. We got this." Hawke laughed. Right at that moment, one of the dancers walked by, and

Hawke called her back. "You free?"

"Sure." She eyed our group before focusing in on Ford. She licked her lips, and I instantly regretted my suggestion of him getting a dance. The way she looked at him was like she wanted to eat him alive. I knew that look. Hell, I couldn't blame her, but I didn't want him disappearing for God knew how long, doing God knew what with her.

"She's not his type. How about someone else?" My tone was calm, but there was no mistaking my intent. I hadn't meant to be so obvious, but I couldn't stop myself. One of the many effects of being drunk. *Say what you want, how you want.*

Ford clenched his jaw, the muscle tic a precursor for yet another argument. I thought he was going to berate me, or his cousins, for trying to push him toward a dance. Instead, he walked up to the stripper, smiled then placed his hand on her lower back. My heart hit my stomach.

"After you." Before he disappeared, he pointed at his family. "Watch she doesn't give you the slip."

The image of that woman getting naked for Ford made my stomach roll. I found it difficult to breathe as my heartbeat became sluggish, but there wasn't a damn thing I could do about my asinine suggestion now.

CHAPTER
THIRTY-SIX

Ford

Under any other circumstance, I would've ignored Cara and stepped to the side, being sure to keep my eyes on her. But I had to walk away before I did or said something I couldn't take back. I needed a moment. Maybe a few of them. Too many things happened at once, and I needed to collect myself, tamp down my brimming anger before it got the best of me.

Pissed off the women had given us the slip, I was relieved when we finally located them. Of course, it wouldn't be a simple task of walking into the club and escorting them out. That would have been too easy, and if I'd learned anything since meeting Cara Dessoye, it was that nothing was easy when it came to her.

Not only was I surprised by the type of club they'd gone into, and us after them, but then I'd discovered that Tripp and Hawke were inside. What the hell were the chances of that? We hadn't seen each other in years, too long, and while I was happy to see them, it wasn't the best time for a family reunion.

One eye was trained on Cara. Therefore, I only had so much attention I could give anyone else. If she acted like a responsible person and stopped trying to ditch me whenever she found an opportunity, I could have a decent conversation with my family, or at the very least try and relax some while watching out for her.

Then she went and pissed me off even more, if that were at all possible, by suggesting that I needed some pussy to relax. Her comment was just one more thing to try and push me over the edge, drive me mad. If she kept it up, it might just be the night it happened. The woman was hellbent on driving me to the brink.

When Hawke called back one of the dancers, I focused on Cara, who was, in turn, watching the stripper. She had the nerve to say she wasn't my type. How the hell did she know what my type was? I most certainly wasn't going to indulge in a dance, it'd been the furthest thing from my mind, but when she made that comment, and I saw the way her lip rose in disapproval, it pushed me to do something I normally wouldn't.

She crossed her arms over her chest and mumbled something, but I didn't hear what she'd said.

But I knew one thing.

She was jealous.

Why? I couldn't say, but she was jealous just the same.

Maybe it was immature and unprofessional, but I decided to have that dance after all. If there was even an inkling of a chance I could get under her skin, the way she burrowed under mine, I was going to take it.

I approached the dancer and placed my hand on the small of her back. "After you." Before we left, though, I pointed toward my family, all three of them, and warned, "Watch she doesn't give you the slip."

Guiding the woman across the room and toward the hallway I'd tried to enter earlier, I realized there could be worse things than having a beautiful woman's attention.

She was significantly shorter than me, but most women

were. Long, red hair fell down her back in waves, swaying with every step of her toned legs. Big tits, a flat stomach, and a round ass made up the rest of her.

"What's your name, honey?" she asked, grabbing my hand and pulling me into one of the private rooms. She locked the door, which triggered an overhead light to come on, indicating the room was in use.

"Owen." I didn't want to use my name.

"Owen," she parroted, flashing me a smile before bending over to turn on the music. After she was all set, she sauntered back toward me. "You're gorgeous, if you don't mind my saying so."

"No, I don't mind." I didn't think I could be any less enthusiastic if I tried.

She straddled my lap before I realized she was that close and grabbed on to my shoulders to anchor herself.

"You have very captivating eyes."

"So, I've been told." I sighed, my loud breath causing her to tilt her head to the side.

"Are you okay? Do you not want to do this? Because we can stop, and you can go back out there to your girlfriend." Her concern surprised me, but I was too focused on the last part of her sentence to appreciate it.

"What girlfriend?" I knew exactly who she was talking about, so I wasn't sure why I bothered to ask.

"The blonde who was standing near you." The thrum of the music played in the background but there wasn't any dancing going on.

"She is most certainly not my girlfriend," I barked, reining in my tone because she didn't deserve my attitude.

She leaned back and stared at me. Intently.

"But you like her." It wasn't a question.

"I don't."

She winked at me and smirked. "Oh, but you do. You just don't want to admit it for some reason."

Placing my hands on her hips, I guided her off me and quickly stood. She studied me for several more seconds before throwing her hands in the air, a sign of surrender. "Okay. Okay. If you say so." She untied the front of her shirt, and her tits spilled out. I looked away and toward the ceiling. "Owen, you can look at me. That's why we're back here. Hell, that's why you're in this place to begin with."

"Can you put your shirt back on, please?" I glanced down at her and saw she held the same tilt to her head she had moments prior. "Please."

"I don't think I've ever had a guy tell me to get dressed before." She laughed, notifying me when she was covered back up.

"Look, I'm sorry I wasted your time by bringing you back here, but I don't want to do this. I was only trying to get back at—"

"That woman," she finished.

"Yeah." I sighed once more, that time long and low. My hands were hidden behind my back, and I was embarrassed by my behavior. Of the lengths I went to in order to stick it to Cara. She was drunk and didn't know what she was doing or saying. I was sober and her security detail. All my actions were inappropriate, and right then, I could've kicked myself for acting the way I had.

"Understood. Say no more." She walked toward the door and unlocked it. "If you change your mind, you know where to find me."

Moments later, I rejoined the group, my cousins laughing at

something Owen had said. Cara and Emily were sitting on bar stools, sandwiched between Tripp and Hawke, my brother standing in front of them all. Karen, Naomi, and Benji were standing on the opposite side of the small group, everyone seeming to enjoy themselves.

"All good?" Tripp asked, his bottle of beer paused halfway to his mouth. "You weren't back there very long. Was Jade not what you were looking for because we can set you up with someone else."

I made the mistake of making eye contact with Cara. She leaned back against the lip of the bar, positioning her elbows behind her which only served to push her tits out farther.

"I think your cousin might bat for the other team," she nonchalantly teased, grinning wide when my mouth dropped open. She knew damn well I wasn't gay, yet she made the comment anyway. Anything to incite a reaction.

Hawke walked up to me and grabbed my shoulder. "That's not true." I didn't answer. "Is it?"

"No." I couldn't care less about the content of the comment. I wasn't offended or anything of the sort. I was pissed Cara seized yet another opportunity to be a bitch. Plain and simple.

"Stop it." Emily smacked her sister's leg and shook her head.

"What? He knows I'm only teasing. Don't you, Ford?" She looked at me briefly before hopping off her stool, grabbing on to Tripp's arm so she didn't fall. She held on a little too long, looking up at him and flashing him a flirty smile.

"I'd be careful if I were you," Hawke laughed. "His ol' lady won't take kindly to you touching her man."

"Is she here?"

"Not yet. But she could show up anytime."

"Until then…" She brazenly ran her hand down his chest.

"Okay, okay. I think someone's had enough to drink," Tripp said, backing away so that Cara's hand fell to her side. He was a good sport about it, no doubt not all offended that a beautiful woman was hitting on him. He probably got that kind of attention a lot being here.

"Where's the ladies' room?" Emily wrapped her arm around her sister's waist and looked around the club, trying to locate the restroom.

"Follow me." Hawke jerked his head to the right. I moved to go with them, but Tripp stopped me.

"I need a word." As soon as they disappeared, he pulled me to the side, out of earshot of the rest of them. "Your woman—"

"She's not my fucking woman."

"You know what I mean." He scratched the side of his head, looking like he didn't want to spill whatever was on his mind. "She asked me if I had any coke."

"And what did you tell her?" My chest puffed up as the last word left my mouth.

"I told her we don't do that shit and neither should she."

Throwing my head back, I inhaled a choppy breath. "Fuck." Needing to take a seat, I situated myself on the same stool Cara had vacated, running my hands through my hair in utter frustration. I swore I was at my wit's end, and if something didn't change soon, I didn't know what I'd do. I didn't even know if I could continue with this assignment, although if I tried to quit, I could forget about Owen talking to me for the foreseeable future.

"She sure is a handful," he said, signaling the bartender he wanted a drink. "You want one?"

"No, still on duty, although I wish I wasn't."

"You and Owen work security, right? I think that's what I

heard." He took a healthy swig of his beer, leaning against the bar and giving me his full attention.

I always got along great with Tripp, and being there with him reminded me of all the fun times we'd had growing up. He'd been the biggest klutz when he was younger, hence the nickname Tripp.

"We do. Actually, we own the firm together."

"Shit. Look at you." He tipped the head of his bottle toward me before taking another sip.

"What the hell are you guys doing here? Do you come here on a regular?"

"Our club owns this place, so yeah, we're here quite a bit. Although Reece would prefer I wasn't." I gave him a blank stare. "My ol' lady."

"Aww. Yeah, I don't have or want one of those."

"You sure?"

"Don't start." I drummed my fingers on the top of the bar, waiting for Cara and Emily to return so we could call it a night and head back to the house. All I wanted was a quiet ride home, then a nice hot shower before collapsing into bed. All things I could bet wouldn't happen. At least not that easily.

"I thought you and Owen were in New York. Are you two in California now?" A woman walked over to Tripp and handed him a piece of paper. He scanned it quickly before sighing, then gave me his attention again.

"Connecticut," I corrected, "and yes we still live there. This assignment is in New York, but they wanted to come out here for a couple of days. A couple of very long days." Defeat ripped through me, and it took every ounce of energy not to hop up from the stool, snatch Cara, and throw her in the back of the Lincoln.

"Yeah, what's the story there?"

"Too long to tell right now. Besides, they're on their way back. I'll tell ya another time."

Tripp placed his hand on my shoulder and leaned in. "Listen, I wanted to tell you how sorry I was to hear about Julia. I would've attended the service, but there was a lot of shit happenin' with the club, and I couldn't get away."

Words failed me, allowing me to respond the best way I could—with a faraway look at the mention of my sister and a shaky nod.

Needing a quick distraction, I watched Hawke stroll back toward us with the women in front of him. He had a big smile on his face, and I knew better than to ask, but I did anyway.

"What's with the shit-eatin' grin?"

"That one"—he pointed to Cara who was already busy chatting with her friends—"is somethin' else."

"What does that mean?" Every muscle in my back locked up, preparing to hear another outlandish story about her.

"You said you're not with her, right?"

"Right?" I answered, the single-word answer strained coming out of my mouth.

"Okay." He looked hesitant. Then his grin returned in full force. "She offered to take me into one of the rooms and show me the time of my life."

How could I be jealous, angry, and disappointed all at the same time? Each emotion reared its ugly head, twisting together to form something I couldn't readily describe.

"And what did you say?" Tripp asked, some sort of silent message passing between them I was all too familiar with since Owen and I did the same thing many times over.

"You know I'm not like that anymore. I told her no thanks."

Hawke balled his fist and hit it against his opposing palm. "Damn, though, if I was, I would've let her do anything she wanted to me. She's fuckin' hot."

"Fuck, man," Tripp admonished, smacking Hawke in the back of the head.

"What the hell was that for?" Hawke was clueless sometimes, had been that way since we were kids. But instead of being pissed off at him, I chuckled at his lack of ability to read a situation. Although to be fair, he didn't say anything wrong.

"Just because."

"You better watch it, brother. Jagger's been showing me the ropes. Soon enough, I'm gonna be able to whip your ass." Hawke punched the air and danced around his brother.

"I'd like to see that happen."

"Yeah, me too," I added, looking over at Owen to see what was going on with the group.

"Where is Jagger anyway?" Tripp craned his neck to look around the corner before scanning the rest of the club.

"He had a fight to get to."

Tripp nodded before tapping the top of the bar. The bartender slid him another beer. "You sure I couldn't interest you in one? It won't kill ya."

"I'm good. Actually, I'm gonna see if they want to head out now."

"Okay. Well, it was great to see you. You'll have to stop by the clubhouse the next time you're out here."

I didn't think I'd be in California again anytime soon, but stranger things have happened. "Sure thing." My answer was both passive and honest. After checking to ensure we all had each other's current numbers, I headed straight for Cara, prepared for her to argue with me, but she hopped off her bar stool when I told her it was time to go.

We said our goodbyes, left the club, filed into the Navigator and drove back to No. 4 to pick up the other SUV before heading back to the cabin. Cara was passed out before we hit the highway.

CHAPTER
THIRTY-SEVEN

Cara

All I heard when I woke up was, "I got her." Then I was lifted into the air, my body weightless. My eyes closed again before I could comprehend what was happening, opening a short time later to find myself lying on top of my bed.

"How are you still awake?" a gruff voice asked, and as the room spun around me, I took a few breaths to focus. I looked over at Ford, and had I not been drunk, I would've fully appreciated the sight of him, even with him scowling.

"I've been drinking a long time," I confessed before scooting back on the bed.

"Why?"

"Why what?"

"Why have you been drinking so long? You're only twenty-five. Way too young to be as jaded as you are."

"How do you know I'm jaded?" I moved to grab a pillow to prop myself up but fell over on my side. I laughed into the covers, slowly rolling back over. For as much as I could hold my liquor, it didn't mean I didn't struggle with simple movements from time to time.

Ford rubbed the back of his neck and flicked his gaze upward, minutely shaking his head. "Because I know you." His tone was sharp, but I ignored the contempt in his voice because I didn't want to get into yet another argument with him, especially when sleep snatched the edges of my consciousness. But I had to correct him.

"You don't know me."

"No?"

"You're arrogant, you know that?" I smacked my lips together, my mouth suddenly very dry. I reached over to the nightstand and grabbed the glass of water I kept there. I thought the lip of the drink was pressed against my mouth, but it was off by two inches. The water dribbled down my chin and on to my chest.

"Why am I arrogant? Because I call you out?"

"You don't call me out on anything. You just make assumptions." I stumbled from the bed and stood on shaky feet. Being drunk and tired wasn't the greatest combination.

He made a move to touch me, but I threw my hand up. "Don't." I couldn't focus on what I wanted to say, but I was getting tired of the snide comments we often shared, even though I was partly to blame.

Ford turned away from me and headed for the door. But of course, in good ol'-fashioned Cara style, I baited him to stay and engage.

"Would you rather I keep everything bottled up inside like you?" He stopped walking but kept his back to me. "Then I could be a moody pain in the ass who tries to stomp out everyone's fun."

"I refuse to do this with you anymore. I can't." His posture straightened before he rolled his shoulders, like he was dismissing me without words. His subtle movements infuriated me beyond reason.

"Look at me." He remained still, the only indication he'd heard me was the flexing of his hands at his sides. "Ford!" I shouted. "Look at me."

He turned slowly, and although he showed no outward signs of any emotion, annoyance and anger flared in his beautiful eyes.

I had no idea what I was going to say to him, but I didn't want him to leave. My fingers played with the zipper on the side of my dress, tugging but getting nowhere. I cursed when the steel teeth still wouldn't budge.

"What are you doing?" He stood stock still, but his eyes traveled the length of me, landing on my face to study me. I hated being the object of his scrutiny. For some inexplicable reason, I felt stripped when he looked at me so intently, as if he could see the scars scorched into my soul. I was vulnerable. Exposed.

"I'm trying to take off my dress." I fiddled with the zipper one more time but gave up five seconds later.

"What did you want to say to me?"

"When?" My short-term memory failed me.

"Thirty seconds ago."

Honestly, I'd never landed on one specific thing to say. Though the booze flowing through my blood didn't help me remember either.

"I need help getting this off." I crept closer to him. "Can you get the zipper?"

"I'll call Emily up to help you."

"Are you scared of me?" The words came unbidden, but I was curious as to what his answer would be.

"Why would I be scared of you?" He shoved his hands into his pockets.

"Because I'm what you can't be." My fingers played with

245

the top of my dress. If I couldn't get the zipper unhooked, then maybe I could just shimmy out of it.

"What does that even mean?"

I waved my arm at him. "You're so… rigid and uptight. You don't know how to have a good time. But not me. I know when to seize the moment and let loose. I'm fun." I managed to loosen the fabric around my chest enough to pull it down a bit. I wasn't wearing a bra because the top of the dress was structured, and a strapless bra would only make the fabric protrude.

"You behaving badly is you having fun? Because if that's the definition, I'd prefer to be rigid and uptight."

I continued to try and free myself from my dress, and after several more seconds of pulling and tugging, I managed to free my breasts, sighing with relief the instant the air hit my nipples.

"Christ, Cara. What is wrong with you?" He looked down at the carpet, the fabric of his pants stretching from him flexing his hands in his pockets. Or was he getting hard?

"I know my tits aren't as big as that stripper's but—"

When his head snapped up, he looked directly into my eyes, not once glancing at my exposed flesh. "You pushed that shit on me. Mocking me. Just to get a reaction. Then when Hawke snagged her, I saw the moment you regretted opening your mouth."

"Wh-what are you ta-talking about?" I stammered. There was no way he could tell I was upset about him sauntering off with a woman whose only job was to get naked for him.

"Don't play dumb."

"You're delusional."

"I'm delusional. I'm arrogant. I'm rigid and uptight. Anything else?" His sarcasm sliced right through me. I wanted to bait him, argue with him, but not like this. He saw too much of me, and I didn't like it. Not one bit. I wasn't in control of the situation.

He advanced, his long strides putting him in front of me before I could process what I wanted to say next. Words failed me, his closeness knocking me off-kilter. My world spun, and it had nothing to do with how much I'd had to drink.

"What did you expect would happen here? You'd get naked and throw yourself at me? Like you did back at the club? Is this how you get a guy's attention?" He peppered me with questions, so many I couldn't focus on which one to answer. He surprised me by grabbing my shoulders and squeezing. "Is this what you want? My hands on you? Is this the drill? What do they do next?" He pulled me so close my breasts brushed across his shirt. "Do you have any idea how dangerous your actions are? Do you have any idea the amount of trouble you could get into being so careless? Not giving a shit about yourself?"

"Why do you care?"

He lowered his face until it was level with mine. "Because you don't only affect your life, you affect those around you who care about you. Yet you don't give them a second thought. Only about what you want." He rose back up to his full height. "You're selfish and immature." He released me and turned to walk away.

"Is that what you said to your sister? Is that the tough-love act you pulled on her?" I knew my mistake as soon as I spoke. If I could rewind time by ten seconds, I would've bitten my tongue and let him walk out of my bedroom.

He whirled around and looked like he was going to charge at me, the intensity on his face sobering. I crossed a line, but it was too late to go back. He stalked toward me, his chest expanding more with each breath he sucked into his lungs.

Ford backed me against the wall and towered over me. His

pupils turned dark, and a bead of sweat broke out on his fore-head. There was barely enough room between our bodies for me to take a full breath.

"What the fuck do you know about my sister?" he growled, the vein in his neck beginning to throb.

"Owen mentioned—"

"I don't care what Owen told you. Don't ever say anything like that again to me. Do you hear me?" he shouted.

"Yes," I mumbled, my response enough for him to back away. He strode across the room then disappeared, grumbling something about his brother.

Immediately, I berated myself for mentioning his sister in such a hostile tone. He didn't deserve that. Even in my drunken state, I realized my harsh and over-the-line statement pushed the boundary of decency. I had no right to talk about his sister, especially when I knew how sensitive a topic it was for him, all details Owen told me.

CHAPTER
THIRTY-EIGHT

Ford

"**W**hat the fuck did you tell Cara about Julia?" I shoved Owen so hard he tripped over the leg of one of the chairs set up around the fire pit. When he got his bearings, I stood so close he could barely look me in the eye.

"Jesus! Back up, will ya?" The anger in his voice was but a fraction of my own.

I'd never wanted to put my hands on my brother more in my life, and it took every ounce of willpower not to slam my fist into his face. What the hell was he thinking? Of all people, he confided in Cara?

"Tell me right now why you told her about our sister. Were you drunk? Tell me!" I shouted, slamming my fist onto the top of the chair so I wouldn't inadvertently break his nose instead.

"Would you please calm down. It's not what you think."

"No? Then what is it?"

"I mentioned Julia as a way to get her to calm down." The scowl on my face drove him to clarify. "I know she's been a handful." That was an understatement. "And I thought if I could give her a sliver of why you act the way you do toward her that she would ease up a bit and…."

"And what?"

"Behave."

"Behave? Do you consider her ditching us, ending up at a strip club, telling me I need either pussy or a drink to calm down, then showing me her tits behaving?"

"She showed you her tits?" Of course, that was the one part he focused on.

"Never mind that." I ran my hands through my hair. "Christ, Owen. I can't believe you said anything at all."

"I'm sorry. I thought it would help." His brows pulled in before he looked downward. "Sorry," he repeated. I believed he had good intentions when he opened up about Julia, but it just went to prove that telling Cara didn't make a bit of difference.

"How much did you tell her?" I braced myself for the worst, concentrating on every breath that escaped.

"Just that she had a problem and that she ended up dying in a car accident. I didn't say anything about the fight you two had beforehand." I flinched at the memory.

"You still told her too much."

He shrugged and nodded simultaneously, a noncommittal response, one I was used to from him every now and then. Part of him agreed with what I'd said, while the other part wanted to disagree. Owen knew when to pick his battles, something I struggled with, especially as of late.

"Help me finish rounds. I'm exhausted and just want this night to be over."

"I'm right there with you," I said, punching him on the arm while we walked back toward the house. I loved Owen, even when I wanted to physically take out my anger on him.

Half of my body disappeared inside the refrigerator trying to search for the mustard, cursing aloud when I turned my head and spotted it on the counter.

I'd woken up in the same sour mood I'd gone to bed with, convincing myself to stay and finish this job and not leave Owen high and dry. I flip-flopped every few minutes. Right then I was on the side of staying.

Slapping my bread on the plate, I finished making my sandwich. I was just about to take a bite when someone entered the kitchen and cleared their throat.

Cara.

"Ford, can I talk to you?"

There wasn't enough patience in the world that would help me get through another conversation with that woman, and I used the word conversation loosely.

She crept closer, careful to keep a respectable distance between us, most likely still unsure of how I'd react. I was borderline explosive last night when she mentioned Julia. I didn't blame her for being cautious.

Placing my hands on the edge of the counter, I dropped my head and tried to garner up the emotional strength to listen to what she wanted to say. I was curious, no doubt, but I was also tired of the needless back and forth between us, even though I was just as guilty in the exchange.

"You don't have to say anything," she started, taking a seat across from me. For the safety of my temperamental mood, I kept my head down and my eyes focused on the sandwich I wanted to devour. "Things got out of hand last night."

"Ya think?" I sniped, raising my eyes to hers. *So much for not engaging.* I geared up to lay into her again, expecting she'd try and convince me, and herself, that whatever happened wasn't her fault. That she'd try and blame it on the alcohol or come up with another asinine excuse. I never knew what was going to come flying out of her mouth. I tried not to project, but it was hard to do when she let me down at every turn. Strike that. She didn't let me down because that would've indicated I cared.

"I deserve that." Her eyebrows gathered inward, and she sighed. "I wanted to apologize. I should've never brought up your sister." My posture locked up at the mention of Julia. "That was crossing the line... and I'm sorry." She placed her hand on her chest, and if I didn't know any better, I would've said she was being sincere. "I was drunk and not thinking straight."

"Or acting right."

"Or acting right," she agreed. Cara looked every bit her age when she was all done up, but right then, she looked younger. With her hair pulled into a ponytail and a clean face, void of makeup, she looked almost innocent.

This was the first time I'd witnessed the genuine side of her. Every other encounter seemed forced and inconvenient, and that was putting it mildly. I was shocked she'd apologized, and while I appreciated the effort of her regret, I couldn't help but keep my guard up.

"Okay, well, that's all I wanted to say." She shrugged before standing, the bottom of her tank top riding up to expose her belly. Images of her pulling her dress down and exposing herself to me filtered in, and while I'd been beyond livid, my emotion didn't deter me from filing away the mental picture for another time.

CHAPTER
THIRTY-NINE

Cara

Since our return home two days ago, all was quiet. I didn't pester Ford to accompany me on needless shopping trips. Instead, I was oddly content to lounge by the pool, read, or watch television. Emily, on the other hand, jumped back into her charity work. I believed she was volunteering at one of the homeless shelters in the city so she'd be gone all day, as would Owen. Which left me and Ford all alone.

We'd crossed paths several times while he busied himself with his rounds, but we didn't speak. The only acknowledgment I received from him was a curt nod. The tension between us persisted, but it was of a different nature. It was hard to explain. I didn't want to antagonize him or lure him for a reaction. Instead, I wanted to keep my distance for fear he'd twist whatever emotion he'd elicited from me into something more.

For the first time in a long time, I was embarrassed by my behavior, specifically hitting him where I knew it would cause the most damage. Bringing up his sister, especially after Owen had discussed her with me in hopes I'd take it easy on Ford, was a low blow, even for me.

There was a moment when he backed me against the wall and towered over me, my nakedness pressing into him, when

I hated the person I'd become. Someone willing to tear into another just to feel the rush of life pump through me. Only, it wasn't life at all. It was disappointment and regret and... shame.

My phone vibrated on the table next to me, my eyes squinting at the screen because of the bright sun overhead. I'd been lazing by the pool for the past hour, thinking about everything that had gone down in California. In addition, I was contemplating making a major change in my life but wasn't sure I had enough gumption to pull it off. I felt like I was lost in limbo, torn between the only way I knew how to be and eager for the life I'd dreamt about when I was younger.

Naomi: Meet me at Blush in an hour. New line just came out.

Blush was a trendy boutique we loved to shop at. The owner, Audrey Filip, had finished her new line early and apparently it was now out for sale. The place was on a smaller scale but quaint. Charming yet classy. Exactly the type of store I hoped to own one day to showcase my own designs.

Random thoughts like that popped into my head more recently, eliciting an emotion akin to hope. Not wanting to dash the image of a future I could have, I focused on the text from my bestie.

Me: Not sure I'm up for it today. Raincheck?

Naomi: Did you not read my text? New line. Out today. Will be gone if you don't get your butt there.

Scrunching my nose, I leaned back against my lounge chair and talked myself into going.

Me: Be there in an hour

No response from Naomi because there was no need to

reply. When it came to shopping, I kept my word and was always on time. It was everything else in life that had to wait.

Clutching my phone, I stood and walked toward the house, and that was when I saw Ford. He was coming out of the guest house, looking at something on his cell when he stopped right before crashing into me, his fingers typing feverishly over the keys.

Whatever he was reading had stolen his attention enough to almost knock me on my ass.

"You done out here?" he asked, picking his head up to look at me.

"Yeah." I took a few steps, then turned back to face him. "I'm meeting Naomi for some shopping. I wanna leave in a half hour." He nodded before disappearing back inside the guest house.

I contemplated being nicer about it, asking him if that was enough notice for him, but old habits were hard to break.

An hour later and I hugged Naomi right before we walked into Blush. Audrey came over to greet us, directing us toward the clothes she'd put out earlier that day, and after some idle chitchat, we lost ourselves to the feel of the material, admiring the lines and cut of the designs. Okay, that was all me. Naomi simply snatched the clothing off the rack and handed it to one of the salesgirls so she could start a dressing room for her.

Because of my love for fashion, I'd grown to appreciate all the intricate details that went into creating a piece. I had numerous sketchbooks at home filled with original designs, although I'd just recently taken them out of storage to look at them. The creative bug nipped at my heels as the days passed, more so ever since Ford had sneaked a peek at some of them one day while I'd been engrossed with one of our home movies. I'd been furious with him that day, but it drove me to follow through with a goal I had years ago.

"How much longer do you think Ford will be around?" Naomi asked from the dressing room next to mine. He stood right outside, so I knew he heard her question. Normally, I would've commented back with sarcasm, even making fun of him in some way, but all I gave her was the honest truth.

"I suppose once we find out where the threats are coming from and deal with it."

"Hey, did you hear about what happened to Kurt?" The clanking of a dropped hanger startled me. Naomi's question about Ford made me think that, in fact, one day, probably soon, he'd be gone. For as infuriated as he made me, I couldn't imagine not seeing him every day. Ask him, and I was sure he'd say he was counting down the seconds until he didn't have to deal with me any longer.

"No."

"His dad threw him in rehab and said that if he didn't follow through this time, he was cut off."

There was a time I would've had some reaction toward what she'd told me. I'd sympathize with Kurt about how unfair his father was being. That it was Kurt's life and he should live it how he wanted to or that his father was blowing shit out of proportion. But the only thought I had was... nothing. I had no thoughts of Kurt or reaction to the news. I hated to admit such a thing, but I was happy my dad had made his ludicrous demand about me staying away from him. Not sure if this was the right word, but I believed I was even thankful Ford had interfered in that debacle of a situation.

Things between me and Kurt hadn't been serious, and I'd planned to end things once and for all between us as soon as I'd gotten bored. I reacted the way I had because I didn't like being told what to do. Tell me to do something, and I'd go to extremes to do the opposite. That had been my mantra for as long as I could remember.

"No reaction to what I just said?"

Naomi stepped into the foyer of the dressing area and I soon joined her. She wore a pair of high-waisted, satin black pants that boasted a slit on each side. Paired with a cream-colored top, she looked amazing. With her slim build, she could wear almost anything and look great. She often complained about not being able to gain weight, though, and wished she could have more of an ass to fill out her jeans. I thought her ass looked good.

I pointed at her outfit. "Love that."

"Thanks, but still nothing?" She twirled around so she could catch all angles in the mirror.

"About?"

"About Kurt?"

"I'm surprised he gave him another chance." She stared at me like I had two heads. "What? If his father felt he was going down the wrong path, then kudos to him for stepping in." I had no other words on the subject.

Looking at my image in the opposing mirror, I smiled. A turquoise tank with the bodice covered in lace felt exquisite against my skin. I tried on the same pair of pants Naomi had on, but they looked better on her. Instead, I reached inside my dressing room and pulled out a simple, yet classic, black mini skirt. I placed it over my lower half.

"What do you think of this?"

"I like both pieces but not together." She took a step closer and touched my arm. "Care to explain why you're on my uncle's side?"

"You don't agree with him?"

"I do. I'm just shocked you do."

I turned from side to side before exhaling. "No more talk about your cousin. Let's finish up here and grab something to eat."

After we'd paid for the items we'd chosen, Naomi and I agreed on a quaint Italian restaurant. I asked her if she wanted to ride with me, but she said she'd meet me there, needing to leave afterward for an appointment. We said our goodbyes toward the front of the store, and as I was about to walk outside, Ford stepped in front of me to block me from exiting.

Truth be told, he startled me. "What?"

"I need to use the restroom before we go."

"There's one at the restaurant you can use. We'll be there in fifteen minutes." I attempted to move around him, but he blocked me again.

"I can't wait." He pinned me with his eyes, waiting for me to either give him a problem or comply. I chose the latter, having no energy to fight with him.

"Fine. Hurry up."

"Don't. Go. Anywhere." He raised his brows, and we entered into a staring contest. I narrowed my eyes before shaking my head.

"I'll stay put," I sang, flashing him a fake smile, my grin slipping as soon as he turned away from me. He asked Audrey if she had a restroom he could use, and she was all too willing to accommodate him. She batted her lashes at him before showing him where it was located.

"Typical," I murmured, pulling out my phone to occupy me while I waited for him.

While I stood near the entrance, three women walked into

the shop, laughing and having a good time. For some reason, though, their voices annoyed me, particularly the blonde in the middle, whose pitch was a level too high for my ears.

I wasn't in a skip-down-the-street type mood, but before my mood did turn sour I decided to exit the shop and get some fresh air. I expected Ford to chastise me for leaving the store, but at least I wasn't trying to ditch him like I had in the past.

The warmth from the sun kissed my skin as I stepped outside, the temperature of eighty-two degrees perfect, especially for late July in New York. Despite it being a gorgeous afternoon, there weren't many people on the sidewalk, only a few stragglers across the street who entered two of the other stores.

Placing my bags on the ground, I rooted through my oversized purse for my sunglasses. While I was preoccupied with my search, I saw a man approach in my peripheral. When he stopped a few feet from me, I didn't think anything of it, not until he stepped closer. His presence made me uneasy, which I blamed Ford for constantly freaking me out by saying I wasn't safe without him. *Where the hell is he anyway? How long does it take to pee?*

"Cara?"

I picked my head up at the mention of my name and locked eyes with the man.

"Yeah?"

I didn't recognize him, but that didn't mean he didn't know me. Or *of* me, to be more clear. Before I had the chance to ask him what he wanted, he rushed toward me and grabbed me around the waist, hoisting me from the ground and placing his free hand over my mouth to keep me from screaming. My legs and arms instinctually flailed around me, but he was too strong for my feeble attempts at escape.

A large black SUV blocked the sight of us from any vehicles passing by. Otherwise, I was sure someone would've stopped to help. Or at the very least, called 911.

I heard the driver-side door open, and within seconds I saw another man approach, the glare in his eyes telling me I was in serious danger. Not that I hadn't already gotten that hint from the man clutching me and covering my mouth.

Again, I attempted to escape but it was futile. I was no match for either of the kidnappers. Seconds later, they shoved me into the back of their vehicle and sped off down the road and toward my possible demise.

CHAPTER
FORTY

Cara

The moment the first kidnapper put his hands on me, my blood froze inside my veins. My lungs snatched my breath and I swore my heart stopped. Regret for all my past behavior flooded over me. I should've listened to Ford when he told me to stay put. I thought he was just being his usual, overbearing self, but he was just doing his job.

I should've never walked outside without him, but deep down I truly thought the threat toward our family wasn't real. How dangerously wrong I'd been.

I could only hope that once he realized I hadn't shut my phone off, that I hadn't tried to take off on him, that he'd pick up on the tracker on my cell and find me before anything bad happened.

As soon as I was thrown into the SUV, I was bound and gagged, the rope tightening around my wrists the more I struggled to escape. Being restrained against my will played tricks on my psyche. A feeling of helplessness sliced away at the survival instincts I was born with and taunted me with the worst possible images of what could happen if I wasn't rescued, and soon.

We'd driven for what seemed like an hour, although it could've been longer. I tried to pay attention to any bumps in the road, or times the vehicle slowed then resumed speed. I had no idea what to do with the information, not having a clue as how to piece any of it together, but I did it just the same.

When the SUV came to a screeching stop, I counted the seconds until the back door flung open. As soon as I saw the two of them standing in front of me, a lone tear escaped and traveled down my cheek, only to be absorbed by the rag still clenched between my teeth. I threw myself back but one of them grabbed my arm and pulled me forward, tossing a smelly sack over my head before hauling me from the vehicle. They barely gave me time to find my footing before hastily ushering me into some sort of building. Through the tiny spaces in the sack I couldn't see much, but the smell of mildew and dirt told me that wherever we were, the place hadn't been occupied in a long time.

We traveled down two hallways and a flight of steps before they shoved me into a room, removing the bag and my restraints before slamming the door behind them when they left.

As I paced back and forth, I tried to figure out how to escape from the windowless room, my eyes welling with tears at the unknown. The two men who'd snatched me never bothered to hide their faces, which I thought was odd. Then again, what the hell did I know about kidnappers? Maybe that only happened in movies.

Alone with only my thoughts, I tried as hard as I could to remember every possible detail about them. They were both large, close to Ford's height, and menacing-looking as fuck. Ford had a similar intensity about him, but he also showcased another side. Not a softer side, per se, and not an approachable side, but there was something about him that indicated he wasn't a brute. Not by nature, at least.

But those two... they were a different story altogether. The one who first grabbed me had a scar on his cheek. It ran from his jawline to his temple, making him scary as hell, all without him uttering a single word. His hair was dark and cut short. I didn't have a chance to study him, but I didn't want to stare too long, either, for fear he'd believe there was no other option than to get rid of me because I could ID him.

The other one didn't appear as menacing, but he gave off the I'll-do-what-I-have-to vibe just the same. His hair was lighter in color, the length hitting just above his shoulders. He didn't have any distinguishable scars that I could see, but he had at least one tattoo that covered the left side of his neck. Again, because my intuition told me not to stare too hard, I couldn't determine what the tattoo was, looking away as soon as I'd seen it.

My thoughts jumbled together. I tried to recall anything I'd seen in movies or in television shows about what to do in this type of situation. If they'd thrown me in the trunk of a car, I would've searched for a release latch. Or if they'd tossed me in a room that had windows, I could've at least seen where I was, do my best to identify anything surrounding the building. None of those things happened, however, and now all I could do was wait. Wait to see if they were going to leave me to starve to death. Wait to see if they were going to rape or torture me, or both. Wait to see if my life would end by either of their hands.

Backing myself into a corner, I closed my eyes and leaned my head against the wall, sucking in a lungful of damp air. Memories of me and Emily playing together flooded in, much like I'd recalled in the home movie I'd watched not long ago, reminding me of a time when I was happy. Innocent. Trusting. I wasn't sure why my mind recalled that particular time in my life, but it was better to have something positive to focus on instead of what was happening now.

My mom and dad's faces appeared next, the love in their eyes comforting me, but their expressions quickly turned to concern and disappointment. I shook my head and opened my eyes, focusing back on the room I was in, staring at the door and willing it to open. Locked away stole my options, but if the door would just open, just a crack, then maybe I'd have a chance.

Logically, I understood that the opening of the door meant that one or both of the men who'd stolen me would enter and do God only knew what to me. But being closed off with only my thoughts seemed to be the worst of the two options. Not knowing was horrible. At least, if I could determine the foreseeable future, I could deal with it. In what way, I didn't know, but to have options was certainly more comforting.

Hell, my thoughts were all jumbled, barely making sense.

I contemplated bashing my head against the concrete. Maybe if I knocked myself out, I could protect myself by allowing the darkness to take over. I decided against it in the end because, quite simply, it was an asinine thing to do. I needed to be alert and ready for anything to happen.

Voices outside the door drew my attention. The hair on the back of my neck lifted and my hands became clammy. Gone were the fantasies of attacking whoever entered the room. There was no way I'd be able to overpower one of them, let alone both.

The handle of the door jiggled, and my heart slammed against my ribcage, my breath stolen before my lungs inflated once more. I waited to see who would enter. There were no more images racing through my mind. There was no more planning on how to escape. There was nothing. Nothing but numbness engulfed me, which was more terrifying than what I anticipated I'd be experiencing in the wake of confronting my kidnappers again.

The creak of the door opening blasted away my remaining courage, and all I could hope for was either a quick death or an explanation. Two extremes and nonsensical options but they were the only two that raced through my muddled mind.

A black shoe appeared first, followed by the leg of someone dressed in dark-colored pants. Then his arm came into view, covered by a white shirt, the sleeves rolled up to the elbows. Finally, the entire man emerged and came into full view. He stood near the door and placed his hands behind his back, the hint of a scheming smirk lifting the corners of his mouth.

I closed my eyes tightly before opening them again. I repeated the action over and over until I made myself dizzy. There was no way the man standing before me was really there. The guys who took me must've drugged me. It was the only explanation.

He looked behind him and nodded to someone. The two culprits who snatched me walked in and flanked him on either side. The three of them together unnerved me, and while my brain tried to wrap around what scenario made sense, my heart fluttered before hitting my stomach.

Nausea racked my body, and I was moments away from getting sick if someone didn't start explaining.

"This couldn't have gone better."

Ford released his hands from behind his back and clenched his fists at his sides seconds before he walked toward me, the most wicked of grins spreading across his deceptive face.

The Score, book 2 in the Massey Security Duet, will be released on July 8, 2019. So, if you're cursing me for this cliffhanger, you won't have to wait long to find out what happens next.

NOTE TO READER

If you are a new reader of my work, thank you so much for taking a chance on me. If I'm old news to you, thank you for continuing to support me. It truly means the world to me.

If you've enjoyed this book, or any of my other stories, please consider leaving a review. It doesn't have to be long at all. A sentence or two will do just fine. Of course, if you wish to elaborate, feel free to write as much as you want.

If you would like to be notified of my upcoming releases, cover reveals, giveaways, etc, be sure to sign up for my newsletter: www.subscribepage.com/snelsonnewsletter

ACKNOWLEDGEMENTS

Thank you to my husband for allowing me to forget about everything else while I lost myself to this story, not coming up for air until it was finished. I love you!

A huge thank you to my family and friends for your continued love and support.

Becky, you continue to push and challenge me. The direction I thought I wanted for this book altered because of your insight. Ford and Cara's story is more polished because of it. Thank you for everything!

Clarise, CT Cover Creations, I'm in love with this cover. You hit it out of the park again, woman. Thank you for indulging me whenever I have one of my many last minute requests. Love you!

To all of the bloggers who have shared my work, I'm forever indebted to you. You ladies are simply wonderful!

To all of you who have reached out to me to let me know how much you love my stories, I'm truly humbled.

And last but not least, I would like to thank you, the reader. Without you, I'd just be some crazy lady with a bunch of characters in my head. I hope you enjoyed the first book in the Massey Security duet. And please don't kill me for the cliffhanger. The next book, The Score, will be out in less than two months' time.

ABOUT THE AUTHOR

S. Nelson grew up with a love of reading and a very active imagination, never putting pen to paper, or fingers to keyboard until 2013.

Her passion to create was overwhelming, and within a few months she'd written her first novel. When she isn't engrossed in creating one of the many stories rattling around inside her head, she loves to read and travel as much as she can. She lives in the Northeast with her husband and two dogs, enjoying the ever changing seasons.

If you would like to follow or contact her,
please feel free to do so at the following:

Email Address: snelsonauthor8@gmail.com

Website: www.snelsonauthor.com

Facebook

Nelson's Novels (Facebook VIP group)

Goodreads

Amazon

Instagram: snelsonauthor

Twitter: authorsnelson1

Newsletter: www.subscribepage.com/snelsonnewsletter

ALSO BY

S. NELSON

Standalones

Stolen Fate
Redemption
Torn
Blind Devotion

The Addicted Trilogy

Addicted
Shattered
Wanted

The Knights Corruption MC Series

Marek
Stone
Jagger
Tripp
Ryder

Knights Corruption Complete Series (all 5 MC books in one:
Marek, Stone, Jagger, Tripp, Ryder)

ALSO AVAILABLE

She intrigues him. She challenges him. She threatens the secret he's been hiding for years. Will a promise make long ago be the very same thing that destroys their chance for happiness?

Grab your copy of *Addicted* today

With the weight of the club on his shoulders, Cole Marek, president of the Knights Corruption MC, had only one choice:

Turn their livelihood legit.

Everything was falling into place until one unexpected, fateful night. With an attack on his fellow brothers, Marek had no choice but to retaliate against their sworn enemy.

Swarming their compound, he comes face-to-face with the infamous daughter of his rival club, making an astonishing decision which would change his life forever.

Grab your copy of *Marek* today

Made in the USA
Middletown, DE
07 July 2019